SOME everly

ENTWINED IN YOU, BOOK THREE
ASHLEE ROSE

SOMETHING EVERLASTING
Copyright © 2018 Ashlee Rose

First Edition

The author has asserted their moral right under the Copyright, Designs and Patents Act, 1988, to be identified as the author of this work.

All rights reserved. No part of this publication may be reproduced, copied, stored in a retrieval system, or transmitted, in any form by or by any means, without the prior written consent of the copyright holder, nor be otherwise circulated in any form of binding or cover other than that in which it is published and without a similar condition being imposed on the subsequent purchaser.

This is a work of fiction. Names, characters, businesses, places, events and incidents are either the products of the authors imagination or used in a fictitious manner. Any resemblance to actual persons, living or dead, or actual events is purely coincidental.

*To my little following, this is for you.
Thank you for the continued support X*

CHAPTER ONE

As I laid a single white, long-stemmed rose at Chloe's grave, I thought, how much of a waste of such a young life. A single tear escaped, rolling down my cheek. Even though we had our moment in Paris, she didn't deserve this. I quickly wiped my stray tear away before looking over my shoulder at Carter. I gave him a heart-breaking smile. He stood with his hands in his pockets, staring at me with a frosty glare. He wouldn't admit it just yet, but this was breaking his heart. I walked slowly over to him with glassy eyes and placed my hand in his, squeezing it tight as we walked in silence to our car.

James shut the door behind us and pulled away. I sat silently thinking about everything that had happened the last few months. The loss of our baby, the death of Chloe, the realization that I was bringing up a baby that my husband-to-be is the father of. Before I could stop them, my eyes were filled to the brim. I blinked, looking at my sparkling engagement ring as the tears fell, landing on my lap. I felt so overwhelmed by everything. Everything was out of my control and I hated it. I didn't know what was going to happen and I was scared. The funeral tipped my emotions over the edge. Everything had been building up, and it all came crashing down. Carter looked worriedly at me and grabbed my hands, slowly moving them to his lips, softly brushing them over the back of my knuckles before planting soft kisses along each one. It was like he read my mind.

"We will be okay, Freya. We will get through this," he said quietly, looking at me with a hopeful look on his face. He then furrowed his brow.

I nodded in silence and put my hands in my lap, nibbling my bottom lip before knotting my fingers and calming my breathing. He pulled his phone out and started working through his work emails.

We slowed outside our beautiful home as the black iron gates slowly started to open. It was so quiet, the only noise I could hear was the tyres on the shingled drive. It made a nice change instead of hearing the hustle and bustle of London.

James pulled up outside and opened Carter's door.

"Thank you, James." Carter nodded at him. He held his hand out for me to take. As our fingers touched, that spark of electricity coursed through me. I stood in front of him as James shut the door behind us and slipped back into the driver's door then pulled away.

I smiled as Carter wrapped his arm around me and pulled me into him, his breath on my face. I tucked a loose bit of hair behind my ear, looking up at him. He placed his free hand around the back of my head, pulling me gently into his lips. As soon as our lips touched, I felt him relax, and I relaxed too. I had been so wanting him. His touch, his kiss, but due to the baby coming along, we rarely had any time for just us. I stood and savoured the moment, enjoying every second. I wrapped my arms around his neck, putting my weight on him as our kiss grew hungrier, my tongue stroking his with every move. He groaned in his throat as I ran my hands through his mousy, tousled hair, gently tugging at it. All of our emotions were put into this kiss. He slowly pulled away as I tried to catch my breath. I rubbed my lips together, not taking my eyes off his. We embraced for a few minutes before we had to be pulled from our quiet moment.

"I miss us," he said, sounding exhausted

"I miss us too."

He took my face into his hands and stared into my eyes, his gaze burning into my soul. "We need a date night," he said with a smirk on his face. "I need you to myself. I can't cope with these little ten minute moments we get."

I started to reply but chose not to. I just nodded in agreement.

We walked up the stairs to our double oak front doors when we were greeted by Elsie. She had such a soft, beautiful face. Elsie had moved in with us to help with the baby, and we were so grateful to her.

"Hey, loves. You two hungry? I've made lunch," she asked softly as we walked past her.

"I am famished," I admitted. I hadn't eaten since the night before.

Carter grabbed my hand as we walked into our hallway and pulled me back into him. "I love you, Freya," he said quietly.

"I love you," I replied, standing on my tiptoes to kiss him on his full lips.

I let go of his hand and hung my beige trench coat up in the cloak closet. I walked through to the kitchen to find Elsie serving up spaghetti carbonara. I blushed as my belly rumbled loudly as soon as the smell hit me. "Excuse me." I smiled.

Carter and I were sitting at the breakfast bar finishing our lunch when Elsie walked round the corner with the baby. I watched Carter as Elsie walked over to him. His eyes lit up, full of love. Elsie handed her over as Carter took her gently and held her up to his shoulder, snuggling into her.

"Hey, baby girl," he whispered, kissing her hair.

She was still so tiny. I watched in awe the love he had for this little girl. She had completely turned our world upside down.

I excused myself from the table and placed my bowl in the sink. I walked back out to the hallway and tiptoed up our sweeping staircase. I needed a moment, a moment to breathe. The high emotions of today had just got too much. Walking into our bedroom, I quietly shut the door behind me. I crumbled as soon as the door was closed, sliding down it to the floor. I brought my knees up to my chest and rested my head on them, quietly sobbing.

I was interrupted by a soft knock on the door. "Freya, sweetie." Elsie's sweet voice took me from my crying. "Are you okay?" she asked.

I cleared my throat. "I'm fine." I couldn't even convince myself.

"Can I come in?"

"Of course," I mumbled through choked sobs.

I slowly stood up, taking a deep breath as I opened the bedroom door.

"Oh, Freya," she whispered, scooping me into a motherly embrace when she saw my raw eyes and smudged mascara.

I couldn't stop as the tears started to fall again. We walked over to mine and Carter's bed and sat. I felt so guilty for letting myself get into that state. I pressed my lips into a thin line and held my hands on my lap.

Elsie wrapped her arm around me and pulled me into her. "I know this is hard, darling," she said, kissing the side of my head delicately before continuing. "This is a massive change, what with everything you and Carter have been through already. But, this baby is now in your life as well as Carter's. I know it's easier for him as she is his flesh and blood. You are taking on and bringing up another woman's baby, but this baby is as much yours as she is Carter's. She needs both of you."

I sniffed and bit my lip, nodding at her comments. She let go of me and started to stand as she took a step forward towards the door.

"It's just hard for me to see," I mumbled. She took a step back and sat down next to me in silence, just listening while I spoke. "I'm still not over our baby loss. I wake up every morning thinking about it, and then go to sleep every night thinking about it. I just can't escape. I miss Carter. I feel like we aren't together, even though we are. Just like passing ships in the night." I sighed, trying to swallow the lump back down my throat. "I'm just finding this adjustment hard. I feel so blessed to have Esme in our lives. I know I don't seem it, but I am, it's just been a lot to take in within such a small timeframe."

She nodded at me and put her hand on my thigh. "You need to take each day as it comes. I remember this feeling well. Even having my own two children with Carter's father was still overwhelming and hard, but we got through it. You two need each other more than you know at the moment. I will deal with Esme tonight. You two have some alone time, and in a few weeks, maybe look at taking a weekend away. It will help. I promise. You two are stronger than you know, but you need to stick together." She smiled sympathetically at me. She stood up and walked to the bedroom door, opening it quietly.

"Elsie," I said in a low, almost whisper of a voice "Thank you. It means a lot. I'll see you at bed time. I have to have my Esme cuddle before she sleeps." I smiled at her, dabbing under my eyes with my ring finger.

"Always here, sweetie. Love you," she said as she disappeared out of the room, shutting the door behind her.

I flopped down on the bed and let out a massive sigh when I heard the bedroom door handle go. I propped myself up on my elbows to see Carter walking towards me.

"Hey, baby," he said as he sat down beside me on the bed. "I would ask if you're okay, but that's a silly question, isn't it?" He pushed some loose hair away from my face.

"I'm sorry. I'm just finding this a lot to take in. I know it's not been a walk in the park for you either, but everything seems to have come crashing down on me today and I'm struggling to lift this heavy weight off my shoulders," I muttered, twiddling a loose strand of hair between my fingers. He sighed and lay on his belly next to me. I turned my face to the side to look at him, searching his eyes for something, but he gave me nothing. "I'm sorry, Carter." A tear rolled down my face, dissolving into our duvet cover.

"Oh, Freya," he replied with a sigh. "Don't say sorry. It's me who should be saying sorry to you." He slid himself closer to me, our faces nearly touching.

"You shouldn't be saying sorry, Carter. I just didn't think our life would pan out this way," I whispered back at him with a guilty look on my face, looking at his lips the whole time. They were parted slightly, his breathing quiet.

"Neither did I," he replied, pulling his brows together. "But we have to deal with the cards we've been dealt." He ran his hand through his tousled hair before continuing. "But, I am sorry as well. You've taken on so much for me. I will forever be in your debt. You are an amazing mummy to Esme-Blu and an amazing fiancée to me."

My eyes started welling up as I leant up and kissed him, lingering slightly.

As I pulled away, he drew in a deep breath and bit his lip before slowly releasing it. "I understand it's just us tonight, that my mum is going to sort Esme out." He slowly ran his index finger from my collarbone down to my hip. I couldn't remember the last time we were alone like this. I couldn't remember the last time we had sex. I wanted him.

I sat up and pushed him up towards the headboard. His eyes were burning into me as I crawled onto his lap.

A devilish smile spread across his face. "Well, hello there." He growled at me.

I forced myself into him, my hands up in his hair, tugging it hard as my mouth covered his. A deep groan came from his throat as he ran his hands up the side of my sleeveless shirt. He pulled away and rested his forehead on mine, catching his breath. His want was as strong as mine. He pressed his full lips onto my neck, nipping at it occasionally. I moaned, throwing my head back as the sweet pang of desire hit me deep in my belly. Carter ran his hands to the top of my shirt and ripped the buttons open hungrily. I gasped as a few of the buttons flew across the room. Carter just smirked at me, as I smirked back at him before meeting with his lips again. I gently tugged his bottom lip with my teeth. I felt like I had a caged animal inside me, ready to be released. He slipped my shirt down my arms, kissing my collarbone and shoulders as he exposed them. His hands found my hip as my shirt fell to the bed. I reached around and undid my bra, sliding it off. As I did, he kissed my lips with force and hunger, pushing his hands through my hair. I pulled myself away and stood up, keeping my eyes on his the whole time. I undid the button to my jeans and slid them down past my bum and thighs then stepped out of them as elegantly as I could.

There I stood, in only my white lacy thong. My long, wavy auburn hair was loose over one shoulder, sitting just underneath my ribs. My skin felt like it was alight from Carter's stare; he was burning into me.

"Fuck," he muttered under his breath as I slowly skulked back over to him. I smirked as I knelt on the bed in front of him. "How did I get so lucky?" he said in a husky voice as he knelt up with me.

"I'm the lucky one."

He pushed my arms up into the air as he kissed my neck, then started making his way down my collarbone whilst still holding my arms in the air with one of his hands. The other found my breast as he took it into his mouth, slowly caressing it then sucking hard. I whimpered as the sting left my body, my breathing getting heavier. His free hand pushed me back onto the bed.

"Keep your arms where they are," he demanded. I did as he said. He knelt up and pushed my legs apart and smiled. "Oh, I've missed you." He growled as he looked down at me, admiring my every curve.

He slowly lay down in between my legs as his fingers started caressing me, slowly running over my lace thong. He released his hand from my arms and ran it under my bum, tilting my pelvis slightly. I slowly moved my arms down by my sides as I watched him, his sage green eyes looking up at me through his long lashes as he tutted. I bit my lip. He was such a turn on. He broke his stare as he put his index and middle finger underneath my thong and gently brushed over my sweet spot, making me moan. He loved the reaction. He did it once more before hooking his fingers through a small hole in the lace and ripping them. I gasped as my knickers disintegrated under his touch. He grinned as he pulled my thong away and threw it on the floor beside the bed. He dipped back down in between my legs and slowly slipped his finger into me. As he did, I arched my back slightly as he pushed his finger deeper. I looked down at him, still fully dressed, and there was me, completely naked, being intoxicated by this god of a man. My man.

He continued to plunge his finger in and out of me in a slow, teasing rhythm. Just as I was about to ask him to stop, he covered my sex with his mouth, carefully licking and flicking his tongue against me, again and again, matching his strokes with his finger. I propped myself up on my elbows to watch him, his tongue making me fall apart each time it hit me in my delicate spot. I moved one of my hands into his hair, grabbing it tightly.

"Tut tut. I told you to keep your arms up." He scowled at me.

"Carter, baby, please. I need you," I begged, panting.

"How much do you want me?" he said in a seductive voice, stopping everything he was doing.

"So bad."

He leant up, slowly wiping my arousal off his face. He took his top off and flung it over the other side of the room, then pulled his jogging bottoms and boxers down, freeing himself.

He made my mouth go dry every time I saw him.

He moved towards me, flipping me over onto all fours. I arched my back slightly and looked over my shoulder, watching him.

"What a view," he said, licking his bottom lip before pulling it behind his teeth, drawing a deep breath. He grabbed my hips forcefully and pulled me back, slamming into me hard. I moaned out as he hit me.

It was rage sex. Full of pent up frustration, emotions, and lust. He grabbed onto my hair and bunched it into a ponytail with his fist and pulled my head back as he continued to slam himself into me. He started moaning as he picked up the pace, my body getting ready for her climb. I moved my hips with him which only made him want me even more.

"Shit, Freya, baby. Come for me," he spat through gritted teeth.

He hit into me one last time before sending me into a hard orgasm, calling his name as I peaked, which brought him to his own release. We slowed, him still holding my hips. He pulled me back into him and cradled me as we lay back onto the bed.

We lay for a few moments, catching our breath. I looked up at him and kissed him softly on the lips. "I love you, Carter," I said quietly as I pulled myself away from him.

"I love you, my queen," he responded in a silky voice. "Forever and always."

CHAPTER TWO

I rolled over and stretched out while gazing at Esme. I couldn't believe she had been in our lives for six weeks. We named her Esme after Chloe's middle name, and Blu because Chloe's favourite flowers were bluebells. I watched her breathing softly in her Moses basket. Her long eyelashes rested on her perfectly pink skin. Her full lips were like her daddy's, pouting as the breath left them. I rolled over, just lying there, watching her. It was getting easier, just like Elsie had said a few weeks ago after Chloe's funeral. I still had my down days, but there were more good than bad. I had to remember who was watching me now. This innocent little girl that depended on me and Carter.

I was distracted as I felt Carter's hand across my belly, pulling me into him, as he nuzzled into my hair.

"Good morning, beautiful," he mumbled with a tired but sexy voice. I loved it when he had just woken up. He was all sleepy, loving, and so utterly handsome.

"What you doing?" he asked while still burying his face in my long mane of auburn hair.

"Just watching her. I could watch her forever." I smiled slightly.

"So could I, but right now I want to look at you, and you know, do everything else in between," he said teasingly as he rolled me over to face him, planting a soft kiss on my lips.

"Erm, not with madam in the room," I scolded him.

"She is six weeks old. She won't remember," he replied as he dived into my neck, kissing it.

As much as I wanted him, it took all my strength to push him off me. "Later," I whispered. "She will want her bottle soon." I smiled then kissed him on the forehead, and like clockwork, she started stirring, making little grunting noises and reaching up for an almighty stretch. I leant up and looked over at her in awe.

"Okay, sweetie. Mummy is going to do your bottle." I smiled down at her.

"Baby, stay in bed. I'll do it. I'm back to work tomorrow so I want to make the most of today." He winked at me as he slipped out of the room. I shuffled back up against my headboard, propping myself up so I was comfortable before leaning over and picking our tiny doll up delicately.

"Morning, princess." I kissed her forehead. Her soft

cries started just as Carter walked into the room with her bottle and a cup of tea for me. We sat in silence while I fed her, listening to the little suckling noises and moans she made as she filled her tiny belly with milk. Elsie was due back here for three days a week so I could go back to work. Carter wanted me to stay home and play mum, but I wasn't ready to give my job up just yet. I still wanted to be selfish.

We originally looked into getting a childminder, but Elsie refused and offered to have Esme so she could have some bonding time with her granddaughter. She gets so lonely, so it's nice that she has Esme to give her a purpose again.

I walked into Esme-Blu's nursery. We decided to use the other spare room at the opposite end of the house instead of using the one that we planned for our first baby. The memories and emotions were still too raw. Her nursery was cream with hints of blush pinks throughout. It overlooked our garden and had a big beautiful window where the morning sun beamed through. I laid her on her changing table and put a clean nappy and baby-grow on her. She cooed at me while staring at me with her big blue eyes. I secretly hoped they'd change to Carter's sage green. Her hair was light blonde, thin, and wispy. She started getting restless so I gave her a kiss and put her down to sleep.

I walked out of her nursery with the baby monitor in my hand and closed the door quietly. I ran my hand down our beautiful oak bannisters as I quickly stepped down the stairs. Our house was finished to perfection. I looked back up the sweeping staircase and smiled as I saw Carter walking down the stairs. I waited at the bottom for him, watching him through the glass balustrades.

"Hey, wifey," he teased with a big smile on his face.

"Hey, you. I'm not wifey yet," I said with a sarcastic smirk, still clutching the monitor.

"Well, you will be soon." He beamed before taking me in his arms and kissing me on the lips, hard. I grabbed his arm to balance myself.

Oh my, Carter.

"How are you? Did Esme go down okay?" he questioned, slowly letting me go and taking my hand as we walked through the hallway.

"I'm hungry, and yeah, she went down well." I smiled, squeezing his hand

"Well, let's do something about your hunger," he said, stopping me before we got to the kitchen. He devoured me with his eyes then pulled me close to him, his breath on my face.

"As much as I want you, Mr Cole, I meant food hunger," I whispered, scared to breathe. He completely took over me.

"Fine." He sulked, pouting his lips then leading me into our open plan kitchen. Oh, he was such a sulker. I let out a titter of a laugh as I followed him.

"All right, stroppy. What do you want for lunch?" I asked. He didn't take his eyes off me, following me up and down our kitchen.

"I want you," he said bluntly.

I bit my lip. "I want you too, but I also want food. I'm hungry and I would like to eat before madam wakes up and wants me all to herself."

"Well, I want you all to myself. Why does she get you to herself and I have to wait?" He held his face up with his right hand. I looked at his Rolex on his wrist, the one I bought him for Christmas. I sighed. That felt like a lifetime ago.

"Because, Mr Cole, she is six weeks old. You are thirty-three. Well, nearly thirty-four," I teased. "Anyway, Grandpa, you get me to yourself. Stop being a grump. I fancy an egg sandwich, quick and filling. You want one?" I asked him, quickly changing the subject and batting my eyelids at him as I held the frying pan in my hand.

"Yes. Then you are fulfilling my wants and needs," he muttered, biting his lip.

My insides squealed. I tried to swallow but my mouth had gone dry. I coughed, trying to clear my throat so I could respond, but words escaped me.

I slid his sandwich across the granite breakfast bar, his hand touching mine as he took it from me; my breathing stilled.

How does he have this effect on me all the goddamn

time? I stood on the opposite side of the breakfast bar, watching him as I tucked into my sandwich. As I took a bite, the yolk escaped and ran down my chin. Before I could wipe it, Carter's thumb had cleaned it away. I stared at him as he put his thumb into his mouth and sucked it clean, staring into my eyes the whole time. *Tease*.

We sat quietly as we finished our lunch. Just as I went to take my last bite, he slid his plate across the worktop then climbed over the top of it. My God of a man stood in front of me, his gorgeous sage eyes burning deep into my soul. He took my plate from me and placed it on the worktop behind me.

"I wanted that," I mumbled, searching his face.

"I want you," he said. He pushed his hands through my messy ponytail and tugged slightly so my head tilted back. I purred as his lips touched my neck before he found my eyes again.

I was so overwhelmed by him. He was my drug. I was addicted to him and how he made me feel.

He pushed me into the worktop behind me before lifting me up effortlessly and resting me on the edge. He spread my legs gently as he stood between them.

"Freya, my love. You intoxicate me. I am completely lost in you," he whispered in my ear. My belly knotted. He took my face in his hands and kissed me as if this was our last kiss. I rested my hand on his chest, his t-shirt between me and his sun-kissed skin. He pushed my hands away as he lifted my grey t-shirt over my head and dropped it to the floor.

"Did you not fancy wearing a bra today?" He raised his eyebrow while looking at me with a smouldering look.

"No. Only me and you here. The housekeepers are in their home, so why not?" I shrugged, smiling at him.

"Easier for me." He cupped my breast with his left hand before taking my mouth over with his again, pushing his tongue deep into my mouth as my tongue caressed his. I ran my hands down his toned torso before tugging at his jogging bottoms. With his right hand, he started pulling the waistband of my leggings. I let go of his jogging bottoms and put my weight onto my hands which were now holding me up on the worktop as he slid my leggings off. I sat back down and marvelled at him as he slid his bottoms down. I bit my lip.

Oh, what a sight. I still couldn't believe this man was mine.

I grabbed the front of his t-shirt and pulled him back into me. Now I wanted him. I pushed his t-shirt up, exposing his glorious, toned stomach as I pulled it over his head. His neatly trimmed snail trail led down to his large, thick shaft. As I took him into my hands, he breathed in through his teeth. I started slowly moving, consuming him with every stroke. His arousal started to show at his tip. I grinned up at him. I loved that I could make him so turned on.

"Baby, stop. I want to devour you," he said, panting.

He removed my hand and forced my legs even wider apart. He wrapped two of his chunky fingers around my delicate white frenchies and tugged them to the side, exposing me. He let his fingers explore and slowly plunged them into me. I gasped as he did it, the exquisite feeling of him working his magic inside me sent my body into overdrive. He buried his head in between my neck and shoulder while he continued his tantalizing rhythm. I moaned as he ran his thumb across my sweet spot. I put my right hand into his hair and tugged him back so we were looking at each other. The fire in his eyes was setting me alight with passion. I moved closer to him, ready to kiss him, when we were interrupted by the monitor screaming at us.

I bit my lip as he slowly took his fingers out of me and pulled my knickers back over.

"Well, that's a shame." He sighed as he sucked his breath through his teeth. He leant in and kissed me hard. "This isn't over."

He pulled his bottoms back up and washed his hands. I slipped off of the worktop, grabbing my t-shirt and pulling up my leggings as I went to make my way upstairs.

"Don't go, I will. Go and have a bath. Have some Freya time, baby." He smiled and kissed my forehead as he passed me, slipping his t-shirt on as he left the kitchen.

I tightened my hair back into its ponytail and made

my way to the fridge. I grabbed a bottle of Vouvray and reached up to get a large wine glass. A bath sounded like a wonderful idea. I had been up a few times with Esme, so having some alone time was just what the doctor ordered.

Carter was amazing. He did so much with Esme so it wasn't all on me. I shut the fridge with my foot and made my way upstairs. Before heading to the bathroom, I tiptoed down the landing and poked my head around the door, watching Carter and Esme.

My heart wanted to burst with love. He was such a natural, wonderful father to her.

I entered our bathroom; the large, white, shiny floor tiles had the afternoon sun beaming across them. The freestanding bath sat in the middle of the large window overlooking our beautifully landscaped garden. I placed my glass on the bath tray and poured the wine. I put the bottle of wine on the sink unit before turning the taps on. A few moments later, my bath was brimming with bubbles, a soft aroma filling the room. I slid my leggings down and took my t-shirt off, throwing them into the wash basket.

I stepped into the hot bath and smiled as I sank down. I reached out for my mobile and put my Spotify playlist on. Within seconds, mellow sounds were echoing round our bathroom thanks to our speakers that were dotted around. I slid down slightly so the nape of my neck was just under the water, then reached for my large glass of wine, taking a big sip.

I closed my eyes for a few moments when I heard the bathroom door open.

"Where's Mummy?" I heard his excited voice as he came striding across the bathroom like the god that he was, with our beautiful Esme.

"Hey, baby girl," I crooned as he knelt down next to the bath. She cooed before expressing a big, gummy smile "Oh, Es. You are adorable, you little pickle." I rested my arm on the roll-top edge of the bath and kissed her on the nose.

"Enjoying your bath?" Carter asked, standing up and bouncing Esme up and down in his arms.

"It could be better," I said in a silky, teasing voice, running my index finger tip up and down the roll-top edge.

"Well, once this little chicken is settled for the night, maybe we can take a dip in the hot tub in the spa room with a glass of champagne. What do you think?"

"That sounds amazing. Oh, and we can have chocolate as well as champagne," I said, trying not to salivate while thinking of chocolate.

"Deal," he said, winking at me. "Come on, Princess Esme. Let's leave Mummy to it. Say bye Mummy." He picked her little arm up and moved it up and down gently in a waving gesture.

"Bye bye, baby," I said while smiling and scrunching up my nose.

He blew me a kiss. I reached my hand up and grabbed

it and kissed my clenched hand. He smiled as he closed the door quietly and left me be.

I was sitting at my dressing table as I threw my hair into a messy bun and slipped on a pair of shorts and my *Friends* t-shirt. No sexy pyjamas now little miss was here. I walked into our bedroom and looked at my phone. I had missed calls from my mum and Laura. I sat on the bed as I dialled my mum's number.

"Hey, darling."

"Hey, Mum. You okay? I had a missed call."

"All okay here, sweetie. Me and Daddy were just wondering how you, Carter, and our beautiful granddaughter Esme-Blu are getting on."

I smiled. I loved that she treated Esme as her own.

"We're fine. I'm tired today. Didn't have a great night with her last night. I've just got out of the bath. That's why I missed your call. Carter took over for a bit."

"That's good that he's helping with the responsibility. The tiredness will go, my love. All part and parcel, darling. Are you eating okay? I know what you're like if you miss a meal." She turned stern.

"Yes, Mother. To be honest, it's good as I am losing weight. Esme seems to know every time I'm sitting down to eat." I laughed. "She either wants a bottle or a nappy change."

"Well, make sure you are eating enough. You'll be exhausted otherwise."

"Okay, Mum." I rolled my eyes. "You and Daddy okay?"

"We're fine. Booked some winter sun yesterday. We're going to Lanzarote for a week at the end of February. I'm missing the sun, love. I hate the winter."

"I know you do. I'm desperate for a holiday." I sighed. "Maybe I'll look in the next couple of days."

"Me and Daddy were thinking of coming to spend a weekend with you in a couple of weeks, if that's okay? Give you and Carter some time for each other. And yes, you should look at a holiday. What about Greece? Not too far for Esme-Blu and a beautiful island."

"Yeah, I could do. I would love to go Greece. I'll have a look tonight maybe. And, yes, please come for the weekend. I miss you both. Just let me know dates so I can pencil it in the calendar. Not that we have many social plans now." I sighed.

"Anyway, love, got to go. Your dad's dinner is done. Liver and bacon. His favourite."

"Okay, Mum. Thanks for calling. Send my love to Daddy and give him a kiss for me, please."

"Will do, my darling. Give Carter and Esme-Blu a kiss from me too. Love you, sweetie. Love to you all."

"Love you, Mum. Bye."

"Bye, my love."

I tried calling Laura but got no answer. I hoped she was okay. It was five thirty p.m. already; the day had flown.

I flopped down on our bed for a moment, and before I could stop them, my eyes fell shut.

Just five minutes, I thought to myself.

CHAPTER THREE

"Hey, sleepy head. Wake up." I heard Carter's silky voice.

"Oh my God. What's the time?" I groaned as I rolled over.

"It's seven," he said with a silly grin on his face.

"What? I only wanted to lie down for five minutes. Where's Esme?"

"She's asleep, babe. She had her bath and her night bottle." He sat next to me.

"I missed her bed time. I never miss bed time." I sulked, throwing myself into our duck feather pillows.

"Don't sulk, baby. She'll be awake at midnight for her bottle. You can see her then." He smiled. He leant over and kissed my forehead, inhaling my scent as he did. "You smell divine. I've sorted dinner. Are you hungry?"

"Yeah, I am. I didn't get to finish my egg sandwich earlier." I threw him an evil look. "I'm hangry."

"Oh, princess. Don't be a brat. Dinner is on the table. Let's eat," he said, laughing.

"Sorry."

"It's okay. I don't like getting in between you and your food," he teased.

"Hey, I want you in between me and my food. I'm not that bad." I scowled at him.

"Oh my God, Freya, I'm joking. The sooner we get food in you the better." He chuckled.

We walked down the stairs, and the aromas of a curry hit my nose. My belly rumbled. It smelled delicious. As we walked into the dining room, I saw six place settings.

"Babe, why are there six place settings?" I asked him with a confused expression on my face.

He pulled me in and kissed the side of my head. "Because," he said quietly in my ear. As soon as that word left his mouth, I heard a noise behind me. As I turned around, there was Laura, Tyler, Brooke, and Peter strolling into the dining room.

"Oh my God!" I squealed as I threw my arms around Laura and Brooke. Carter shook Tyler and Peter's hands.

"Good to see you," he said.

"Girls, I can't believe you're here. I also can't believe my husband-to-be didn't think it was a good idea to tell me that I should get changed!" I threw a stern look at him.

"Baby, you are fine as you are," he reassured me.

Brooke and Laura's facial expressions didn't agree.

"I'm going to get changed. Girls, come with me. I'll give you a quick tour." I smiled at them.

"Babe, get the boys a beer and get a bottle of wine out, and the non-alcoholic one we had stocked from…" I stopped mid-sentence.

"Of course, baby." He nodded with a weak smile. Carter had bought a few bottles of non-alcoholic wine when I was pregnant, but obviously, no need for it now.

"Anyway, girls, follow me," I said as we headed up the stairs. "Quiet though. Esme is soundo."

"No worries, Frey Frey. We won't wake her up, but I do wanna sneak peek at her. Photos just don't do her justice. You never know, we might accidently wake her then I can have a broody cuddle." She beamed at me.

"Lau, you never wake a sleeping baby!" Brooke said abruptly. "You wait. You wake Esme, I'll wake this little one up when she's here." She pointed at Laura's growing bump.

I felt immense pain as I looked at her bump in awe. My hand automatically went to my belly. I wondered what my little bump would have looked like. I may have not even had a bump. I let out a deep sigh. I felt Laura's arm wrap around my shoulders.

"I'm fine," I said bluntly, shrugging Laura off. I saw Laura side eye Brooke with an 'oh shit' expression. I ignored it.

"Okay, so this is Carter's study." I opened the heavy

oak door on Carter's beautiful workspace. The floor to ceiling windows just made the house. Every room had its own sunshine trap. His white high gloss desk sat on steel legs with a huge, high-back leather chair behind it. There were bookcases along the right side of the wall, filing cabinets along the left. Opposite the back wall where Carter would sit was a large framed photo of us. The one that Ava took when we had dinner together. It was one of many photos now, but it was a favourite.

"Have you shagged on here?" Laura blurted out.

"Lau!" Brooke exclaimed. "What the fuck is wrong with you?" she questioned, holding her hand out, waiting for Laura's explanation.

"Nothing is wrong with me. It's just a fantasy of mine." She blushed.

"Well, after dinner you are more than welcome to live out your fantasy. Just make sure you disinfect the desk." I roared loudly, and so did they. Oh, it felt good to laugh.

We walked out of the study and into the spare bedrooms.

"These are pretty self-explanatory." I rolled my eyes, smirking at them.

"Is this where we will be staying tonight?" Brooke asked me, eyes twinkling at the shabby chic décor.

"You're staying? It's a Thursday. What about work? What about Lola?" I asked her, confused again.

"Yeah. Carter thought it would be nice for us to spend

the day with you and Esme tomorrow while he is at work. Boys are going to go golfing, apparently, and meet Carter at lunchtime. Lola is with my parents."

I squealed. "I can't believe you're here for the night and day!" I jumped up and down on the landing. "Oh, I'm so happy." I beamed at both of them, my Trunchbull bun flopping around.

"On with the tour!"

We whizzed around the girls' en-suites which were located off the spare rooms then showed them our main bathroom.

I swung the door open to our lavish bedroom. They both gasped as the door opened.

"Oh, wow," Laura said, astonished. "This room. Why do you ever wanna leave?"

"I don't," I replied, giving her a little elbow in the arm.

We had a queen, grey crushed velvet headboard, with crisp white duvet covers and four pillows either side. We had big peony pink square cushions sitting in front of the two big piles of pillows. At the end of the bed lay a thick, knitted peony pink throw which hung delicately off the bed. By the foot of the bed we had a matching grey crushed velvet ottoman. The carpet was off white which complemented the room perfectly. Our big window had long, white curtains hanging off a delicate silver curtain pole with a vase of pink peonies sitting there, looking pretty. I sighed to myself as I looked at it; it really was a beautiful room.

"Come and see the best bit," I said.

I walked them through the bedroom, past our double bed. We walked through an archway which revealed our walk-in wardrobe. Mirrored wardrobes either side, a chest of drawers next to the wardrobes then, sat in the middle, was an island with all of our jewellery underneath a glass panel. My mirrored dressing table faced out to the window. I couldn't get enough of the views. I looked behind me and saw the girls' jaws hit the floor.

"It's something, eh?" I said, running one of my silk gowns through my index and middle fingers.

"I need to marry a millionaire," Laura blurted out.

"So do I!" Brooke piped up. "Wanna swap me Carter for Peter?" she asked seriously. "He is pretty good at doing the housework, and a rocket in bed." She laughed.

"Erm, sorry, but no. He's not for sharing."

"I wouldn't swap him either if he was mine." Brooke snorted before giggling to herself.

"Ahh, poor Pete!" I giggled along with her.

I gave them a quick tour of our en-suite before heading back out onto the landing.

"What's that room?" Laura quizzed, pointing to the door on the left of ours.

"Oh," I said, catching my breath. She took me by surprise. "Erm, that was our nursery," I said quietly, staring at the closed door.

"Oh. Sorry, hun," she muttered.

"Don't be silly. It's okay." I smiled weakly at her as I made my way down to Esme's nursery. As I got to her door, I turned to face the girls, putting my finger up to my mouth. I quietly opened the door and tiptoed into the room, the girls following me. My heart burst when I saw how cute Esme looked, snoozing on her back, arms resting up by her head while snug in her tiny gro-bag.

"Isn't she the cutest?" I said, giddy, running the tip of my index finger across her forehead, pushing her little wispy hair away.

"Oh, Freya. She is beautiful," Laura whispered.

"She's like a little doll. How is she six weeks old already?" Brooke questioned.

"I know. It's gone so quickly. It was such a whirlwind, but we finally seem to have found our feet a bit," I whispered again. "Come on. I'm starving. If you're still awake at midnight you can come and join me on her feed," I joked.

"Night, my little bluebell." I kissed my index and middle finger and pressed it onto her head.

We all walked out of the room, pulling the door to.

"Give me five. I'm just going to get changed out of my pyjamas. I'll meet you downstairs." I watched them walk down the stairs, nattering to themselves.

I re-joined them all at the table five minutes later. Carter pulled my chair out and took my hand and kissed it before I sat down.

"Thank you so much for all of this, Carter. I am so happy, but not going to lie, I was looking forward to the hot tub," I said quietly, smirking to him amongst the chatter.

"Anything to make you smile, my queen. Don't worry, we can do that tomorrow." He smiled at me, his sage eyes twinkling. "Now, eat. You must be starving." He nodded at the food. It all looked amazing. I helped myself to the vegetable jalfrezi and rice. There was no way Carter cooked this; he obviously got a takeaway. *Cheeky.*

After an amazing meal, we all retired to the lounge where we sat losing ourselves in easy chat.

"Your house is amazing, Carter. You and Freya have made it look beautiful," Laura complimented us.

"Thank you, Laura, but all the finer details and décor are down to her." He smiled at her, the whole time holding my hand tightly while rubbing his thumb over the back of my knuckles. He could sense my emotions were a bit all over the place.

"So, guys. What time are we hitting the holes tomorrow?" Carter asked Tyler and Peter. Brooke spat out her wine then started coughing while she caught her breath.

"Brooke, are you okay?" I asked, concerned.

After she coughed and spluttered, she answered. "I'm fine. Sorry. Carter's sentence just took me by surprise."

She sniggered.

"You dirty bitch, Brooke!" Laura belly laughed, holding her delicate bump as she did.

"What did I do?" Carter questioned, surprised. "Because I said hitting the holes? Brooke, seriously," he roared a deep laugh.

Oh, it's such a wonderful sound. I just fall in love with him a little bit more every day.

I took a big sip of wine as I listened to the men talk about their jobs while Laura and Brooke spoke about pregnancy. I know they probably didn't realize, but it was hard to listen to.

"Excuse me," I muttered as I got up and walked into the kitchen. I didn't want to go upstairs; I just wanted to hide away for a few moments. I walked to the other side of the kitchen and opened the pantry cupboard. I closed the door quietly behind me, taking a deep breath as I looked around. The shelves were filled with goodies. I grabbed some chilli tortilla chips and some chocolate. I sat on the floor against the wall, facing the door. I opened my crisps and chocolate and started to eat while pondering, why was I being such a bitch? Was I being a bitch?

Not really. These were normal feelings, right? I felt resentful of her and her bump. I sighed. I was a bitch. Just as I shoved a big handful of tortillas into my mouth, I saw the door handle move. *Shit.*

I saw Carter's broken-hearted expression.

"Baby," he said, deflated, as he sat down on the floor next to me.

"Hey, I'm sorry. Just got a bit too much for me," I said, staring into my crisp bag.

"So you decided to come in here, out of all of our rooms?" He chuckled softly.

"There was food."

He leant into me and kissed my forehead, lingering a little longer. As he pulled away, he stayed close. As I went to stand, he pulled me onto his lap so I was facing him.

"Why did you take the shorts off?" he whispered.

"Because, Mr Cole, we have guests and I didn't deem it appropriate to wear little shorts." I smirked at him.

"Want me to make you feel better?" he teased before kissing my earlobe then going down to my neck. My hands found his hair before I moaned out to him in agreement.

"Take me," I panted. "Take me, please," I begged him.

I stood up on top of him, sliding my skinny jeans down my thighs and kicking them off.

"Take your bottoms off," I demanded. He took a deep breath while he did, staring up at me while I was standing over him, watching his every move.

"You are a goddess." He ran his hands up to my hips then he bit his lip as he pulled me back down on him.

I moaned as he took me. I felt like I had gone to heaven with each slow movement hitting me again and again. I had my arm wrapped around his neck, pulling him into me. I started moving with him, savouring every moment. I could never get enough of him.

He grabbed my face and pulled me down to him, kissing me hard while he began his climb. I bit his lip hard in the moment as his thrusts got harder and deeper.

"Oh, God, Carter," I said into his kiss while my body started reaching her peak. I ran my hands over his shoulders, digging my nails into his back. My kiss got hungrier as I felt him tighten his grip around me.

"Oh, baby, I'm going to come." He groaned continuing moving my hips faster with his movements and I hit my peak with him. I threw my head back as my body exploded around him. He sat with his arms tightly around me, trying to still our breathing.

"Feel better?" he asked smugly, leaning up and kissing me.

"I do." I smiled, reaching for my chocolate. "Want some?" I held a strip of chocolate out to him.

"Chocolate and sex? What a night," he teased, taking it from me and slowly entering it into his mouth.

"It's not as tasty as you." He winked at me as I got up and dressed, and he got dressed after me.

"Come on. Let's go and join the party." I grinned at him.

"Be brave. Think of the positives, darling. Not the negatives." He pulled me in and kissed me hard. He made my lips feel bruised, but in a good way. He took my hand

and led me out of the pantry.

"Where the bloody hell have you two been?" Laura quizzed us.

"She needed help getting something out of the pantry cupboard." Carter looked down at his feet, trying to hide his smile.

"Mmhmm. I smell a rat." She shook her head in disbelief. I blushed as I tightened my grip on Carter's hand as I swung on his arm, trying to hide my face.

"You had sex!" she screamed.

"Shh! Esme!" I scowled at her.

"You had sex!" she whispered. Just as I was about to answer, I was distracted by Esme crying through the monitor. *She's early.*

"Saved by the bell," I whispered to Carter. "I'll change her, you do her bottle." I smiled at him.

"Okay, wifey." He squeezed my bum before walking into the kitchen.

"Won't be long. If you want to go to bed I won't be offended." I smiled.

I ran upstairs into Esme's nursery and kissed her. "Hey, sweetie. Let's get you changed and fed," I said, laying her down on her changing table. Her little smile brightened my world.

I had just finished changing her when I felt Carter's big hands wrap around my waist, his head nuzzling into my neck. "Oh, I love my girls," he whispered in my ear.

"We are so lucky, but unfortunately there will always be heartbreak surrounding you, my angel," I said quietly, looking over my shoulder to the picture of Chloe that we put in Esme's room. We always said we wanted her to know her real mummy and her story.

Carter handed me the bottle. "Want me to feed her?"

"No, it's okay. I'll feed her. I love this feed. She is still snuggly and sleepy." I smiled.

"Want me to stay with you?" he offered.

"Yeah, that would be nice." I kissed him on the cheek before picking Esme up off the changing table and sitting in the nursing chair in the corner of the room. I cradled her as I fed her. I felt Carter looking at me with such admiration and love. "What are you looking at?" I asked him, giggling.

"I'm looking at you." He ran his hand over his chin. "And just how perfect you are." He smiled before resting his elbows on his knees. I puckered my lips and kissed the air; he caught it and held it to his heart. "I am so in love with you, Freya. I don't know what my life was before you. I can't wait to make you mine officially." He flashed his big smile, and his sage eyes creased slightly as he did. "You are the most perfect mummy to Esme, and I am dreaming of the day when we welcome our own bundle of joy into our world." He walked over to me and kissed me and Esme on the forehead.

"Even though I am her mummy, I will never be her

mum, and I think I'm okay with that now. This happened for a reason." A happy tear rolled down my face as I looked at our sweet, precious Esme-Blu Cole.

CHAPTER FOUR

I stretched as I started to wake. What a long night. I rolled over to see Carter still blissfully sleeping. I was jealous. Esme had me up four times in the night. In the end, I put her in her Moses basket by our room. She slept so well during the day in her cot, but hated it at night.

I closed my eyes, trying to fall back to sleep, but my body wasn't having any of it. Maybe I was anxious because Carter was going back to work full-time. I'd been lucky that he had worked from home for the last six weeks, popping to the odd meeting here and there. I sighed as I lay awake, staring at the ceiling. It was three-thirty a.m., I was exhausted, but I couldn't sleep.

Half an hour had passed and I still couldn't doze off. I quietly shuffled down the bed and slipped my slippers on, heading for the door and grabbing my silk dressing gown as I left the room. I closed the door quietly and tiptoed downstairs. I noticed the kitchen light was on. Intrigued, I walked cautiously into the kitchen to find Julia prepping food.

"Freya?" she asked. "Is everything okay? It's four in the morning." She looked concerned.

"Oh, I'm fine, Julia. Just couldn't sleep. Been awake for half an hour just staring at the ceiling." I sighed.

"I'm sorry to hear that. Would you like a cup of warm milk and cinnamon?" she offered, a warm smile spreading across her face.

"That would be lovely." I smiled back at her, tucking my hair behind my ears. I watched as she made my milk over the copper saucepans. I remember when my mum used to make me warm milk when I was a little girl.

"Here we go, love. A nice hot cup of milk to help." She handed me the mug.

I held it up to my nose and sniffed. It smelt amazing. I pressed the mug against my lips and let the warm milk slide down my throat.

"Tell me to mind my own business, love, but is everything all right?" she asked while continuing to prep the meals for the day.

"It's okay." I looked over at her. "I'm not sure if it's the thought of Carter going back to work tomorrow and leaving me alone with Esme. It's still hard to get my head round it all, if I'm honest." I frowned, looking back down into my mug full of milk. I was interrupted when I heard her pull up a stool next to me, slowly putting her hand on mine.

"We are all here to help you. You won't be alone in this. It was quite a shock for us all. We're still getting used to having a baby around the house," she said, still holding onto my hand. "Please try not to worry. Mr Cole is only a phone call away. It's only one day then it's the weekend." She smiled as she let go.

"Thank you, Julia. I asked if he could just start back on Monday but he's got a big meeting that he can't get out of." I realized I was mumbling on. "I'm sorry. You're busy and I'm keeping you. I can't believe how early you have to get up to do all this." I felt extremely guilty for how much Julia did for us.

"It's my job. I enjoy it. Mr Cole is a wonderful boss. We are all very well looked after," she replied with a big smile on her face, she was blushing slightly under the dimmed kitchen lights.

"Anyway, I will leave you be. Thank you for the chat, Julia." I slid off the bar stool, taking my mug of warm milk with me to finish off.

"You are most welcome, Freya." She turned back and continued prepping the food.

As I walked out of the kitchen, I bumped into Carter. "Oh, shit," I muttered as I spilled warm milk down myself and him. "Sorry." I bit my lip as I slowly looked up at him.

"What are you sorry for? It was an accident. You don't always have to say sorry," he said quietly, his eyes still hazy from sleep, his hands holding the baby monitor. He took the cup out of my hand and took it into the kitchen. I turned and followed him.

"Good morning, Julia. Mmm, all looks good. I can't wait for dinner," he praised her before walking back out of the kitchen. "Why are you awake?"

"I, erm, I couldn't sleep," I responded, knotting my fingers before looking at him. My heart was thumping. He put his hand on the side of my face, my hand meeting his and resting on top of it. I leaned my face into it, closing my eyes for a moment.

"What's on your mind?" he whispered, not moving.

"A lot of things, but mainly you going back to work."

He took a deep breath and sighed. "It's one day, baby."

"I know it is. I'm just a bit worried. Being left alone with Esme is a big thing." I moved his hand from my face and let it go gently before crossing my arms and leaning up against the wall as I dropped my eyes to the floor.

He put his index finger on my chin and lifted it up so I was looking at him. "You won't be alone. You have Julia, Laura, and Brooke. Like I said, it's one day. You will survive. You have survived much worse," he said with a sarcastic smirk. "Anyway, come back to bed. It's too early." He kissed my cheek.

"I'm not tired. I'm going to jump in the shower before Esme wants me and I won't have a minute to myself," I hissed at him.

"Hey, are you pissed off with me?" He grabbed my hand as I went to walk away.

"Yeah, I am." I frowned as I faced him then pulled my hand out of his. "Just put yourself in my shoes for a bit and have a think!" I raised my voice as I stormed up the stairs. I heard him behind me. "And don't follow me!" I shouted as I walked into the main bathroom and locked the door. I didn't care that we had guests and I didn't care that Julia had heard that conversation.

I was furious. Why was he being insensitive? I turned the shower on and got undressed as I walked into the level shower, letting the water hit my skin. Why was I getting myself so worked up over this? I was back to work the next week myself. Elsie would be having Esme three days a week, and I'd only be having her for two. I was such an idiot. I lashed out at Carter for no reason at all, all because I was having a strop.

I left the shower and wrung out my hair before wrapping it in a towel, then wrapping another towel round me. I opened the bathroom door to find Carter sitting opposite, on the floor with his head in his hands. He looked up as I stood in front of him. He looked broken. His face withdrawn, his sage eyes dull. I dropped to my knees in front of him.

"What's wrong?" I asked in a hushed voice, mindful that our guests were still sleeping.

"I don't want to fight with you. This is how it starts," he said with anguish.

"How what starts?" I asked him. My brow furrowed, my eyes looking for my Carter who had somehow disappeared in the space of half an hour.

"Us breaking up," he said bluntly as he looked at his feet.

"What? We aren't breaking up." I put my hands either side of his face and lifted his head up to look at me.

"Then what is this? I never had a moment like this with the *others*." He spat the last word as if it was bitter.

"It's bickering," I said calmly. "Carter, we will fight, we will disagree, but one thing is for certain. I love you. More than you love yourself. We have been through hell and back and I'm sure we will visit there plenty more times, but this, this was a little argument because I'm in a mood. I'm tired, and I'm scared. I'm still getting to grips with this. I need you now more than ever, the same as you need me. I want to be able to confide in you, to be able to tell you when I'm scared, excited, worried, or hurt. There will be times we don't agree on things, and that's okay," I replied, his head still in my hands.

"I don't like it."

"I don't like it either, but it's called being an adult. Carter, our falling out after your 'Number Seven' comment was worse than this." I laughed.

"But you weren't mine then. You weren't my fiancée,"

he replied bleakly. "Freya, this battered old heart of mine is yours and yours only." He took my left hand from his face and placed it on his chest. *Boom, boom, boom.* "This is all for you, my sweet Freya. You have made this cold-hearted man feel love. I feel like you have thawed my heart from its icy cage. I have never felt love. I *thought* I was in love, but you, you have shown me feelings I could never have for anyone else. The last thing I want is for us to fight over something so silly." He took a breath, his eyes on mine the whole time.

"You aren't going to lose me," I whispered. "You are my world, everything I have ever wanted. I'm so glad you fell in love with me." I lifted my left hand up and touched the side of his face, leaning up and kissing him so delicately.

"I'm so glad I fell in love with you." He kissed me back, then took my left hand with my sparkling engagement ring and kissed it. "Soon, you'll be mine, in sickness and in health – 'til death do us part," he whispered.

"Come on. Let's go back to the bedroom. Esme will be up soon and you have to get ready for work." I held onto his knees as I pushed myself up off the floor then took his hand as he climbed up from the floor.

My heart. My Carter. My love.

I was sitting in bed feeding Esme when Carter walked

out of our dressing room in a light grey suit, white shirt, and a light pink tie. His tousled hair was styled, and his cologne smelt amazing.

"Hey, beautiful," he purred as he walked over to the bed before kissing me on the forehead and taking in my scent. He then leant down to kiss Esme.

"We like your tie, don't we, Esme?" I cooed at her.

"I chose it for my girls," he said as he sat down on the bed next to me. "So, I've been thinking," he started, placing his hand on my leg.

"I'm nervous," I muttered, smirking at him.

"Don't be nervous." He laughed. Oh, it was nice hearing his laugh again; it was a lot better than how I found him earlier.

"Anyway, I've been thinking." He winked at me. "Seeing as we weren't together on your thirtieth and, no doubt, you sat at home with your parents, Tilly, a bottle or two of wine, and *Friends*." He chuckled.

"Hey! Nothing wrong with that!" Little did he know that is exactly what I did. *I miss Tilly, but she's a lot happier at Mum's. She wouldn't like having Esme around.*

"I'm joking, baby." He smiled. "I want to take you away, just me and you." His eyes lit up as he was telling me. "What do you think?" He was like an excited kid.

"Yes!" I screamed. "Yes! Oh, Carter, I can't wait. Where are we going? When?" I asked. Now I was the excited kid.

"I'm not telling," he whispered as he leant into me and kissed me on the nose. "I've got to go, baby. I'll be home soon. Love you." He then kissed me on the lips.

"Have a good day. We love you." Esme was gurgling and cooing at Carter as he walked out of the room. I sighed. "Come on, baby girl. Just me and you. Well... and my friends. We can do this." I kissed her on the nose as she smiled at me. I got out of bed and walked towards her nursery.

"Hey! Freya, morning!" I turned around and smiled at Laura.

"Hey, hun!" I waited as she caught me up. "Did you sleep okay?"

"I slept like a log. These beds are amazing. Tyler has just left for golf with Peter." She smiled. "OMG, look at her." Laura beamed. "Can I hold her?"

"Of course!" I handed Esme to her as we walked into the nursery.

"She is like a doll. Are you not scared you're going to break her?" she questioned with worry all over her face. There was sheer panic in her eyes.

I leant towards her and whispered in her ear. "Every fucking day." I giggled. "Honestly, I get so scared that she will just break on me." I put my hands into my face.

"Well, Freya, you are doing such an amazing job. Given the circumstances and everything." She grumbled the last sentence. I looked over at Chloe's photo and my heart broke for her, and for Esme.

"I know, but I need to be the best mum I can be to that little girl. For her and Chloe's sake." I took Esme from Laura as I laid her down on her changing mat. "Mad to think in three months this will be you." I smiled at Laura.

"I know," she whispered. "I'm scared."

"Don't be scared. God, if I can do it, so can you," I reassured her. "At least you have time to get your head around it. It was like, BAM, here's a baby. But you know what, she was the best gift." I looked at Esme. "Aren't you?" I said in a high pitch baby-like voice, and she giggled. I put a new baby grow on her and laid her down for her nap. We walked out of the room and pulled the door to.

"You're dressed early. I thought most new mums spend most of their lives in PJs?" she joked.

"Oh, I've been up since four, so I managed to get an early shower." I laughed.

"Why didn't you sleep? Or don't I wanna know?" She nudged me.

"Oh, God. I wish! No, I just couldn't sleep. I think the fact that Carter left me today for the first time in six weeks was bothering me." I bit my lip. "But I need to get used to it. I'm back at work from Monday for three days and then I have her Thursday and Friday, which will be nice. Do you want a coffee? Or tea?" I asked Laura.

"Tea, please," she said as she struggled to get on the bar stool.

"Lau! Go and sit on the sofa in the lounge. Don't try and get on them," I said, trying not to laugh. She reminded me of a beetle on its back.

She went into the lounge and slumped down on the sofa. "I'm so fat!" she wailed.

"You are not fat!" I rolled my eyes. "You are pregnant. It's a gift."

Julia interrupted us by walking round the corner. "Morning, Freya. Would you like a coffee?" she asked politely.

"Thank you, Julia, but I was just about to make one, and a tea." I smiled at her.

"Don't be silly. Go join your friend. I will bring them in, along with breakfast."

I smiled at her and did as I was told.

I sat down on the sofa next to Laura and hovered my hands over her bump. "Can I?"

"Of course!" She beamed at me.

I placed both hands on her growing tummy. "Isn't it a miracle?" I sighed.

"It is." She placed her hand over mine. "Your time will come, babe."

"Oh, I know. I know." Just as I went to move my hand, I felt a thud against it. "Oh my God. Did she just kick me?" I asked excitedly.

"She did."

"That's amazing." I wiped my eyes; I felt so

emotional. "Auntie Freya loves you, baby Smythe." I automatically kissed her bump. I noticed Julia from the corner of my eye. I sat up as she walked over. "Thank you, Julia." I smiled and nodded at her.

She placed the tray down; one latte for me and a china cup of tea for Laura. Then she unloaded three plates of pancakes, bacon, and maple syrup.

"Let me know what your other friend would like to drink when she joins you. If she isn't here in five minutes, let me know and I will re-do her pancakes. Enjoy ladies." She nodded and walked out of the living room.

I picked up my latte and took a big mouthful. Oh, it was amazing. I needed it after being up most of the night.

"Morning, bitches!" Brooke walked into the living room. "Ohhh, are they my pancakes?" She licked her lips. "I'm starving."

"What would you like to drink, Brooke?" I asked before tucking into my pancakes.

"A coffee would be lovely. White Americano, please."

I walked into the kitchen but Julia wasn't there, I flicked the switch on the coffee machine and grabbed the milk out of the fridge. I walked back into the lounge with Brooke's coffee.

"Enjoy." I smiled as I gave it to her. I sat back down and put my pancakes on my lap and tucked in. They were good. We lightly chatted while stuffing our faces and drinking our coffees and tea. I had missed those girls, and

I was so glad they were there.

The wolf pack was back together. I smiled at the thought. I was so lucky.

CHAPTER FIVE

We had just got in from a walk around our grounds; there was still a lot of work to be done but it was nice having it all on our doorstep. I just loved how quiet it was.

"What time you all heading back?" I asked Laura and Brooke as I hung their coats up in the cloak closet.

Julia had taken Esme for her bottle and to put her down. We walked into the kitchen so I could put the kettle on; it was freezing out there.

"We will probably leave around dinner time. I don't want to leave." Laura groaned. "Can't I just move in with you?"

I laughed. "We have enough room for you all!" I said, boasting. I handed them both a cup of tea and pulled up a stool next to them.

"I hope the guys are having fun on the golf course," Brooke said.

"I'm sure they are. No work, no wives, just them and

the golf course," Laura piped up, nodding her head.

"I'm glad Carter gets on with Tyler and Peter. He hasn't seen his friends in so long. I've only met them once." I wrapped my fingers around my cup. "Thank you for coming again, girls. It was such a lovely surprise." I smiled.

"It was all Carter's idea." Brooke beamed.

"He is very thoughtful," I said to them both. "Always looks out for me."

"How's he finding fatherhood?" Brooke asked.

"He doesn't really say, but he is amazing with Esme. I think he has days like I do, but he never complains," I replied, tucking a loose strand of hair behind my ear. "We just take each day as it comes." I took a big sip of my tea.

I heard Julia come down the stairs and into the kitchen. "Ladies," she greeted us, smiling at us and putting the baby monitor on the worktop.

"Hey. Is Esme okay?" I asked.

"Fine. She took a little while to settle. She keeps putting her fists in her mouth. I think she's teething," she replied before walking to the fridge.

"Oh. Is she not too young?" I sighed.

Julia laughed. "No, of course not. It's quite normal for her age. I'm going to the shops in a little while to do our weekly shop. I will see if I can get her some teething gel. It might just help her settle a little easier in the night." She smiled at me gently before leaving.

"I am useless. I don't know anything about babies.

How could I not know she was teething?" I asked with defeat in my voice.

"Freya, you aren't useless!" Brooke slid off her stool and wrapped her arm around me. "I was the same when we had Lola. I didn't know she was teething until a tooth popped through!" She let go of me and leant on the breakfast bar. "You don't get a textbook telling you what to expect when you have a baby, you just have to learn. Even all those expensive baby classes I took before Lola was here didn't prepare me for motherhood. It is such a grey area. You are doing a great job. You only learn from not knowing. Now you know." She grinned at me.

"Honestly, Freya, don't beat yourself up over this. You are doing great." She kissed me on the cheek.

Once Esme was up, we all sat on the sofa binging on *Friends* when we heard the front door open. It was Carter.

"Hey, baby." He beamed at me, Tyler and Peter following him.

"Hey! I'm glad you're home. We've missed you." I smiled at him.

"I missed you both too." He walked over to me, kissing me passionately, then kissing Esme. "Come to Daddy," he said softly as he picked her up. She looked like a little doll in his big arms. She cooed and gave him her biggest, gummiest smile.

"Daddy's girl already. She's got him wrapped around her little finger," I said to the girls, smiling at them.

"Don't be jealous, sweetheart. You still have me wrapped around your little finger." He winked at me then wandered out of the room. *So cocky*.

"We really should be getting ready to make a move, Lau. Are you okay with that?" Tyler asked, standing with his hands in his pockets, waiting for her answer.

"Oh, okay. I'm ready when you are then," she said bluntly. She clearly didn't want to go.

"Fine by me," Peter said.

"Oh, I'm so sad to go." Brooke sulked, sticking out her bottom lip.

"I don't want you to go either, but you are always welcome over," I replied sadly.

Carter re-appeared with Esme's playmat and laid it down on the living room floor before laying her down gently on it. I looked at her lying there, kicking away happily.

"You leaving? I was going to sort some dinner out," he asked Tyler.

"Yeah, mate. We've got to get back, but thank you for the offer. We've had a great time." He walked over to Carter and shook his hand while putting his other arm round his broad shoulders. "I'll whip your arse at golf next time." He laughed and slapped Carter on the back before running up the stairs to get their bags.

I stood up and took Carter's hand in mine then wrapped my other hand around his arm.

Laura walked over to us and gave us both a cuddle. "Thank you for having us. Hopefully see you before your princess is here." She let go of us and rubbed her bump, smiling.

"I can't wait to meet her." I beamed.

"I can't wait either. Three months to go! I can't believe we're in February already," she said, shaking her head. "Time is flying."

"It really is." I sighed.

I looked up to see Tyler coming down the stairs with Peter in tow.

"See ya later, Freya. Hope to see you all soon." Tyler gave me a hug and a kiss on the cheek, and Peter did the same. I hugged Laura and Brooke before waving them off at the front door.

"Let's go and have some chill time," Carter said, leading me back to the lounge where Esme was gurgling and cooing at her playmat toys.

Bless her. Such a happy baby.

***

Monday morning soon rolled around. I couldn't believe the weekend was over already and Carter and I were back to work. We had a bad night with Esme, but we'd learned that we would be tired for the next eighteen years. I dragged myself out of bed and walked straight into the shower.

Elsie came down on Sunday evening, ready for her

three days with Esme. She had already taken her downstairs to feed her which was a nice treat. Selfish as it sounds, I was looking forward to going back to work for some 'me' time, as well as adult conversation.

I let the water hit my skin as I began to wash my hair when I felt Carter's arms wrap around my waist.

"Good morning, beautiful."

"Good morning," I replied.

Once I had finished lathering my hair, he turned me round gently and planted a kiss on my lips. "Hurry up. I need to shower," he teased.

"Well, you shouldn't have got in with me as I'm going to take even longer now," I said in a silky voice before pulling his hands off me and stepping back under the shower, rinsing my hair. When I looked up, he had a hungry look on his face, his eyes wide and his lips parted. "What are you looking at?" I asked, knowing exactly what he was looking at.

"You," he said bluntly.

Just as I reached for my conditioner bottle, his hands were on my face, pushing me against the wall of the shower. He slowly moved his hands from my face and ran his fingers down my arms before pushing them up above my head. Holding both of my wrists with his left hand, his right one moved down to my hips. His kisses trailed from my mouth down to my neck, before he looked back into my eyes. I looked at him, the water dripping off his head; he looked so hot. His left hand clasped my cheeks, his tongue invading my mouth hungrily, wanting me. He released my hands and took a handful of my hair, tilting my head back, his lips placing hot, wet, kisses down my throat. I wanted to look at him but his grip was too tight. His lips continued their trail down to my breast. I felt his wicked grin on my wet skin before he nipped my nipples with his teeth, then kissed them gently before taking my left one straight into his mouth, licking and flicking his tongue over it while still holding my head back against the wall and out of the water, the shower water hitting my sensitive breasts. I moaned out as I unclasped his grip from my hair and shook my head so my hair cascaded down my body.

"You minx," he teased before finding my mouth again. I hung my arms round his neck as his hands clenched my bum before lifting me up and slamming me back against the shower wall.

He held me effortlessly with one hand, while his other one maneuvered his hard, thick girth deep into me. I moaned as he filled me; I could never, ever get enough of him. He thrust into me hard as my back continued to hit the wall; it hurt, but I didn't complain. Removing my arms from his neck, I placed them on his chest and pushed myself off of him. He looked at me, confused.

"What are you doing?" he questioned me, out of breath.

"I want to be in control," I said seductively. I turned

him around so he was against the shower wall and pushed him to the floor. He dropped to his knees.

"I like this view," he said. He reached up and turned the shower pressure down slightly, and his fingers ran slowly up the inside of my right leg before stroking them between my thighs, bringing me back to life.

Ha, he was turning the tables. Not happening.

I grabbed his hand before he could take my body over with his tantalizing strokes. While holding his hands, I looked down at him and shook my head. "Tut tut." I dropped his hand to his side and smirked at him. "Sit with your back against the wall," I demanded.

This was hot. I liked telling him what to do.

"Oh, isn't someone bossy today?" he teased, then slowly bit his lips. "I like it."

I moved forward and stood over him so a leg was either side of his. I reached forward and turned the shower pressure back on, I smiled down at him.

"I like it too," I muttered before lowering myself down onto him. He groaned as he filled me once more. The water was hitting both of us. My hands were up around his face as I pulled his lips to mine, kissing him firmly as I started to move. His hands were on my hips, gripping them tightly. I threw my head back as the pleasure started to overtake my body. He sat forward as he started kissing my neck and my collarbone. I was getting hot. I ran my hands up into my hair, pulled it off my face, and held it in a ponytail. I started rotating my hips as he wrapped his arms around my waist and started to thrust up into me, matching my rhythm.

"Oh, Carter," I moaned as he sat back against the wall and watched me, waiting for me to unravel over him.

His left hand was back on my hip, his right was making its way to my sweet spot, slowly caressing me. I could feel my climb, the feeling of him deep inside me and the exquisite sensation of his strokes over my sex. I couldn't hold on anymore.

"Carter, I'm going to come."

"Don't," he growled. "I'm not finished with you yet, Miss Greene."

He lifted me off of him and turned me over onto my knees. Carter sat on his knees behind me before grabbing my hips and pulling me down back onto him so I was resting on his thighs. All my senses were heightened. I wanted to release myself. I needed to release myself. He kept one hand splayed against my stomach, the other back in my hair, pulling my head back. His lips were on my neck, this time nipping at each thrust into me. His splayed hand moved down in between my legs and started slowly rubbing me in my sensitive spot. It only took a few strokes before I moaned; I couldn't hold back. I started moving against his thrusts, building myself back up, ready for my release, then with one more hard tug of my hair and another nip, I cried out his name. "Carter, please. Don't stop," I said, panting.

"Come, Freya," he demanded.

As soon as the words were off his tongue, I came hard around him, not holding back on my moaning. He let go of my hair before finding his own high. I had to catch my breath. I slowly moved onto all fours and looked at him over my shoulder as he was coming down from his high. I bit my lip, not taking my eyes off him.

"What a delightful view," he said as he kneeled behind me, taking my hips and pulling me into him before leaning down on my back and whispering in my ear. "Round two?"

"No, Mr Cole. I have to go to work. It's my first day back and I can't be late," I said sternly.

My heart was thumping. I didn't want to say no to him. Of course I wanted him again; I always wanted him. He removed his hand from one of my hips and ran his finger down my buttocks and slid his index finger deep into me. "You don't want this?" he teased.

I nipped my arm and moaned as the pleasure hit me deep in my stomach. "No," I whispered under my breath. I lied.

"Are you sure?" He grinned as he slid a second finger in and continued his slow, teasing movements. He tightened his grip on my hip as he carried on. Before I knew what I was doing, I started moving my hips with him, moans slipping from me. "Enjoying that, baby?"

"Mmm," was all I could reply with. I could feel my legs beginning to tremble, a second wave about to hit me, yet he didn't stop. He kept the same rhythm.

"Let it go," he said. I could hear the grin in his voice. "Come," he whispered. He tipped my body over the edge. I was already on the brink but he gave me the last nudge I needed.

How could he do this to me? He owned me, my body, my heart, my soul. With one last, tantalizing stroke, I came again, this time harder than before.

"Fuck," I whispered while looking over my shoulder at his smug expression that was spread across his face. He slowly removed his fingers before putting them both in his mouth and sucking them dry.

My insides squirmed. *Shit, he is so hot.* His eyes focused on me, his wicked grin spreading across his face, then his teeth sank into his bottom lip and pulled it in before giving me a hard slap on the arse. "Go get ready, wifey. You will be really late if you stay in that position. I can keep going, especially with you. I never tire of you. You are intoxicating. I could fuck you all day long, and one day, I am going to. I want you begging." He smirked.

He helped me up from the shower floor. I frowned when I realized I hadn't conditioned my hair. Messy bun it was.

"I'm looking forward to that day." I blushed.

"I'll get it sorted," he replied before kissing me on my

sensitive lips. I wrapped myself in a towel and brushed my teeth while watching Carter enter the shower again. I winked at him as I walked into our dressing room. *This man. My God.*

I rummaged through my underwear drawer and picked out black, lacy French knickers and a matching balcony bra. I slipped the knickers up my thighs and over my bum, then put my beautiful bra on. I slowly slid black stockings up to my thighs before connecting them onto my suspender belt. I was interrupted by a wolf whistle. I looked in the mirror at Carter.

"I'm a lucky son of a bitch," he said smugly as he walked over slowly, wrapping his arms around my waist and burrowing his head in my neck, planting a soft kiss. "You look beautiful, but please don't go to work like that," he joked.

"This is only for you, baby." I winked at him as he walked over to his side of the wardrobe and pondered over which suit to wear.

"Go for the grey one," I suggested. "You look hot in grey." I smirked at him. "And go for the pink tie, then maybe you can tie me up with it later." I giggled and blushed. I wasn't normally so forward.

"Oh, I will, you just wait," he teased before disappearing into the bedroom. I slipped my black, capped sleeve shirt on and my leather pencil skirt which I tucked my shirt into. I put my Rolex on then pushed my engagement ring onto my finger and smiled. I quickly dried my hair before pulling it up into a messy bun. I applied a light dusting of bronzer and mascara then applied a red lipstick. *Perfect*, I thought, before spraying my Chanel No. 5. I slipped my Louboutins on and grabbed my Neverfull bag then entered the bedroom to grab my phone.

Carter walked back into the bedroom. "Wow, you look wonderful, Freya. I can't wait to get you home tonight."

"I look forward to it, Mr Cole. I've got to go."

He interrupted me. "Give me five and James and I will drop you to work."

"Okay, hurry up." I smirked before leaving the bedroom.

I saw Elsie sitting in the lounge with Esme.

"Morning, Elsie. I'm leaving in five minutes. Is everything okay?" I asked.

"Everything is fine. Freya, you look radiant. You're glowing." She smiled at me.

"Thank you, Elsie." I blushed again. I knelt down and picked Esme up off her playmat.

"Hey, bubba. Mummy and Daddy have got to go to work. Be a good girl for Nanny," I told her, her beautiful gummy smile appearing, then I realized she was looking at Carter over my shoulder.

"Hey, baby girl." He leaned in and gave her a kiss,

then I kissed her.

"Any problems, Elsie, please call. I can get home as soon as possible." I smiled warily. I was nervous about leaving her.

"Enjoy your break, Freya. She will be fine," she reassured me.

My eyes searched Carter's face.

"She will be fine, baby." He agreed with his mum. "Come on, we need to go." He gave his mum a kiss on the cheek before grabbing my hand and leading me to the front door. "Stop worrying. She will be fine."

"I know, just nervous." I smiled at him.

"I know, baby," he replied, kissing me on my forehead before walking out the door and closing it behind us.

It'll be fine.

CHAPTER SIX

It was nice being back in the office. The last six weeks had gone so quickly. I sat and watched the office while I waited for my computer to load.

"Welcome back, bestie." Courtney came bounding over like an excited puppy. "I've missed you." She beamed at me as she flicked her long, gold locks over her shoulder before sitting on the corner of my desk.

"I've missed you too." I smiled at her. "It's good to be back. So, are you going to bring me up to speed or shall I go and sit with Morgan?"

"No, I'll do it. I'll go make you a coffee. Meet me in the meeting room in five." She smacked the desk as she got up and walked towards the kitchen.

I took a deep breath. The last time I sat there, I was pregnant. My hand slowly moved across my tummy before I quickly moved it away. I checked my phone, smiling when I saw a message from Carter.

Enjoy your day baby. I can't wait for tonight.

I love you xx

I smiled as I typed a quick response back to him before walking into the meeting room. I took my seat and waited for Courtney to appear.

"Hey, sorry. Here," she said, passing me the coffee she made.

"Everything okay?" I asked her.

"Yeah, fine, just some issues at reception," she assured me. "Okay, so let me brief you." She smiled.

An hour later, I sat back at my desk, my brain numb from the amount of information I had just taken in. Everything was going well. We had signed five new authors which now made me busy, but I preferred to be busy than twiddling my thumbs. I flicked through the paperwork she had given me and started reading one of the manuscripts while I waited for my mailbox to download all my unread messages. After a few minutes, I could use my computer. I started reading the old messages, just to make sure nothing had been missed, then lost myself in my work.

I stretched my arms above my head then rolled my neck. It was five p.m. already. I wrote a few notes of things that I had to get completed for the next day before logging out of my computer.

"Freya, we're going for a drink tomorrow night in the local bar. Fancy it?" Courtney asked.

"I will check with Carter, but I don't think we have anything on. That will be nice. I haven't been out in so long." I smiled at her.

"Good. If you can get Esme looked after, bring Carter along. I bet he could do with a drink. How are you feeling being back?"

"Yeah, okay." I laughed. "Just trying to get my head around it all again," I said, eyeing up my growing pile of paperwork.

"You'll get there. I will help where I can anyway. I am your assistant, after all."

"Thank you, Courtney. I'll see you tomorrow. Carter should be outside." I picked my bag up and gave Courtney a quick hug.

"Bye, hun. See you tomorrow." She let me go and walked back over to her desk.

I walked down to reception and waited in the lobby for James to arrive. I checked my phone and flicked through Facebook to kill some time when I could feel someone's eyes on me. I looked up around the reception area; there was only Josh, the new security guard, and Alex on reception. I shook my head and looked back at my phone, but I felt uneasy. I looked up again out of the reception windows when I saw someone standing on the opposite side of the road, watching me. I walked slowly towards the window. It was hard to focus on him as the London rush hour traffic was crawling along. I pushed myself through the doors but he was gone. It could have just been my imagination, but he looked like Jake, only he had light hair. I threw my arm down and looked down the street, left and right, but he had vanished, as if into thin air.

I watched as James pulled up outside our offices. He stepped out and opened my door. "Thank you, James," I said politely.

"Hey, beautiful," Carter purred.

"Hey" I replied as I slid into the car next to him, leaning over and kissing him on the lips.

"You okay?" I asked him.

"I'm even better now I'm with you." He smiled, taking my hand in his. "You?"

"Yeah. Busy already." I laughed. "It feels like I never left. But, as I left the office today, I felt someone looking at me. When I looked up, I saw a man." Carter's face turned serious, his eyes focused on mine. "It looked like Jake."

I felt his grip tightening around my hand. "Jake!" He growled. "What the fuck, Freya?"

"It may not have been him, I'm just saying it…"

He cut me off. "It obviously was him," he said bitterly.

"Carter," I said quietly, trying to calm him down.

"What?" he snapped at me.

"Nothing," I said bluntly, pulling my hand from his

and burying it in my lap.

"Freya," he said, defeated.

"I don't want to hear it," I replied before looking out the window. I heard him mutter *fuck* under his breath before taking a deep breath. We sat in silence for the car journey home.

Once we pulled up outside, I didn't wait for James to open my door. I bolted straight for our front door and ran up to our bedroom. I was so angry. How fucking dare he speak to me like that? I slammed the bedroom door behind me then threw my bag down onto the floor and collapsed on the bed. My insides were boiling.

Carter came storming through the door shortly after me. "Don't walk away from me," he growled, still seething.

"Well, don't speak to me like that," I bit back, crossing my arms as I stood from the bed.

His face softened as he got closer to me. "I just saw red," he said quietly, slowly pulling my arms from their crossed position.

"Okay, you saw red, but what just happened wasn't my fault. I told you I *thought* I saw Jake, then you just blew up," I said, frowning at him.

"Because I hate him."

"So do I, Carter, but going off on me isn't going to change that, is it? I told you because I don't like keeping anything from you." I bit my lip as my eyes searched his.

"I'm sorry. But I swear, Freya, if it is him," he said

disgusted, "and he comes anywhere near you, I will kill him, do you understand?"

"He isn't going to come anywhere near me. Please believe me."

"You don't know that," he hissed.

"Yes, I do." The truth is, if it was Jake, he was only coming for me. "Carter, please can you drop this? I told you because I wanted you to know. It could have been someone that looks like him. Don't let this ruin our evening," I said as I placed my hands on his tie, running it in between my index and middle finger before pulling it gently.

He let out a deep sigh before leaning down and kissing me on the lips. "Fine, but I won't forget this. You will be coming with me every day to work, and coming home every night with me." He winked at me, trying to soften his little demand.

"That's fine," I said, "but, you should know…"

"Oh, here we go." He rolled his eyes.

"I've been invited out with Courtney and the girls tomorrow for a few drinks after work." I watched his facial expression change.

"Well, I can't stop you, can I? But do you have to?"

"How about, Mr Cole, you come with me? See if your mum would mind watching Esme for a couple more hours than you can join us," I asked, hoping he would take me up on my offer.

"Fine. Now let's go see our little girl." He pulled me into him and kissed me once more. His kiss was hungry, fierce. He was clearly still angry.

Carter was feeding Esme as I finished my dinner. Elsie had excused herself for the evening. He hadn't said anything, but I could see he was stewing over what had happened.

"I'm taking her up. Are you going to say goodnight?" he asked bluntly. I finished my mouthful before getting up and kissing her goodnight, and he disappeared without a word. I loaded my plate into the dishwasher and poured myself a glass of wine. I heard Carter talking to Elsie upstairs as I walked out of the kitchen, asking if she would take over with Esme for the rest of the night.

I tiptoed up the stairs when I saw Carter walking along the landing. "Why are you sulking?" I questioned him as I got to the top of the stairs.

"I'm not," he said harshly.

"Yes, you are! You're acting like a child." I scowled at him.

"Am I?" he said in a low voice.

"Yes," I said, before taking a sip of my wine.

"Oh, really." He walked over to me, his eyes dark. I grabbed the oak bannister behind me as he pushed himself up against me, trying to steady myself. "How about I show you how I'm feeling?" he whispered in my ear.

My heart jumped up my throat. I couldn't answer him

back. I had lost my voice.

"Come," he demanded as he took my hand and walked me to the bedroom then took my wine glass and placed it on the bedside cabinet before standing in front of me. I was nervous. I had never seen this side of him. I felt like I did when he first stepped into my office; intimidated.

He twirled a loose strand of my auburn hair around his finger and smirked before taking my hair out of its messy bun. His eyes burned into mine. Shit, I was in trouble. I was excited and terrified at the same time. Was I about to meet 'old Carter?' The one I never got to meet?

I stilled my breath as he stroked his finger down my cheek, along my jaw, and down to my collarbone. He stopped at the buttons of my black shirt, slowly undoing them then pushing my shirt off my shoulders and letting it drop to the floor, biting his lip. He grabbed my chin and pulled my face up towards his, then pulled my bottom lip in between his teeth and breathed in. He dropped his hand from my face, releasing it before smoothing both hands down my leather pencil skirt. I kept my eyes on him the whole time, afraid to move, but so wanting him at the same time. He undid my zip and let my skirt fall to the floor.

"Step out," he whispered while taking my hand to steady me. I still had my Louboutins on. I did as he said. "You look..." He stopped and let out a deep breath. "Beautiful," he whispered, with a dark, devilish look. He stepped back to marvel at me, and I felt myself blush.

"Such a lucky bastard," he muttered under his breath.

He loosened the pink tie I chose for him that morning and wrapped it around his hand before throwing it on the bed, his eyes devouring me. He took a step towards me then ran his finger under my suspender belt.

"I like this." His lips twitched before the corners broke into a little smile. He dropped to his knees in front of me and spread my legs slightly with his hand as he planted soft kisses along the lace of my stockings, nipping at my hot, sensitive skin.

We had hardly touched, yet my skin was on fire. I looked down at him as he continued to plant wet kisses along my thigh, his right hand making its way between my legs, brushing my sex as he did before grasping my right arse cheek and giving it a squeeze. I moaned out of frustration.

"Be patient," he said, pressing his smile against my thigh. His hand slowly moved back around to my front as he pressed his thumb firmly against my sweet spot, making me moan again. His fingers slowly made their way inside my black thong and slipped straight into me. I was so ready for him, but he wasn't going to make it that easy. He moved his face against my naval and kissed it while his fingers caressed me inside. My fingers found his tousled hair and lost themselves in it as they grabbed it, tugging it gently in response to his pleasure. My breath caught; I wanted him to take me now. My body needed a release.

"Stop," he commanded as he slipped his fingers out. "Go wait by the bed." His eyes were still dark. He wasn't letting this go.

I slipped my shoes off and walked over to the foot of the bed. I caught my reflection in the wall mirror. I was flushed. I bit my lip as I saw Carter walking around the corner with a duffle bag. *What the fuck is that?* I thought. *Oh, shit. Maybe he's going to kill me.* I rolled my eyes at my stupid thought. He dumped the duffle bag on the floor and smirked at me. He undid his shirt and threw it across the room, then unbuttoned his suit trousers and dropped them to his ankles before softly kicking them away. The god was standing there, tanned, toned, and sexy. His sex lines made my mouth go dry. Why was he making me wait?

He crouched down, reached inside the duffle bag and pulled out some handcuffs.

"Cuffs?" I questioned him, trying not to show the fear that was slowly tearing away at my insides.

He skulked over to me. "If you would have taken me up on my offer of being one of my '*flavours*' then you would know what this was all about. This is the old me. The old me that likes to make appearance when certain arseholes piss me off, so, for that, I am now going to take my anger out on you, like this." He reached into the bag again, this time pulling out a crop. "This will be a pleasure you have never felt before," he said, a twisted smile appearing across his gorgeous, strained face. "Put your arms behind your back," he demanded.

I did as he said. The cuffs nipped my wrists, but in a good way. My heart was racing, I didn't know what to expect. He spun me around so my knees were resting on the ottoman at the end of our bed. He stood close behind me; I could feel how aroused he was. He splayed his hand out over my bare stomach, then worked his way into my thong before stroking me gently on my sweet spot. I threw my head back onto his chest, letting out a quiet moan. His free hand found my throat as he delicately wrapped his fingers around it. I felt his lips on my ear.

"I am going to fuck you. So hard." He growled.

He pulled his hand back out of my thong, leaving me wanting even more. He reached for his pink tie that was thrown on the bed and placed it gently over my eyes before tying it round the back of my head. His hand found my hip then squeezed it before he pushed me forward, pushing my knees up onto the ottoman. He ran his finger down my back and slowly over my backside. I felt exposed. My face was on the bed, my backside in the air, and still in my full underwear set.

"What a beautiful sight," he said.

I tried to move my hands, but that only made the cuffs nip my skin more. I felt the tip of the crop on my spine as he slowly moved it down again to my backside before giving it a snap on my right cheek.

"Ah," I moaned.

He did the same routine again, another snap of the crop but now on my left cheek. I heard him take a deep breath as he dropped the crop to the floor then dropped down to his knees and planted kisses on both of my cheeks before pulling my thong to the side. I was so hot for him; I needed him now. He slowly filled me with two fingers, and I moaned against him. I couldn't do anything, I was helpless, but I was loving every minute as he continued to pleasure me with his strokes. I was building, so close to my tipping point. I didn't want him to stop. After a few more strokes, he slowly withdrew his fingers then bent over my body, putting his fingers in my mouth, I had never done anything like this before, but it was hot. He smirked as he took his fingers from my mouth then stood behind me. I felt his hard shaft on me. He reached forward and grabbed my loose auburn hair and wrapped it around his fist, pulling my head up and making my back arch, still completely helpless and bounded by the cuffs. My senses were heightened, every movement so much more intense. He tightened his grip on my hair as he buried himself into me, filling me. I cried out as he smashed into me again, hard. I felt the anger and release in every movement into me as he growled. He was full of frustration that he was taking out on me again and again; he wasn't letting up. He tugged my head back again with force as he sped up. He needed a release and I wanted to give it him and bring him down from the anger that he was feeling. I started moving my hips back into him. He grabbed my hip with his free hand, forcing me into him.

"Fuck." He sucked air through his teeth. "I'm getting close, Freya," he growled as he continued his forceful movements in and out of me.

Not going to lie, I loved not having control. I loved that he had taken over my mind, body, and soul. I wanted to give my man everything. My climb had begun. I was so close to erupting from his delicious and raw rhythm. I moaned out loudly as my orgasm was about to crash around him.

"Oh, Carter. I'm going to come," I cried out as he slapped my arse cheek hard as he hit his climb, us both shattering around each other.

We stilled for a moment, taking the last few moments in. He leant across my back and kissed the side of my head, releasing my hair and un-doing the tie. He stood and undid the handcuffs. Oh, it felt good to have my arms back. They felt dead. I put my hands on my thighs and pushed myself up off the ottoman. My legs were trembling; everything was so intense. I touched my lips as I thought about what just happened, and smiled.

"Hey, are you okay?" he asked, pushing my hair away from my face before placing his hand on my cheek, and cupping it softly.

"I'm fine." I placed my hand over his and smiled. I was sore, but I was okay.

"I went soft on you. That was nothing," he teased before smirking at me. "You wait 'til next time. I have plenty more hidden toys." He kissed me. "I'm sorry for my mood."

"Me too. I just wanted to tell you."

"I know, baby, and if we see him again then we will deal with it," he said bluntly. "I'm not having that prick coming back into our lives."

I wanted to respond but decided not to. "I love you," I whispered.

"I love you more, my queen," he said before finding my mouth again and losing himself in me once more.

CHAPTER SEVEN

I lay awake, the moonlight beaming through our window. I couldn't settle, I just lay and watched him. My God. He was so, distractingly good-looking. I could never get enough of him. I wanted to grow old with him. I wanted him to be my forever and always.

I sighed as I lifted his dead, heavy arm and snuggled underneath it. I gently ran my fingertips over his toned chest, slowly back and forth while my mind wandered. I was dreading work in the morning. Carter wouldn't let me go alone if he thought it was Jake that I saw. It surely wouldn't be him after all this time. I hadn't heard from him since I left Elsworth. I shook the thoughts away. I needed to sleep.

Thirty minutes later, I was still tossing and turning. Elsie had taken Esme into her room so Carter and I could have a break. I had to be up in a few hours, but by that point, I was mentally exhausted but too over-tired to sleep.

My mind kept going over everything. I couldn't seem to shut off. I rolled over and watched Carter, jealous that he was so settled. *Bastard*. I bit my lip as I propped myself up on my left arm, watching him for a moment as he slumbered on his back. I kneeled up and sat myself on top of him, reaching down and planting a kiss on his full, soft lips as my fingers slowly wrapped around his strong, chiselled jaw. He stirred underneath me, slowly opening his eyes.

"Freya, what's wrong?" he asked sleepily, but panicked.

"I can't sleep." I leaned back down, kissing him again. "I need you to keep me busy," I said as I sat up on him after kicking my white, silky shorts off. My auburn hair was loose and tumbling past my breasts.

"Do you now?" he muttered, his lips twisting up slightly.

I lifted myself as I put my hand down his boxers and started pleasuring him slowly. He growled as he started to awaken from his deep sleep. He reached his hand around the back of my head and pulled me down to him, crashing his mouth into mine as our tongues entwined with each other. His other hand slowly and gently slipped down the spaghetti strap of my white, silky vest. His hand was on my breast instantly, rolling my nipple between his fingers, bringing my body to life. I moaned into his mouth. I lifted myself up as he pulled his boxers down, freeing himself. I smirked at him as his sage eyes started to devour me. I lowered myself onto him, taking every inch of him in. Would I ever have enough of this feeling? His hands were on my hips, guiding me with his rhythm. I already felt drugged by him.

"Make love to me," I whispered as a slight moan left my lips.

He sat up and cradled me as his hips thrusted up into me, my hips moving with his every move. I threw my head back as I placed my hands behind me and held onto his knees. The pleasure was overwhelming. I loved being fucked by him, but him making love to me was so much more intense. He trailed his wet kisses down my neck and collarbone before finding my breasts then taking them into his mouth, one at a time. He slowly nipped and sucked on my nipple as he caressed the inside of me with each thrust. That wonderful, deep pleasure pool was starting to fill. I wanted it to overflow and intoxicate us. His slow, teasing thrusts were getting too much.

"You drive me fucking insane," Carter whispered against me as he kissed my throat.

"The feeling is mutual," I teased, panting while my fingers got lost in his hair. I was there already, my peak about to shatter around him, consuming every bit of him I could, as always. It was like he could read my mind. One final, deep thrust into me sent me spiralling into heaven as I started my comedown from this beautiful, addictive high, with him following. I smirked as he pulled me down on top of him, his arms wrapped around my back, his fingers slowly making their way up and down my spine. My hair splayed out to the side of me, while my head rested gently on his chest.

"Please sleep, princess," he demanded, but his voice was soft.

"I will. I'm exhausted now." I lifted my head and grinned at him.

"Good," he mumbled sleepily before kissing my forehead. I lay my head back down onto his chest and nuzzled into him. As much as I wanted to move, I couldn't. I needed to hear his heartbeat. I needed to feel all of him. My eyes started feeling heavy before I drifted off into a deep sleep.

I woke with a jolt when I realized Carter wasn't next to me. I rolled over and looked at my phone. It had gone seven. I stretched out and took a moment to wake up. I saw Carter strolling out of the dressing room.

"Morning, baby," he said as he walked over, kneeling on the bed and kissing me.

"Morning to you too." I smiled at him, and his eyes glistened. "You feeling better today?" I teased.

"Hmm," he mumbled as he sat up, twiddling his thumb as his mouth twitched before breaking into a little smile. "I am." He winked at me as he stood up. "Now, Ms Greene, get out of bed and get dressed. You don't want to be late for work." He kissed me on the head before disappearing back into the dressing room.

I slowly got out of bed and made my way to the en-suite. I showered quickly and brushed my teeth before making my way back into the dressing room. I threw on a pair of high waist trousers and a black ruffled front shirt which I tucked in then slipped into my black stiletto heels. I brushed my knotty hair then tucked it behind my ears before putting on a light dusting of bronzer. I applied some soft, red lipstick. I heard the sound of Carter's shoes along the hardwood floor of the dressing room.

"Your butt looks fantastic in them." I heard the smile in his voice as he wrapped his arms around my waist and kissed my neck. "I can't wait for you to be my wife," he whispered.

I laughed as I turned to face him, his arms firmly around my waist. "Well, Mr Cole, we actually need to set a date and plan," I said sarcastically as I admired my engagement ring.

"Well, isn't that down to you, baby?"

"It's up to both of us. Anyway, I don't want a big wedding. I just want me, you, Esme, our parents and Ava, a couple of our close friends. Oh, and Julia and James."

"Really?" He didn't sound convinced.

"Yes. Really. Why would I want a lavish wedding when all I want is to show you how much I love you? It's me and you remember?" I reached up and kissed him.

"I love you. Okay, so if you want intimate, let's do intimate. I need you to be my wife now. I've waited long enough." He lifted me up and squeezed me. "Come on. Let's go say our goodbyes to Esme and get you to work." He took my hand as we left the bedroom and made our way downstairs.

"Morning, baby girl," I cooed as I took Esme from Elsie. "Oh, Mummy misses you. One more day at work tomorrow then we have two days just me and you, bubba!" Her beautiful gummy smile melted my heart.

Carter stood next to us and kissed Esme on the head. "Love you, baby girl." He smiled as she wrapped her fingers round his. We stood there taking the perfect moment in. We heard Elsie ahhing as she snapped a picture on her phone. "Oh, Carter, you need to get this printed and framed." She smiled at her phone.

"We will, Mum. Thank you for taking that. Now, come on, queen. We really need to go." He sighed.

I kissed Esme again before handing her back to Elsie. "See you tonight."

"See you tonight, darling. Dinner will be ready for six."

"Oh, Mum. Sorry, I forgot to say. Freya and I are popping out for an hour after work. I know I mentioned that we *might* be going, but we decided to go. Can we push dinner back until seven? I'll owe you." He flashed her his perfect smile, his eyes twinkling as he worked his magic on her.

"Of course," she said, still smiling. "You two need some time out. Enjoy it." She walked out of the lounge into the kitchen without saying another word.

We sat in the car on the way to our offices in silence. Carter was rubbing his thumb over my knuckles while scrolling through his work emails. James slowed up outside my office and pulled into a parking space.

I turned to face Carter. "Have a good day." I leant over to kiss him, our lips touching. I didn't want to stop.

"Have a good day, baby."

I bent down and looked through the door, his eyes devouring me while looking me up and down. "Bye, God." I winked as James shut the door behind me. Oh, that man.

I walked into the office and wished Alex good morning as I made my way to the lift. I smiled as I entered our main office and slipped into my little room. I dumped my bag down and placed my phone on my desk then put my coat on my coat hook.

Courtney popped in. "Hey, you." She beamed at me. "Are you coming for drinks tonight? Please say yes!"

"Yes, we are coming." I looked up from my computer screen and smiled at her.

"Yay! And Carter? Ohh, it'll be so good. Morgan will be there as well." She held her hands together in front of her face while smiling. "Anyway, I'll leave you to it." She walked towards the door, grabbing the doorframe on her way out and turning to face me. "Oh, there's someone in the meeting room for you." Before I could ask who it was, she was gone.

I opened my emails and put my ever-growing pile of paperwork in front of my computer. I checked my phone before standing up and making my way into the meeting room. As I walked in, I saw a young man sitting there, nibbling on his nails anxiously. I looked at him, confused, then stepped back out into the main office and threw Courtney a puzzled look. She just shrugged at me. I looked back into the meeting room before going in and sitting down in front of him. I studied him for a minute. His crystal blue eyes looked glazed. His light brown hair had speckles of blonde running through it; his long fringe flopped onto his forehead. He was slim and tall, his face gaunt with blonde stubble. I couldn't work out why he looked so familiar. Then it dawned on me. This was the guy I saw the day before, watching me from across the road.

"Hey. I'm Freya Greene. I've been told you wanted to see me? Are you an author who has submitted a manuscript?" I asked him, confused but confident.

He was still nibbling at his nails. He looked up at me, his blue eyes searching mine, wide with worry. "I need to talk to you," he said with a serious tone in his voice.

I smiled at him. "Well, I'm here. What do you need to talk to me about?" I asked, sitting back in my chair and crossing my legs.

"I want to see my baby," he said bluntly, with authority. He dropped his hands to the table.

"Sorry?" I stifled a laugh, but it was more from the shock of what he had just said.

"Esme, right?" A wicked twist in his mouth appeared. I felt sick.

"Esme is mine and my fiancé's daughter," I corrected him. I placed my hands on my thighs and rubbed them slowly down to my knees. My palms were sweaty.

"No." He smirked, looking up at me through his floppy fringe. "No, she's not. She is nothing to do with you or Carter."

"Is this some sick joke? Tell me what's going on before I call security and have you arrested!" I pushed myself up and stood, hands on my hips.

He stood up too and walked slowly over to me, running his long, skinny index finger along the edge of the meeting room table before standing in front of me. I backed myself against the wall. His breath smelt stale. He towered over me, even though I had my heels on. He placed one hand up against the wall next to my head and the other came up to my face, grabbing my chin hard while his fingers were on my cheeks. I winced.

"That baby you are bringing up isn't yours," he snarled, his eyes not leaving mine. "Can you not give Carter a baby of his own?" he spat as his voice got louder.

"Please, get off me. You must be confused. We were

told Esme was ours." I placed my right hand on his wrist, trying to pull his hand from my face, but that only made his grip tighter. I looked to the office door, praying that someone would burst through.

He laughed as he watched me. "Pathetic," he whispered in my ear. "You know why I'm here. This was all part of the plan. Me and Chloe had it all sussed out. The 'doctor' was in on it. Chloe knew she was pregnant. She lied. The only thing we didn't foresee was her dying. Now I want to do what I promised." His mouth was still close to my ear. His free hand ran down to my hip, then slowly down to my thigh when he stopped and gave it a squeeze. "Carter broke Chloe's heart. So now I'm breaking his," he said with a wicked grin.

I was petrified. I didn't know what he was going to do. I didn't want to scream as I didn't know what he was capable of. My heart was beating so fast. His hand that was on my hip started its trail again, slowly wandering and exploring my body. I closed my eyes as a tear rolled down my cheek.

"I'm taking my daughter. She is mine, but not before I take you," he said, his breathing fast as his fingers continued trailing across my body.

My eyes opened wide when I heard the office door go, my eyes meeting his. My Carter.

He flew through the door and tackled the man to the floor, throwing a punch at his face.

"Who are you?" he shouted as he threw another punch at him. "WHO THE FUCK ARE YOU?"

The man didn't say anything. He just lay there smirking and antagonizing Carter.

"Carter, he's not worth it. Get off him," I pleaded.

Carter looked over his shoulder at me, his eyes dark, full of anger. He had this man by the scruff of his t-shirt, one fist still hovering over his face. I breathed when I saw that security had arrived along with Morgan. Morgan walked over to where Carter still had the man pinned down and shook his head before placing his brogues on the man's chest, pushing down slightly and grinning. He patted Carter on the shoulder as Carter climbed off him.

"Pathetic piece of shit," Carter growled at him. "Get him the fuck out of here."

I had my hand over my mouth, trying to register and take everything in that had just happened.

"Freya, baby." He took me into his embrace, kissing my head before inspecting my face. My cheeks felt bruised from his grip. "Did that bastard hurt you?"

"I'm fine." I sniffed as I threw myself into Carter's chest. "How did you know?" I asked him quietly.

"Courtney called me. She said some random man demanded a meeting, so I came as soon as I could. Come on. Let's get out of here," he said, kissing me on my head again. "Everything okay, Morgan?" Carter asked.

Morgan was still standing there with his foot on the

man's chest. "Yeah, mate. All sorted. Get Freya home. I'll call you later." He nodded at Carter as we walked out of the meeting room.

Just as we got to the door, the man shouted out, grinning like the Cheshire Cat. "I'm not finished with you yet, Freya. I will come back for you. You owe me that."

Carter grabbed my hand and pulled me in front of him. His hand moved to the small of my back as we made our way through the main office. I could feel everyone's eyes on me. "Go get your things and don't worry about him. He won't get near you again," he whispered as he ushered me into my office. I shut my computer down and grabbed my phone, bag, and coat.

On the way home, I kept playing the scenario over and over. Carter was on the phone to his doctor. He wanted a DNA test carried out on Esme and himself. I was too busy daydreaming to hear what he was saying but came back around once I heard him snap.

"Just get it fucking sorted. This needs to be dealt with," he said as he cut his phone off. His hand, clenched into a fist, was pressed against his forehead as his elbow rested on his knee.

"Carter, this man is probably doing this just to hurt you," I said quietly.

"I don't fucking care. Why would someone just say that? If she is his baby then that's that," he said bluntly.

"What do you mean?" I asked him, brows furrowed.

"Exactly that. If Esme is his baby, she goes out of our care, Freya."

"But she's our daughter." I bit my lip, trying to take the focus off the fact that my eyes were welling up.

"If this prick is right, then no, she's not. She never was!" he snapped at me, regret all over his face as soon as he said it. "Freya, I'm sorry. I've got so many emotions coursing through me at the moment I just don't know how to deal with them all." He moved closer to me. "What if he had hurt you? What if he had done something to you?" His eyes flitted back and forth to mine.

"But he didn't. I'm okay. Shaken, worried, and heartbroken, but okay," I said, my voice shaking slightly. "When are you in with the doctor?"

"I'm waiting for a call back," he said quietly as he took my hands in his. "I would never have forgiven myself if something had happened." He kissed my hands. His phone started ringing, and he dropped my hands into my lap before answering.

"Yes!" he snapped. "Perfect, we will be there in an hour." He didn't even say bye, just cut them off. "We are going to get Esme, then going straight to Dr Cox's office."

"Okay."

We sat quietly for the duration of the journey. I just wanted this nightmare over with. I wanted to cuddle my baby girl and forget this day ever happened.

CHAPTER EIGHT

Carter jumped out of the car as soon as it pulled up outside our house. "Stay there. I won't be a second," he ordered as he ran up the stairs and through the front door.

Shit.

I couldn't believe this was actually happening. I pulled my phone out and checked for messages. Two from Courtney and one from Morgan. I sighed. What a great second day back after six weeks off. Surely what that man was saying couldn't be true. Esme is Carter's. Why would the doctor tell us that if she wasn't? Was he in on the plan as well? Thinking about it, he never did give us his name. We should have asked for it, but I suppose we were in such shock with the news we had been given that asking his name was the last thing on either of our minds.

I saw Carter with Esme in her car chair coming towards the car. He leaned in and placed her car chair on the iso-fix base. He then moved to the front seat and nodded his head for James to leave. I kept my eyes on Esme the whole time, studying her tiny features. My heart hurt knowing this could be one of the last times I saw her. I softly stroked her little hand. Her fingers opened and she wrapped them back around my index finger. I didn't want her to let me go. I didn't want to let her go. I felt Carter looking at me, and my eyes met his. I knew he felt the same as me but wouldn't admit it. He just gave me a weak smile before turning back around to continue his quiet chatter with James.

After what felt like forever, we finally arrived outside the doctor's office. I took a deep breath as I got out of the car. The last time we were there, everything happened with us. Carter took my hand as he joined me with Esme still snuggling in her car chair. I gave it a tight squeeze as we walked slowly up the stairs to the building. We walked in silence until we reached the reception. I took a seat with Esme while Carter spoke to the receptionist and booked us in.

"It'll all be okay, sweetheart," I whispered as she was still in her peaceful slumber, completely unaware of anything that was going on around her. Carter came and sat down next to me, taking my hand in his. "You okay?" I asked him, worried, my eyes darting over his face.

"I'm fine." He sighed. He wasn't fine.

"Carter, I know you're not okay. You are allowed to feel something. Please don't bottle this up," I told him, keeping my eyes on him the whole time. I could tell that this was eating him up but he wouldn't admit it or show any emotion. I didn't press it with him. I didn't want to keep on at him. I was sure he would talk to me when he was ready.

Esme started to stir just as Dr Cox walked into the waiting room.

"Mr Cole, Miss Greene, please come through," he said with his usual polite smile.

Carter picked Esme up out of her car chair and left it at reception, while I took her nappy bag.

This was it, the moment of truth. My heart was in my throat, and I felt sick. *Please let this all be okay.*

"Take a seat," Dr Cox said as he held his hand out in a gesture for us to sit on the two chairs opposite his desk.

His office was so cold; it was dark and grey. It needed some colour. This was the first time I had actually studied him. His hair was grey and swept off his face, his eyes hazel and dark. He looked in his late fifties. I imagined he was very handsome in his younger years.

I was distracted when he started talking again.

"I wish we were meeting on better terms," he said with a grimace. "Okay, so let's get started. Carter, if we take you through next door to carry out your part of the DNA test. Then, once you are done, we will do Esme's. That okay?" he asked, tapping his fingers on his desk.

"That's fine," he mumbled as he pushed himself off

his chair. He leant over and gave me a kiss on the head, then leant down and kissed Esme, lingering a little longer than he normally would. My heart broke right there. *Oh, my poor Carter.*

I sat nervously while I waited. I was grateful that Esme was moaning for her bottle, it kept my hands occupied. I sat just staring into space when I heard the office door open behind me. I looked over my shoulder to see Carter walking towards us. "Hey. All okay?" I asked him as he stood next to me.

"Mmm, not bad. I need Esme," he said quietly.

"Okay, let me just wind her," I replied. I sat her on my knee as I winded her. I didn't want her screaming because she had trapped wind while Dr Cox did what he needed to do. After a few minutes and some tiny burps, she was good to go. I kissed her on her button nose and handed her over to Carter. He smiled gently as he made his way out of Dr Cox's office.

I didn't look over my shoulder, I just waited until I heard the door shut before crumbling. I couldn't hold it in anymore. My heart was breaking. I just didn't know how much more I could take. My heart had been put together so much over the last few months. I grabbed a tissue off of the desk and dried my eyes. We didn't deserve this, we really didn't. We needed a chance to be together, to live our lives without this nonstop hurt that we'd both been through.

I sighed as I sat back in the office chair and tilted my head back, staring at the ceiling. I jumped as I heard the door open again. I stood up and looked at Carter and Esme. I walked towards them and threw my arms round his neck. I laid my head on his chest and I stared at our beautiful Esme.

"Where's Dr Cox?" I asked.

"He is waiting on the results. He said we should have them shortly. If they don't match, then Dr Cox should be able to get the details of who to call." He breathed in while running his hand down my back and squeezing me before kissing me on the top of my head.

"It'll be okay, won't it?" I asked him.

"I don't know, I really don't." He sighed. "We can just hope, baby. That's all we can do."

We didn't move. We stood in the middle of the office while we were waiting for Dr Cox to appear.

"Hey, do you want a coffee?" I asked, trying to break the silence.

"Please." His eyes were glazed, dull. He had lost his sparkle.

"Okay, baby. I'll be back soon." I touched his chest as I reached up and kissed him, my stomach knotting as our lips touched, that familiar electricity coursing through my veins. I always wondered whether he felt it like I did. He consumed every part of me with just a look. I smiled at him before walking out of the office and into the reception area.

I stood reading the posters while the hospital coffee machine did its thing, before grabbing the two coffees and walking back towards Dr Cox's office. I could instantly feel the atmosphere. I looked to Carter who had turned as I opened the door, then I saw his eyes were glassy and red raw. *Oh.*

I stood next to Carter and slipped my hand into his already open hand, squeezing it tightly. I turned my face into his arm and kissed him, trying to steady myself for the blow we were about to get.

"Carter, please take a seat," Dr Cox said. I walked with Carter to our seats. Esme was snoozing again in his big arms. She looked lost.

"Okay, so as I said when I walked in..." He stopped and looked at me. "Sorry, Freya. You were out getting coffee." He smiled weakly before facing Carter again. "So, as I was saying the results came back. I'm so sorry, Carter, Freya, but Esme is not yours. I'm not sure what happened or who it was who told you this information but you are definitely not a match. I can't believe I'm giving you such bad news again within a few weeks." He looked down at his desk, his fingers knotted together.

"I, I..." I choked. I tried to get my words out but I couldn't. They were stuck, stuck behind this lump in my throat. Carter grabbed my hand, pulling it up to his mouth. He didn't kiss it, just rested it in front of his lips. I faced him, his eyes swollen as the tears escaped. He didn't look at me; he was fixated on Dr Cox.

"Carter," I whispered. Nothing. He closed his eyes and bowed his head in defeat. "Dr Cox," I said quietly. "These results are one-hundred percent correct?" I asked, hoping, praying that there was some hope for us.

"Yes, Freya. Unfortunately so." He nodded his head before his eyes moved back to Carter.

"So, what now?" I asked, my eyes now also on Carter. His eyes were still closed, tears still escaping him. My broken Carter.

"Well, after running some details through the system, we have found the father. I got Claire on reception to call but it seems the father hasn't been seen since earlier today. His mother answered his phone. She will be here shortly to collect her grandchild." He sat back in his chair, clearly feeling gutted for us.

"What?" I exclaimed, my voice getting louder. My eyes stung, and my heart felt as if somebody had torn it out of my chest and obliterated it in front of me. "We don't even get to say goodbye? To get her stuff?"

"No. She legally isn't yours. She needs to go to her grandmother."

"But the father is clearly unstable. He attacked me at work earlier which is why we're here!" I shouted back at him. The pent up rage that had been brewing for months had finally erupted.

"Freya, I know you're upset..." he trailed off.

"Upset? UPSET?" I growled at him, standing from my chair and leaning over his desk, resting my hands down. "I am more than upset. I am devastated. Not only have we recently grieved the loss of our own baby, we are now mourning the loss of our daughter who we have brought up for the last six weeks! And now, now she is literally being taken from us. We don't have any rights, nothing. Our life is being destroyed right in front of our eyes!" I lowered my head and shook it.

"Please, calm down."

"Calm down?" Carter piped up, his eyes raw with hurt and betrayal. "How the fuck can we calm down?" He also stood up, wrapping his arm round my waist. "How would you feel if this was you? TELL ME! HOW WOULD YOU FEEL?" He let go of me and passed me Esme. "We have just had our whole world shattered once more!" he shouted as he hit his hand down on Dr Cox's desk.

"Carter, please don't make me call security. I have known you and your family for years. Do you think I wanted to tell you this? Do you think I wanted these results to come back as they did? This is out of my control, and I really am truly sorry for you and Freya. But this is the end of the road. Esme needs to go to her family. Her real family." He slowly stood from his chair. "I'm sorry, I really am." He walked around from his desk and patted Carter on the back as he walked towards the door. "She will be here soon. Say your goodbyes. Again, I'm sorry," he said before closing the door behind him.

"But we are her family," he mumbled to the closed door.

"Carter," I said as I wrapped my arm round him. Esme snuggled into my chest. He kissed me on the head, his tears beginning to fall once more.

This wasn't fair. He didn't deserve this. I know he upset Chloe, but this, this plan of hers. This was another level. She didn't just break his heart, she fucking destroyed it. Completely and utterly obliterated it. I really didn't know how I was going to get him back from this.

We were interrupted when we heard the office door open again. "Hello?" A soft, posh female voice came around the door. "Carter? Freya?"

I looked towards the door and saw an impeccably dressed lady, in her mid-forties if I had to guess, bleached blonde hair in a neat bob. She had the same crystal blue eyes as her son, and her make-up looked flawless. She was dressed in a two-piece grey suit which consisted of a blazer and skirt with kitten-heeled black shoes. She removed her leather driving gloves and put them into her Chanel bag.

"I'm Mya, Philip's mother," she said in a low voice as she closed the door quietly. She walked over to us. She looked nervous.

Carter turned to her, defeat all over his face.

"I'm Freya. This is Carter, my fiancé, and erm, this is Esme." I had to bite my lip to stop myself crying. "Esme-

Blu, after Chloe's favourite flowers, bluebells." I sniffed.

"She is beautiful," Mya said as she walked over. Unfortunately, Carter wasn't as pleasant.

"Your fucking son needs help. He attacked my wife-to-be earlier today. Where is he now? I don't want him in Esme's life!" Carter raged at her. His fists were clenched, a vein bulging in the side of his head.

"My son, Philip, is what I like to call damaged. Philip's father and I had no idea about any of this, or Chloe. He is in custody at the moment, but I promise he won't get to her. Not without a fight from me and his father. Esme will have a wonderful life. She will never want for anything. If you don't mind, we could swap numbers? I would like to still keep in contact, for her sake," she said as she stopped for a breath. "I know how hard this must be for you." Her eyes didn't leave Carter's at all.

"You don't have a clue what we're feeling" he snarled at her. I took his arm and clung onto it.

"Thank you, Mya. As you can understand, we are heartbroken at this news. I would love to exchange numbers with you, but please be mindful that we need time to heal."

She smiled at me before taking a step closer towards me, Carter, and Esme. "May I?" she asked, again in her soft voice.

I nodded as I gently handed Esme to her. As soon as she was out of my arms, the tears began to fall. Carter wrapped his arm around my waist and pulled me into him as I sobbed into his chest. Carter stood still, watching everything Mya did.

"She is beautiful," she cooed as Esme started to stir. I pulled my face away from his chest and just watched.

Esme fixated on Mya's face straight away, a little smile appearing on her face. It was like she knew who Mya was. I knew that she didn't, but it did bring some comfort to me.

"Can we say goodbye?" Carter asked, still watching her every move.

"Oh, of course. Please, you don't have to ask," Mya said kindly as she walked towards us. She handed Esme to him and took a step back to give him some privacy. I stayed next to him, clinging onto his arm, sniffling, tears escaping and streaming down my face.

"Hey, baby girl," he said in a soothing, quiet voice. "I know this makes no sense to you right now, and it probably never will, but these past six weeks have been the most amazing six weeks of my life. You have brought so much joy to me and your mummy and I know your real mummy is shining down on you. I'm not quite sure what I did wrong to deserve this, but please know that I will always love you and remember you. My darling Esme-Blue, you have lightened our lives. We are going to miss you. Your nannies and grandad love you so much." He sniffed as a tear ran down his nose and dripped onto her bib.

"Goodbye, baby girl." He kissed her forehead, taking in those last precious moments. I then leant in and kissed her.

"Mama loves you so much. I'm so sad that we're not going to see the beautiful woman you will become. We will never forget you, our little bluebell," I said before kissing her one final time, taking in her scent as I sniffed her hair.

Carter handed her back over to Mya. "Fucking take care of her," he said before walking out of the office.

Mya sighed as she watched him leave before looking back at me. "I'm so sorry again," she whispered.

"It is what it is. We've learnt that everything happens for a reason, but this, this is just heartbreaking," I said biting my lip.

"I know." She started to walk towards me. "This is my business card. Write your number down, and please do check in on her. I promise to tell her of you and Carter. If you can send me your address we will be over later tonight to collect her things." She smiled weakly at me. I took the card from her and gave it a quick glance. *She's a paediatrician.* I grabbed a pen from Cox's desk and jotted my number down, with our address.

"We will text in a few days. I don't want to make her settling in process any harder. Please, if you do have any questions just call us. There is no need for unnecessary upset if we can help it." I smiled back at her, another stray tear rolling down the side of my face.

"Of course. Goodbye, Freya. Please say goodbye to your husband for me." She nodded, grabbed Esme's car chair, and turned for the office door. I started to correct her about Carter being my husband but I didn't have the energy. I watched her open the door, ready to leave, but she turned back once more and smiled at me before disappearing with our baby girl.

I put my hand over my mouth as my caged sobs left my body. Carter walked back into the room once she had left and fell to his knees in front of me. I slowly lowered myself down to the floor in front of him as he sobbed silently into his hands. I couldn't bear to see him like that. I placed my hands on his knees and rested my head against his. "I love you," I whispered. I didn't want anything back, I just wanted him to know.

Forever & always.

CHAPTER NINE

We walked through our front door in silence. Carter hadn't said a word the whole way home. Elsie stood in the hallway, hands over her mouth when she saw us without Esme.

"No," she stammered. "It can't be." She shook her head in complete disbelief.

"Unfortunately so," I mumbled, my eyes on Carter the whole time. He stood in front of his mum and wrapped his arms around her. He towered over her as she snuggled into his chest, trying to comfort him. I ran my hand over his back slowly before escaping upstairs. I didn't want to invade their moment.

I walked into Esme's nursery and stood looking around. I couldn't believe this had happened. I shook my head before running my fingers along her chest of drawers. Without thinking, I opened the drawers slowly and started taking her clothes out, putting them in a neat pile. Mya was going to be here later to collect her bits. Might as well make a start on it.

A few hours had passed. I had black bags and boxes all around me. Luckily, we had some left in our garage from when we moved. I had placed all her delicate things in the boxes, wrapped up so they were safe. I stood up and took a deep breath. Carter hadn't been up to see me. He hadn't even come looking. If this was how he wanted to deal with it then that was fine.

I looked around the room again. Her cot was dismantled. Her Moses basket was resting on its stand, and everything else of hers was in bags and boxes. I couldn't believe this was it. The last we had of her was packed away, apart from her blanket which she was wrapped in from the hospital. They weren't having that.

Elsie appeared in the doorway and cleared her throat. "Freya," she said quietly.

"Hey" I replied, trying to keep focused, because if I stopped, I would cry. "Where's Carter?"

"He's sitting quietly in his office with a bottle of whisky," she said, pulling her brows together while holding her hand to her chest.

"How do I deal with this, Elsie?" I asked, pleading for some advice.

"Leave him. I know he didn't react like this when you both lost the baby, but he has had this little girl in his life for six weeks. He will come to you when he's ready. Trust me on this one, Freya. You don't want to push him away." She smiled softly at me. "He loves you so much. He will come back." She nodded before leaving the room.

I stood up and pulled the door shut as I walked out of the nursery. I crept slowly past his office and saw him sitting there, feet on the desk, leaning back in his chair while cradling a tumbler full of whisky, half a bottle sitting on his desk. I wanted to go in there, wrap myself around him and tell him it was going to be okay, but I thought back to Elsie's advice and moved on.

I made my way into the main bathroom and ran a bath. The house was so quiet. I felt weird not walking around with the baby monitor attached to me. While I was waiting for my bath to run, I text Courtney, letting her know what had happened, and that Carter and I wouldn't be joining them for drinks, and asked her to thank Morgan for his help with our little situation earlier. I put my phone on the vanity unit and slid into the bath. What. A. Day.

It had gone six p.m. I wasn't hungry, so I respectfully declined dinner from Julia. Elsie had retired to her room and Carter was still drinking himself into oblivion. I checked my phone to make sure I hadn't missed a call from Mya. I climbed into our bed and flicked *Friends* on the TV. I was going to call Laura but I just didn't have the energy to go through it all again. I put my phone on charge and turned it onto silent. I didn't want to be interrupted by anyone. My mood was taking a downward spiral. All of a sudden, I was interrupted by vibrating. I sighed as I picked my phone up and saw a number that I didn't recognize.

"Hello?"

"Freya? It's Mya. We will be with you in five. Is that okay?" she asked.

I didn't really have a choice, did I?

"Of course." I nodded to myself. "Is Esme okay?"

"She is a bit fretful, but she's okay," she reassured me. "Ok, we will see you soon," she said before putting the phone down.

I slugged myself out of bed and tiptoed into Carter's office. "Carter?" He didn't reply. "Babe, can you help me? Mya is going to be here in five minutes for Esme's stuff. I need help with the cot and everything." I bit my lip while I waited for his response. Again, nothing. "Fine!" I shouted at him as I slammed his office door.

I marched into Esme's room and started picking up the black bags and running them down the stairs to the front door. I jumped as I saw James walk out of the kitchen.

"Everything okay, Freya?" he asked.

"No. No it's not," I said, defeated. "Could you help me? Carter seems to have lost his ability to speak and I need help bringing stuff down the stairs from Esme's nursery."

"Of course."

He followed me up the stairs, not saying anything. I

didn't even know if he was allowed upstairs, but at that point, I didn't care. I was so annoyed with Carter.

We walked back into the nursery, grabbing some boxes, and placed some bags on top while James lifted the slats of the cot and the sides. After a few more trips, we finally had everything downstairs.

"Thank you so much for your help, James," I said gratefully.

"No problem at all, Freya." He smiled and walked away.

I paced up and down the hallway while I waited for Mya. I was anxious. I couldn't believe this was it. The end.

I heard a car pull up outside. I opened the double oak front doors slowly as I peered out, watching a brand new white Range Rover park up. I opened the door fully and rested against the doorframe as Mya walked slowly up the stairs.

"Is Esme in the car?" I asked.

"No, she is at home, asleep." She smiled weakly.

"I see." I bit my lip and shook my head. "Okay, so here is her stuff. Would you like help to put it in the car?" I asked, hoping she would decline. I just wanted to get back to my bed.

"If you wouldn't mind." She smiled at me again.

"Of course not." I turned to put my shoes on and rolled my eyes.

I started walking her bags out whilst Mya grabbed a

couple of the boxes and followed me out. I placed her bag of belongings delicately in the boot while trying to push the lump back down my throat. I walked back into the house and started moving the cot. After a few minutes, the hallway was empty. Just like that, all trace of her was gone. I walked into the kitchen to pour a glass of water when I saw a bag on the breakfast bar. Intrigued, I opened it and saw the picture that Elsie had taken of me, Carter, and Esme that morning in a delicate, mirrored frame. I wiped a tear away before heading back upstairs.

I wished I could have gone back to my little flat tonight. I really didn't want to be there. I snuggled back into bed and tried to push everything to the back of my mind. I watched a complete series of *Friends* before deciding to call it a night; I still had to get up for work in the morning. I turned off my lamp and rolled over and snuggled into our duvet. Still no sign of Carter. He was probably asleep in his office. I sighed before closing my eyes and trying to get some sleep after an exhausting day.

I woke with a jump when I heard banging on the bedroom door. I ignored it. I wasn't letting him in. I pulled the duvet over my head to try and shut the banging out. Then, I heard the door swing open and crash into the wall.

"Hellooo," he slurred with a stupid grin on his face. "I'm home."

I rolled over and looked at him; he looked a mess. His hair was all over the place, his work shirt open and he was only wearing his boxers. God knows where his trousers were. He stumbled over to the bed, flopping down, face first.

"Wifey for lifey, where are you?" he said into the duvet in a childish voice, then started whacking his hands down, trying to find me.

I threw the covers back. "Go away, Carter."

"I'm not going anywhere." He smirked at me.

"I'm serious. Go away. You're annoying me. You left me to deal with Esme's stuff. I had to get James to help me because you were too busy drowning your sorrows!" I shouted at him as I got out of the bed and stood by the walk-in wardrobe doorway.

He stuck out his bottom lip as I watched him try to undo the buttons on his shirt. He hadn't realized they were already undone. I rolled my eyes and walked over to him. I took his shirt off his shoulders and folded it up, placing it on the ottoman. I used every last bit of strength I had to roll him over to his side of the bed. He was snoring within seconds of his head hitting the pillow. I wanted to wake him up and get things sorted, but there was no point. I huffed as I sank back into bed, turning my back on him. This was the first night we had gone to bed without cuddling or making love. I moved to the edge of the bed and tucked the duvet under my face. I would deal with him in the morning.

I was up before my alarm. Carter was still snoring. I

placed a cup of water and two paracetamols next to the bed. Hopefully it'd help his killer hangover. He hadn't moved all night, still lying on his back with his arms above his head.

I ran the shower for a moment before stepping under it. I thought I would have calmed down by the morning, but nope, I was still angry. I wrung my hair out and brushed my teeth before deciding on what outfit to wear. I dried my hair roughly before putting it in a loose plait.

"Ah, shit." I heard Carter mumble, along with a bang. "Poxy ottoman." He growled.

I sniggered. I looked over my shoulder as he walked into the dressing room. "Morning," he groaned as he walked towards me.

"Morning," I replied bluntly. I sat at my dressing table and started to do my make-up.

"It's early. Where are you going?" he asked, rubbing his fist in his eye.

"I'm going to work, Carter. I'm busy," I snapped.

"What's the matter with you?" he asked, looking around the dressing room as if he didn't know where he was.

"Are you actually joking right now?"

"No, I'm not," he said with a puzzled look on his face.

"You left me to deal with all of this shit while you sat and drank yourself into oblivion! How could you? Just because she was your blood, well, so we thought, didn't mean she wasn't my daughter. This was as heart-breaking for me as it was for you. I had to take her cot apart, sort her clothes, put her toys away, and where were you? Sitting in your stupid office!" I screamed at him.

I was annoyed at myself, but so annoyed at him. He didn't say anything. Just looked at his feet while rubbing the back of his head with his hand.

"Nothing to say?" I said bitterly. "Pathetic." I slammed my hand down on my dressing table. "I'm going to work. Say bye to your mother for me," I said as I walked towards the door, picking up my bag as I went. "Oh, and have a think about how you behaved last night. You left me when I needed you. I know this is hard for you, Carter, but you shut me out last night when we should have been dealing with this together." I bit my lip to stop the tears before they started falling. Carter kept quiet as I barged past him and straight out of the door. I heard him call out when I was at the stairs, but I didn't stop. Julia called to me as I got to the front door but again, I ignored her. James was waiting outside, ready to take us to work.

"Morning, James. Can we go please?" I said quietly.

"But, Freya, Carter isn't here," he said, eyes on me the whole time.

"Carter won't be going to work today," I said bluntly. "Please can we go? I have so much work to do and I don't want to be late."

"Of course, Freya. Sorry for questioning you," he said

apologetically as he started the car.

I caught Carter out of the corner of my eye, standing in the doorway, watching me leave. I hated it, but I wanted him to know just how annoyed I was. I sat back and put my earphones in while shuffling my Spotify playlist. As much as the commute was horrendous, I would rather have sat in the car for an hour than sitting on a sweaty, cramped train. Plus, Carter wouldn't have allowed it. Poor James had to drive him everywhere. The soothing sounds echoed in my ears while I closed my eyes. My phone had beeped a couple of times; it was only Carter, asking for us to talk but I had nothing to say to him at that moment in time.

Finally, we arrived I said bye to James before entering the office. I could feel everyone's eyes on me. I couldn't believe how much happened yesterday. It felt like days ago, yet it hadn't even been twenty-four hours. I kept my head down as I walked to the lift. I didn't want to talk to anyone. I stood quietly as the lift took me to the fifth floor, and my heart dropped when the doors pinged open. I walked slowly to my office, and as I walked in, I saw Courtney heading towards me. I held my hand up, suggesting that I didn't want to talk. I shook my head and entered my office, closing the door behind me. I knew I was being a bitch, but I had to just sit quietly for a moment. I fired up my PC as I sat strumming my fingers on the desk while I waited. I sorted my paperwork into priority piles. I was distracted as Courtney knocked and placed a cup of coffee on my desk. "Hey. Everything okay?" she asked.

"No, it's not," I whispered.

She sat on the corner of my desk and gave me a sympathetic smile. "What's wrong?"

"Well, what with everything with Philip yesterday, and Esme," I started.

"Philip? Who's Philip? The guy who was in here yesterday?" she asked, furrowing her brows.

I nodded. "Esme's biological dad." I puffed my cheeks out after realising I hadn't told her any of this.

"What. The...?" Her jaw hit the floor, her eyes wide with shock.

"Yup, then my wonderful husband-to-be decided to sit in his office, knocking back whisky instead of talking things over with me and dealing with this clusterfuck that had just happened. I don't know what to do, what to feel..." I kicked my shoes off under the table and put my head in my hands. "I'm all over the place. I just want our life to go back to normal, before all of this happened."

I heard Courtney slide off the desk before draping her arms over me and kissing my hair. "Please don't be upset. You and Carter will work this out. Look how far you've both come. This is just another thing to test you." She rubbed my back as she walked around to the front of the desk. "Take your time on that. We seriously need to go out for a drink. It's been too long." She smiled and left the office quietly before closing the door.

I put my head on the desk and groaned before being interrupted by my phone. Carter, again.

Baby, please talk to me. I'm sorry. If you keep ignoring me I will turn up at your office.

C xx

I sighed. I didn't want him coming to my office and bringing more drama. There was only so much Morgan could take before he fired me. Yes, he and Carter were mates now, but he wasn't going to keep someone on who brought drama everywhere she went. I rolled my eyes.

Hey, please don't come to the office. I don't want to talk about it via text message. I am so annoyed with you. We will talk about this tonight. I need to work. I need some alone time. If I could, I would be back at my flat X

Before I could think about my reply, I sent it. I turned my phone on silent and put it in my desk drawer. I needed to just lose myself in my work. I opened my emails and dealt with the most urgent, before turning my attention to my manuscripts. I was starving, but I wasn't stopping. I needed a distraction for a few hours. A few hours of normality before going home to be brought back down to reality. I just wanted this all over with. I wanted me and Carter back. The old us. The fun us. I'm sure we were in there somewhere, we just needed to find ourselves again. We needed a holiday more than ever.

CHAPTER TEN

It had gone four by the time I had five minutes to myself. That moment was soon interrupted by Courtney bounding into my office like an excited puppy. "Hey, bestie." She beamed her angelic smile at me before getting her compact out and checking her make-up. "Want to come back to mine tonight for a bottle?"

I went to decline, but soon retracted that thought from my head. "A bottle is so needed." I smiled at her. "I'll be finished in about half an hour if you can get out early? I'm pretty sure you can work round Morgan," I said, winking at her.

"I'll see what I can do." She winked back. "But yay! You can come to our place and stay if you want? Oh my God," she said too excitedly. "We can have a sleepover!"

I laughed. "As much as that would be fun, I have no clothes and Carter will go mad." I shook my head. "But I am definitely up for wine."

She pouted and sulked then shrugged her shoulders. "Well, at least you're coming." She smiled. "Anyway, see you in half an hour." She waved and left my office.

I typed a quick message to James, telling him not to collect me. That would piss Carter off. I smirked to myself; such a child.

Within minutes, he was calling me. I sent him to voicemail each time. I still didn't want to talk to him.

I opened a website tab and started looking up holidays. I thought back to where my mum had suggested; Greece. I was meant to look at it that night, but what with Laura and Brooke's surprise visit, I completely forgot all about it. After a few moments, I fell in love with Santorini. It seemed perfect for a short break which Carter and I so desperately needed. The only thing was, the weather wasn't warm enough. I sighed as I flicked back through the destinations and researched where the best places were for hot weather in March/April. A few Caribbean islands came up, but they were just too far for a week's break. We couldn't commit to longer than that. I was about to give up when I found Cape Verde. It was a six hour flight and the weather looked great for March. Excited, I looked through my work calendar and messaged Carter's PA, asking for dates that he couldn't miss work and said I needed them back as soon as possible. A few minutes later, she had text me saying the beginning of March was a better time for him with less work commitments. I went back to my calendar to make sure I had no author meetings before hitting the button on our adventure. Seven days of bliss in beautiful Cape Verde. He wouldn't let me pay for anything around the house, so I booked the holiday out of my savings. Might as well use them for something we would both enjoy. I put my card back in my purse and threw it in my bag before shutting my computer down and standing from my desk. It had been a productive day, but the bottle of wine at Courtney's was so needed. I slipped my shoes back on and grabbed my bag before leaving the office to find Courtney waiting for me.

"Come on, woman. I need a drink," she teased before linking her arm in mine and walking towards the lift. We jumped in Morgan's car that was outside waiting for us. Courtney thanked their driver before sliding into the car. I smiled politely, following her.

After a short car ride, we pulled up to some lavish new build flats. I couldn't wait to see inside.

"Wow, Court. This is amazing," I whispered. It really was. It was so modern. I thought Carter's penthouse was modern, but that felt dated compared to this. Of course, they had the penthouse; floor-to-ceiling windows overlooked the beautiful city. It actually wasn't too far from where we used to live.

"White, red, or rosé?" I heard Courtney shout from their open-plan kitchen.

"Er, white please. But only if you're happy with that."

I took my seat on the leather corner sofa.

"It's wine, hun. I'm happy for anything." She smirked as she walked over with a bottle and two glasses.

"Your home is beautiful. I bet you and Morgan love it here," I said, taking my glass from her.

"We really do. I could never see us moving," she said, taking a big sip of her wine. "Anyway, what's going on with you and Carter?"

"Just this Esme situation." I sighed. "I know it's such a hard place for him to be in, but shutting me out isn't helping. I just wanted him to confide in me, not his mum. I know that's selfish." I sighed before taking a swig of wine. "And all she told me to do was leave him alone. Do you know how hard that was when all I wanted to do was comfort him and tell him everything was going to be okay? He just completely shut down. You know Carter. He would have been outside work pleading for me not to come here, but instead, he didn't show." I sighed.

"He knows you're annoyed, and rightly so. You've been through this as well, not just him. He's probably trying to give you some space now." She rolled her eyes. "I still can't believe all this has happened. I still can't believe Esme isn't Carter's. What a bitch that Chloe was. I know Carter broke her heart and chose you, but this, this is evil. Spiteful. I know she didn't choose to die. But she had obviously planned this prior to that. It's not fair. She knew exactly what she was doing," Courtney said, shaking her head in disbelief. "Psycho bitch."

"Can we drop it? I just want to drink and chill." I gave her puppy dog eyes.

"Of course." She smiled as she put the TV on – *Sex and The City* played in the background. Perfect.

We had just finished our Chinese takeaway when Morgan walked through the door. "Hey, ladies." He beamed. "Oh! You've eaten without me."

"We did eat without you, BUT…" she said excitedly, getting up from the sofa, "I left you a plate in the oven." She walked over and wrapped her arms around his neck, planting a kiss on his lips. He pulled her closer.

"Okay," I said, standing up. "I think I'm going to go." I placed my glass down on the coffee table and awkwardly started to walk out.

"No!" Courtney squealed. "Please don't go."

"She's right, don't go," Morgan said. "Honestly, don't mind me. I'm going to kick back with a bottle of red. Been a hell of a day." He pulled his tie loose. "So, where is the wonderful Mr Cole? I have emailed him a few times about some author he's fighting me for," he asked, pouring himself a big glass of red.

"At home still sulking most likely." I flopped back down on the sofa while Courtney poured me another glass of wine.

"Morgs, no work talk!" she demanded. "You did promise." She fluttered her eyelashes at him.

"I know, I know. Sorry. Just hard when my assistant is here." He smirked at me. "One last thing, I promise. Freya, we need a meeting in the morning. I can't be arsed to sit and send you an email seeing as you're here. Ten a.m. Don't be late," he warned, his crystal blue eyes glistening. His jet black hair flopped over them; I wasn't used to seeing him without it being brushed back. It was weird seeing him chilled. He was normally so irate and aggressive when it came to work. We all sat amongst light chatter while *Sex and the City* still played, Morgan's eyes glued to it every time a pair of boobs or a sex scene was shown.

I jumped when I heard the flat buzzer go. I looked at Courtney, confused. She gave Morgan the same look. He shrugged as he got up from the sofa and walked to the front door, pressing the answer button.

"Who is it?" Morgan asked.

"It's me. Let me in. I need to see her."

My heart skipped a beat. He sounded so sad. Morgan looked over at me, waiting for my response. I started biting my nails. I nodded before necking my glass of wine. Courtney was there, topping me up instantly. Morgan pressed the door release button before opening the door and joining us back on the sofa. He gave me a smile while raising his eyebrows. I heard Carter's hand hit the door, his eyes panicked. I stood up to greet him.

"Freya," he breathed as he walked over to me,

cupping his hands around my face. "I'm so sorry," he whispered, kissing me. He looked like hell. I was glad, in a way.

"Drink?" I asked, and he nodded. His eyes were red raw, with dark bags under them.

Morgan walked over to the kitchen then poured him a glass of red and handed it to him before patting him on the back. He thanked Morgan as he sat next to me on the sofa. Courtney cosied up with Morgan as Carter took my hand and squeezed. I needed to speak to him. We needed to go home. Carter didn't do anything except drink his wine. Once I was finished, I stood up, and Carter followed.

"Thank you so much for having us." I smiled at Courtney and Morgan as they followed and stood up to say their goodbyes.

"I'll see you both tomorrow. Thanks again." I gave Courtney a kiss on the cheek, and gave Morgan a hug.

Carter shook Morgan's hand and nodded at Courtney.

"Let's go," I mumbled taking his hand and leaving. James was waiting kerbside for us; he didn't look at me. I felt awful. I must have got him in trouble. Carter didn't say anything to him, just scooted along and sat next to me.

"Freya, I'm sorry," he said as he took my hands in his and kissed them delicately. "Everything got too much. I know that's all I seem to be saying to you at the moment, but I am. I can't lose you. I'm scared I'm going to push you away." He shook his head at me, disappointed in himself.

"Please, let's not talk about this tonight. I'm tired, you're tired. Let's just go home. We can talk about it tomorrow," I whispered, giving his hand a gentle squeeze. He nodded.

When I woke, Carter was nowhere to be seen. I checked my phone for the time before stretching and getting out of bed. I grabbed one of his hoodies and threw it over my head as I made my way downstairs. I heard the radio playing in the kitchen. A faint smile appeared on my face as I saw Carter, cooking breakfast.

"Good morning, beautiful." His gorgeous smile spread across his face, his eyes soft as he looked at me with so much love.

"Morning." I smiled back at him as I wrapped my arms around him from behind. "Breakfast smells good." I kissed the middle of his shoulder blades.

"Thanks. Pancakes and bacon. I remember that's what you ate when we spent the night in the hotel." He grinned at me. "Oh, I've booked us a Valentine's dinner for tonight." He turned his head over his shoulder and puckered up.

I leant round and kissed him. "Thank you. I completely forgot about Valentine's Day with everything going on. Are we going to talk about yesterday?" I questioned him as I walked away and sat at the breakfast bar.

"Let's not for the minute. I know what I did was wrong but I just had to try and deal with it, and that was the only way I knew how. I'm sorry for shutting you out. I will never do that to you again. I promise. I just want us to have a good day. Is that okay?" he asked as he set my pancakes down in front of me.

"Well, I haven't really got a choice, have I?" I shrugged at him, wrinkling my nose.

"You always have a choice, Freya," he said, sitting next to me and pushing his hand through his tousled hair.

"Okay, well… I want to talk about it," I said bitterly before taking a bite of my pancake. Ohh, it was good.

"Okay, go ahead," he said, not looking up from his plate. He knew I was about to go off on one.

"You fucking pissed me off for one," I said. "I know you were hurt, Carter, but I was hurting too. I wanted to be there for you, like you were there for me when we lost our baby, but you shut me out. Left me alone and turned to drink, which is fine – I've been there. But I was next door. I packed our girl's room up, moved everything out of there and gave it to Mya. I needed you. You needed me. Yet I wasn't enough for you. I wanted to go home. I didn't feel like I was wanted here. Even your mother couldn't tell me what to do apart from leave you alone. Well, I'm sorry, but I won't do that ever again. You are going to be my husband soon, and I will not go into a marriage like this. I will not be put in this situation again, do you understand? I will not sit there and wait for you to come out of your downward spiral. I am here for you. Through thick and thin. Me and you, remember?" I took a mouthful of fresh orange juice while watching him.

His jaw was clenched, his eyes cast down to his plate, his hands balled into fists.

"Carter, please, I can't go through that again," I said in a hushed voice as I placed my knife and fork down, waiting for his response.

His beautiful, sage eyes met mine. "I'm sorry," he whispered. "I have nothing else to say apart from I'm sorry." He reached over and took my hand in his. "My heart was finally whole again after the loss of our baby, then it was shattered within minutes all over again." He brought my hand to his lips and kissed it softly. "Sorry," he whispered again into my hand. "Please forgive me." He dropped my hand gently as he started to eat his breakfast. "Eat up. It'll be cold by now and all my hard work has gone to waste." He pressed his lips into a thin line, then winked at me before shovelling a big mouthful of breakfast into his mouth. I smiled at him as I picked up my knife and fork again and started to eat.

Once breakfast was done, we made our way upstairs to get ready for work. One more day to get through then it was the weekend. I was excited for our dinner tomorrow night; our first Valentine's Day together.

We were finally both dressed as we made our way

downstairs to find James waiting for us. "Good morning, Carter, Freya." He smiled at us as he opened our door.

"Good morning, James." I smiled back at him. Hopefully he had forgiven me for getting him into trouble. I took Carter's hand as he sat next to me and squeezed it.

He looked at me and kissed me delicately on the lips. "I love kissing you," he breathed.

"I love you kissing me." I blushed. "I'm sorry I didn't get you anything for Valentine's Day. Like I said, it completely slipped my mind." I shook my head, disappointed with myself.

"Hey, baby. Please don't worry. I have you, that's all I could ever wish for." He kissed me again. "Oh, one little surprise for you," he said, grinning. "Your mum and dad are arriving tomorrow morning for the weekend."

"Are they? Oh, I can't wait to see them. It's been so long." I beamed at him. "Thank you." I bit my lip as I looked into my lap.

"One more thing," he said, his stupid grin still on his face as he reached under the car seat and slid me a small, blue Tiffany box. "Happy Valentine's Day, baby."

I gasped as I undid the delicate ivory ribbon before opening the box slowly to reveal a platinum, diamond infinity necklace. "Oh," I whispered as I held it up in front of my eyes. "It's stunning."

"Us forever. Me and you for infinity, my love," he said, cupping my face and pulling me in, his lips finding mine.

I didn't want to leave him for work. I wanted to stay there, in the perfect moment and forget everything around us. This was what we needed, to just be us. Me and him. It had been so long since we'd had a moment like that. He broke away before taking the necklace out of my hands. I turned so my back was to him as he delicately draped it around my neck before securely clasping it. I felt his hands on my shoulders as he kissed into my neck, taking my scent in. My stomach flipped at his touch, the electricity coursing through my veins. We both sat back as he scooped my hands into his and held them tightly. I loved that man with everything I had.

CHAPTER ELEVEN

I kissed Carter goodbye before I entered my office.

'Morning, bestie." Courtney beamed at me.

"Hey." I smiled at her, accepting my coffee. "Did you get my email before we left last night? There a few bits I need you to sort before my meeting with Jude." I said as I entered my little office.

"I saw it all this morning. I've just got a few things to sort then it will all be ready for you," she said, following me. "How's things with Carter?" she asked as she perched on the corner of my desk, flicking her long blonde hair over her shoulder.

"Yeah, okay. He apologized so that's something," I said as I waited for my computer to start up. I caught her rolling her eyes at me. "What?"

"You let him walk all over you, Freya," she said as she nibbled on her false nail.

"No, I don't."

"Mmhmm, you really do. I would have had Morgan's balls if he did that to me," she said, eyeing me up and down. "And he knows it."

"I'm just not like that. I don't like confrontation. I like to try and get things resolved quickly and quietly." I took a sip of my coffee.

"Just don't be a doormat for him," she said as she whipped a nail file out of her stocking. I shook my head. That woman. "I know you've both been through a lot, but he needs to understand he can't treat you like that. I love you and I'm not having him treat you unfairly." She pointed her nail file at me.

"He treats me fairly," I said defensively. "What is this about?"

"It's not about anything. I just know he'll tell you to roll over and you would do it." She bit her lip to stop her mouth turning into a smirk. "It's not a bad thing, like I said. I just want him to treat you fairly. Anyway, gotta go. My boss is on my arse to get her the things she needs for her meeting." She sighed as she pushed herself off my desk. "Bye, bitch." She winked as she shut the door behind me.

I slumped back in my chair and let out my breath. *Do I let Carter walk all over me?* I shook the thought away before getting lost in my work. I had so much to do, I couldn't let her little outburst stop me.

Five p.m. soon arrived. I smiled as I saw my phone

light up with Carter's name.

Outside baby, hurry, I miss you — C x

I turned my PC off and walked into the main office. Courtney had already gone. I frowned. I wanted to speak to her but would have to do it over the weekend. I walked as quickly as my legs would take me down to reception where he was waiting for me with a single white rose. I couldn't hide the smile on my face as he wrapped his arm around my waist and pulled me into him, his full lips meeting mine, his tongue slowly caressing mine as I melted into him. All pent up anger from yesterday had fizzled out. Couldn't we just skip dinner and go straight back home?

As if he could read my mind, he said, "We will have lots of time tonight for just me and you." He took a deep breath. "You are so beautiful. I fucking love you."

I was distracted when I saw James walking towards us with two big shopping bags. "Here you are," he muttered to Carter. Carter nodded at him as he handed them to me.

"Go get changed," he said in a raspy voice. I blushed as I took the bags and walked towards the bathroom. I looked over my shoulder at him and James, Carter's eyes fixed on me.

A few moments later, I was looking at myself in the

mirror. Thank God I had make-up with me. I touched up my concealer under my eye bags and re-applied some bronzer, then after swiping a bit of blush over my cheekbones, I applied a matte red lipstick, rubbing my lips together then pouting at myself in the mirror. That was better. I brushed my hair, my loose curls still in which I was surprised about. I took a step back and looked in the full length mirror to the side of me and gasped as I saw myself in the dress Carter had chosen. It was a nude midi bodycon dress that sat just under my knees. The neckline was a sweetheart line and clung to my natural curves perfectly. Thank God he had put new underwear in, otherwise I would have had to go commando, it was that tight. I blushed at the thought, but before I could stop myself, I reached up and slipped my thong down and stepped out of it before putting it in my bag. I smirked at my reflection. I was flushed already. I reached down and did up the delicate strap around my ankle to my beautiful black open-toed sandals that he had bought. I felt so lucky to have met him. I couldn't wait for later; it really was needed.

I gave myself one last look and walked back into the lobby, Carter's eyes alight as soon as he set them on me. They slowly moved up and down my body and all of a sudden I felt conscious, especially when I saw James' mouth drop open.

Carter held his hand out for me and gave me a twirl.

"Well, fuck," he muttered. "I done good." He chuckled. "Fuck, Freya." He shook his head then pulled his bottom lip in with his teeth. "Fuck dinner. Let's just go home." He pulled me into him and kissed me once more.

"Come on, you. Let's go. I'm starving." I laughed as I pulled myself away from him, leading him out to the car.

After a short car ride, we pulled up to The Shard. I had never been there before. We walked quietly as we made our way up to the restaurant. After a short lift ride, the air left my lungs as I took in the views of our beautiful city. I took it for granted and forgot just how stunning the city is. I held my hand up to my chest as I took a moment to come back down to Earth. Carter pulled me from my daze as we entered a private dining area. He let go of my hand as he pulled my chair out. I smiled at him as he sat opposite me. "Freya, honestly. You look breath-taking," he said with a delicious grin on his face.

I blushed again. "You don't look too bad yourself, Mr Cole." I bit my lip as I grabbed my glass of water. I felt hot. I wanted to leave and go back home and enjoy every single inch of him. He had such an effect on me.

The waiter approached and poured us both a glass of white wine before putting it in the chiller. "I took the liberty of pre-ordering our food. I hope you don't mind," he said in a low voice, his accent coming across thick as he rubbed his thumb across his bottom lip, his eyes devouring me.

I caught my breath. "Of course not."

"I hope you're ready for tonight," he said as he grinned.

"For?" I sat up, intrigued, taking a sip of my wine.

"I am going to fuck you senseless." I choked on my drink, holding a napkin up to my mouth. He grinned at my response then continued. "I won't stop until you're begging me to. I want your legs shaking while they're gripped around my waist. I can't wait to peel that dress off you."

I pressed my thighs together as the burn coursed through me. I wasn't hungry for food anymore. I was hungry for Carter. My breathing increased, my body flushing. I watched as he slowly ran his finger around the rim of his wine glass, teasing and tormenting. I flashed my grey eyes up at him as he stood up and slowly walked over to the dining room door before walking out. I relaxed and took a deep breath, trying to fill my lungs with the air that had just been knocked out of them. I grabbed my wine glass and took a big mouthful before placing it back down. I heard the door handle as I tried to compose myself. I saw Carter lock the door behind him. My mouth went dry, and a whimper left me as I knew what was coming. I eyed him up and down, his grey suit and crisp white shirt unbuttoned. As he approached, he held his hand out for me. I reached out and touched him. As always, the electricity coursed through my veins. He let go of my hand and cupped my face as his lips came down to meet mine, his kiss hungry. In that moment, I didn't care where we were. I wanted him. He pushed me back towards the table. He was pressed up against me when I felt him growing hard. He pulled his lips from mine and started nipping at my neck then planting soft, wet kisses along my collarbone, his hands gripping onto my hips. I ran my hands into his tousled hair as I gasped when he nipped me right on my collarbone. He looked up at me, his eyes hungry for me. He gripped onto my bum as he lifted me onto the table, pushing everything off as he did.

"Oops," he said in his silky voice. I looked over my shoulder at the mess he had made. The glasses were smashed on the floor. "Fuck it. They can bill me."

He groaned as he pushed my legs apart, scrunching my dress around my waist. My hands were on his waistband as I started unbuckling his belt and pushing his trousers down slightly. He grabbed my hands with his free one as the other one made its slow, tantalizing run up my thigh. I slowed my breathing as he gradually made his way to the apex of my thighs. His face lit up when he realized I had no knickers on.

"Eager, were we?" he teased as his finger started caressing down my core. I grabbed a fistful of his hair and pulled him into me, moaning into his mouth as our lips crashed together. I knew I wouldn't last long, I was climbing already and he had hardly touched me.

"Don't come," he demanded as he pulled away from

me. I watched as he started to kneel down and traced soft kisses down my left thigh until he got to my knee. He then moved to my right leg and started trailing his kisses back up as he reached my apex. He looked up at me through his long eyelashes before his mouth met my sex. I whimpered. I threw my head back and moaned as his expert tongue tasted every part of me. One hand was holding my thigh so hard while the other started to explore, slowly sliding his finger into me as he continued his rhythm. I gripped onto the white tablecloth that was barely on the table as he continued to shatter me with every flick of his tongue. I moaned out as the burn in my stomach started to grow.

"Carter," I whispered. "I... I..." and before I could finish what I was about to say, my orgasm exploded. I felt Carter's grin as he completed his task. I watched as he slowly stood up, my arousal glistening on his plump lips. "You taste amazing, as always."

I blushed a crimson red. I started to slide off the table when he pushed me back and shook his head. "I'm not finished with you yet," he said, licking his lips. He pushed his trousers to his ankles and stood in front of me. I marvelled at him; he was just delicious. He grabbed both my thighs and pulled me into him, gasping as he did. One of his hands found its way into my auburn locks as he wrapped them around his fingers, tugging it back. His mouth fell onto my neck as he kissed and sucked before slamming himself into me. I cried out, still clinging onto the tablecloth, my knuckles white from holding on. His hand held onto my waist to steady himself as he continued slamming into me. This was what we both needed; fast, hard, sex. His eyes burned into me with each movement.

That exquisite feeling in my stomach started to grow. "I'm close." The whisper left my mouth.

"Good, let it go," he whispered back as he increased his speed.

I didn't know how much more I could take; I was at the brink. He tightened his grip on my hair so my chest was pushed out further as his climb had begun. "Oh, fuck," he spat through gritted teeth. "Freya, what do you do to me?" I felt his hand tighten around my waist, and with one last forceful blow, I came undone under him, crying his name out as he followed me.

Panting, I slowly moved myself off the table. I watched as he dressed himself. I held onto the edge of the table as I came back down from my heaven. My legs were trembling. Before I could move, he grabbed my chin. "That was nothing. Wait until you are back in that room," he warned, his eyes glistening. I couldn't talk, my breath completely gone. He had intoxicated me in that moment. I reached around for my bag and pulled my knickers out. I stepped into them.

"Don't do that in front of me unless you want me to take you again," he threatened before smiling at me. I ignored him and slid them up. I lifted my hair off my neck as I looked around at the mess we had made. "Erm, how are you going to explain that?" I joked.

"Don't worry about that." He laughed. "I'll tell them the truth. That I just fucked you on the table." He shrugged as he walked towards the locked door. My mouth went dry. Surely he was joking.

A few moments later, a waiter appeared to re-lay the table and clear the mess. I couldn't help but fidget in my seat as I blushed. I was so embarrassed. Carter thanked the waiter as he left to get our plates. I was so hungry now. Within minutes, he was back with sea bass, potatoes, and vegetables. My stomach growled. We sat having light conversation while we ate, and I devoured mine.

"Oh, guess what," I said with a chirp.

"What?" he asked playfully.

"I booked us a holiday. Happy Valentine's Day." I smiled at him. "We're going to Cape Verde in a couple of weeks. I've already cleared it with Misha." I sat there feeling amazing.

"Are we really? Well, thank you. I wanted to book you a holiday for your thirtieth." He smiled, but his brows furrowed. "We need this. Really, thank you." He kissed me before holding up his glass. "To us."

"Don't worry, you can sort the honeymoon. To us. I love you." I beamed at him.

"I love you more," he replied.

The rest of the evening was pleasant. We sat and

talked about everything and we laughed so much, I felt like I was getting him back. My Carter.

When we walked through the door to our house, I felt exhausted. "Hey, you okay?" Carter asked as he hung up our coats.

"I'm tired." I smirked at him.

"Ha!" He laughed. "You aren't getting out of tonight that easy, Mrs Cole-to-be. I need you."

He winked at me then grabbed me and threw me over his shoulder. "Oh my God, Carter!"

"Quiet you," he said, and playfully slapped my bum as he walked up the stairs. I tried to force my way out, but the more I tried, the tighter he held me.

I laughed as he dropped me to the bed. "Be right back," he said as he disappeared into the dressing room.

I lay quietly and rested my eyes for just a few minutes before Carter came back.

"Hey, sleepy head." I heard Carter's muffled voice. "Wake up lazy."

I rolled over and saw him sitting on the edge of the bed in his jogging bottoms, his gorgeous body on show.

"Sorry," I mumbled guiltily.

"Don't be sorry. You've only been asleep for about half an hour." He smiled as he ran his thumb over my cheek, then slowly moved it down to my lips. "I love these lips," he said quietly, breathing in then leaning down and kissing me softly. I felt the bed move as he kneeled onto it and moved in between my legs. "How about we make a deal?"

"Mmm?" I mutter sleepily.

"Let me explore your wonderful body once more, then I will leave you be," he said, his eyes smouldering. I loved that he wanted me. "I need you," he whispered.

I smiled at him as I sat up and wrapped my arms around his neck, kissing him. I didn't have to say anything. I wanted to give my man everything he wanted. His hands moved around to my back as he unzipped my dress slowly. He pulled away and looked as I slipped it down to my waist.

"You are so fucking beautiful," he breathed into my ear. I continued to slide it past my thighs then fell back as he took it by the hem and pulled it off my legs. "Much better. Don't get me wrong, you looked amazing in that dress. But. This. Now. I'm a lucky bastard." He covered my mouth with his, his hands exploring my every curve. All of a sudden, I wasn't tired. I wanted to spend the night with him, losing myself in him again and again. Our moans and scents filled the room, and I couldn't have wished to be anywhere else.

He was everything to me. All that I wanted. All that I needed. Everything.

CHAPTER TWELVE

I jolted from my sleep and searched the room. I couldn't see Carter. I looked at my phone; it was two a.m. I stumbled out of bed, eyes still full of sleep. I staggered downstairs to find Carter sitting in front of the fire, still with his just-fucked hair, his grey, low jogging bottoms, and he was topless, cradling a tumbler full of whisky. I padded quietly over to him.

"Hey, you," I whispered, searching for his reaction. His eyes were glassy, burning into the roaring fire. "Carter?"

I took his silence to mean that he didn't want to talk. I got up and walked into the kitchen, grabbing a tumbler and joining him back on the floor. I was only wearing one of his t-shirts. I was cold, so being near the fire helped. I grabbed the single malt brown liquor from the coffee table and poured myself a glass, I didn't say anything, just sat next to him. I brought the glass to my lips and the smell hit me, hitting the back of my throat and making me cough. I shook it off and took a sip, the burn stinging my tongue as soon as the liquor hit my taste buds, sending them into an explosion of unfamiliar taste which then slid like silk down my throat. I shuddered once I had finished it, but continued drinking next to Carter. After what felt like a lifetime, Carter took a deep sigh. "Hey," he mumbled.

I was sitting with an empty tumbler in my hand, staring into the fire. "Hey." I turned to face him, giving him a weak smile. "You okay?"

He shook his head, his sage eyes dull and lifeless. He reached out for me and pulled me towards him. I nuzzled into his side, listening to the crackling of the fire which was slowly starting to die. I was beyond tired but I didn't want to leave him. He reached back and poured us both another glass. My stomach turned at the thought of the taste, but I didn't decline. I took another sip, trying to hide my shudder.

I heard him laugh under his breath. "Not a fan of single malt?"

"Not really." I shook my head while swirling the tumbler and watching the brown liquor circle in the opposite direction to my glass. "So, are you going to tell me what's going on?" I asked, trying not to push him. He sat and twitched his mouth from side to side while tapping his long index finger on the rim of his glass.

A few minutes passed of silence before he opened his

mouth. "I'm just sad." I nodded, trying to show that I understood, but I wanted him to elaborate. "I miss her," he whispered, looking at his feet.

"I know you do." I wrapped my arm around his broad shoulders and kissed the top of his arm, "I miss her too."

He took a swig from his glass and winced as the burn travelled down his throat. "It just brings back everything. The loss. The hurt that I've felt my whole life," he muttered. I was confused with where he was going with this but kept quiet. "I miss my dad. We never ended on good terms because business and money took over everything." He shook his head. The more he drank, the more his accent was coming out. "I never made my peace with the way I treated him. He was never there when I was growing up. It was always me, Mum, and Ava. Dad became quite selfish. Money went to his head. I didn't want any of this," he said, waving his hand around in the air. "That's why I like spending it on you. I don't need it. It just reminds me of my childhood. My dad started neglecting us. He never showed my mum love. I didn't know what love was. I grew up thinking I was never capable of love. Which is why I started my 'flavours'." His eyes darted to mine. Nerves panged through my stomach, taking me back to that conversation. The one where I nearly lost him. I swallowed hard; my mouth was so dry. I necked the rest of my whisky, wincing as I poured another glass. He started talking again. "Then there was Aimee. You know..." he trailed off. I knew exactly. "Anyway, I thought I could love her but then she did that to me, betrayed me with him." He tightened his lips. "As I said, no one could love me. Everyone that did, left." He sniffed as he brought his knees up, resting his elbows on them as he shook his glass gently from side to side. "I miss Ava. I haven't seen her in months because she's working like a dog back home in Australia." He sighed as he poured another glass of whisky. "She has no life. I had no life until you." He looked at me and took my hand in his, slowly rubbing the back of my knuckles. "Then I told you I loved you, and you didn't come back. I know I fucked up, baby. I really did. But I got scared. It was all part of a plan, a plan to make myself feel better, but then I fell. I fell so fucking hard for you. Then, like the prick that I am, I fucking left you. Instead of running and grabbing you, I left you." He shook his head in disappointment. "I'm such a wanker. That year was the worse year of my life, without you. I tried to move on and look where that got me." He necked his whisky again; this time he didn't wince. It was like he was numb. His eyes fell soft, and the line above his nose had faded. "Then I saw you in Paris. My heart swelled as soon as I laid eyes on you. You always take my breath away, Freya. If only I could have told you when I first saw you in Jools' office how I felt. I fell in love with you from that moment, I really did. I never stopped loving you, even when I met Chloe." He said her name as if it was a sour taste in his mouth, puckering his lips. "She knew the deal. If you were in Paris and you wanted to see me again that was her cue to leave. But she couldn't just fucking leave it there, could she?" He balled his fist. "She had to fucking destroy me. She couldn't say that I broke her heart; she was fucking someone else. She never loved me. I know I didn't love her. She was sick. Sick in the head for doing that to us. I know she didn't plan to die, but she fucking destroyed everything." He growled as he launched his tumbler into the dying fire. I jumped as I heard the glass shatter, and the fire roared slightly. "She took that baby from us. She was pregnant in Paris, and she didn't even tell me. Then that skinny prick shows up at work and threatens you. What if he had hurt you, Freya?" he asked, looking for my re-assurance.

"But he didn't." My voice was small. My head felt like it was going to explode with everything he was saying, but I didn't want to stop him. He obviously needed to get all of this out.

"If he did, I would have killed him. Then, they took her. Just like that. I couldn't even give you a baby. Maybe this is why. How can something so defenceless love me? Maybe that was our sign. Our sign that maybe I'm not meant to be a dad. Maybe I am being punished. Then, I had a second chance to make you a mother. A wonderful one at that, but, that even fucked up. You weren't even angry. You didn't care that I had a baby. Well, thought I had a baby with someone else. You took it all in your stride.

That's when I knew you must really, really love me. Then, like that, the rug was pulled from under our feet and I broke your heart all over again. I am so, so sorry." He bit his lip to stop it trembling. "I really am. I feel like everything is fighting against me. How can I get out of this black hole? Please don't think it's the whisky talking, I just feel like I can't heal. You know I would give you everything if you would let me, right?" He looked at me. "I'm sitting here, a broken man who needs you. I need your love. Please don't ever leave me. I couldn't go on without you." He turned to face me, his eyes red and brimming with tears.

"Carter," I whispered. It took me a few moments to get the words out. "I am never going to leave you. I love you more than anyone I have ever loved. You are my everything. I don't know what my life would be like without you. I know it wouldn't be worth living. You are my home. My life." I took a deep breath as I moved closer to him, resting my forehead on his. "My heart chose to be with you. I'm scared I will never, ever get enough of you. Like I've said before, my soul was walking this Earth searching for you. If I didn't find you last year, I would have found you eventually. You brought me back to life, Carter. I will forever be in your debt." I kissed his forehead. "How can you say you aren't capable of love? You are the most amazing man I know. You would give your last penny to someone who needed it, and your dying breath to make sure someone you loved survived. I can tell you love me because of the way you look at me, like I'm all you have ever wanted. You are so much more than you think you are, Mr Cole. You have made me the happiest girl in the world, and I love you," I whispered as a tear escaped. "So fucking much."

I ran my hands through his hair, grabbing it as I kissed him, the taste of whisky on his breath. I wanted to kiss all of this away from him. All of the hurt he was feeling. I crawled onto his lap, wrapping my legs either side of him. His hands wrapped around my waist and pulled me closer to him. He moved his hands from my waist onto my thighs, squeezing them as his tongue took over mine. His hand moved to the hem of his t-shirt before bunching it up on one side. He pulled away as he breathed in through his teeth then pulled his bottom lip in. I kneeled up as he quickly pulled his jogging bottoms down, freeing himself. The want between us was too much; we needed each other. I needed to show him how much he was loved. He hooked his finger around my knickers and pulled them to the side as I lowered myself down onto him.

"Always so ready for me." He groaned as he filled me.

I wrapped my arms around his neck as I moved with him, his hips thrusting up with each of my own thrusts. I rested my forehead on his, looking down at him, biting my lip as his lips parted and his breathing increased. He shoved my t-shirt up and took one of my breasts into his hands, gently rubbing and squeezing my hardened nipple. I whimpered as a pang shot through me. My breathing increased as the sweet, sweet release took over my body.

He started to groan as he was building. "Freya, you are just..." He couldn't finish his sentence before breathing in sharply. "I'm going to come," he said as he bit my lip hard as he tipped me over the edge into my orgasm. We both collapsed into each other as we came down from our high.

"I love you," he mumbled as he kissed my hair.

We lay for a while and watched the fire burn out. "Thank you for talking to me. I really appreciate it," I said, lifting my head off his chest. He didn't say anything, just took a deep breath. "Come on. We need to go to bed. It's gone five a.m. and I am so tired." I groaned. I backed up off him and onto my knees before he pulled me back down and kissed me.

"Thank you for listening." He smiled weakly before pulling me up and leading me to bed. As soon as we hit the pillows, we were gone.

I rolled over and saw Cater still snoring; I didn't want to wake him. It was past eleven. My mum and dad were due soon. I put some pyjamas bottoms on underneath Carter's t-shirt. I pulled my now knotty hair into a messy bun and made my way downstairs.

"Freya!" I heard my mum squeal as I walked down the stairs.

"Mum!" I ran off the two bottom steps and threw my arms round her. "I'm so glad you're here. Where's Daddy?" I asked.

"He's walking round the garden. He hasn't been good since the whole Esme thing."

"Neither has Carter," I said with a grimace.

"I'm so sorry, sweetie," she said, taking me in her arms and kissing the side of my head. "It'll be okay." She nodded, as if she was trying to convince herself.

"I need a cuppa. Do you want one?" I asked her.

"No, thank you. Julia made me one while you were still snoozing." She nudged me.

"Sorry. We had a late night." I flicked the kettle on.

"I don't want to know," Mum said, screwing up her nose and covering her ears.

I swatted her. "No! Oh my God. Mum!" I flushed with embarrassment. "We were up talking. Carter couldn't sleep!" I rolled my eyes. "I can't believe you." I laughed as I started to get over her comment.

"How was I to know? You're both young." She shrugged and smiled at me.

I reached up to grab a mug out of the cupboard before pouring the boiling water onto my teabag. I sat down and had a catch up with my mum. My dad was still wandering around the garden. I heard Carter come down the stairs. He walked around the corner, pulling his t-shirt over his head. I stifled a laugh when my mum didn't know where to look.

"Did you sleep okay?" I asked as I stood up to grab a cup.

"Yeah, good. I feel a lot better." He smiled at me as he kissed my forehead.

"Tea?"

"Please," he said as he sat next to my mum. "Morning, Mrs Greene." He smiled at her. "Where's Harry?"

"It's Rose, please. He's gone for a walk around the grounds, trying to clear his head," she said quietly. Carter just nodded. I know he didn't want to ask why, because he knew.

"What do you fancy doing today?" I asked as I handed Carter his tea.

"I know what I fancy doing," Carter mumbled, looking at me and winking. I shook my head and ignored him.

"How about some lunch and a walk?" my mum suggested. "We also need to talk about your wedding."

"Okay, Mum. Enough. I'm going to get dressed." I shut her down and ran upstairs.

I stepped out of the shower when I saw Carter walking in, looking me up and down.

"You're getting out already?" He groaned as he took me in his arms, my soaking wet body pressed against him, making his t-shirt wet.

"I am. I need to get dressed." I laughed as I tried to

push myself out of his grip.

"I don't think so, Greene." He smirked. He picked me up and put me back under the shower with him. He pinned my hands up against the shower wall as his mouth met mine. He dropped one of his hands while the other one was still holding both of my hands in place. He trailed his finger across my breasts, running the tip across both nipples as I gasped out before kissing him again. His finger moved down to my stomach then he ran the tip from hip to hip before going down in between my legs and sliding his finger inside me while his thumb brushed over my sweet spot. I tried to pull my arms away but he shook his head and tightened his grip.

"I don't think so," he teased as he moved down to nip my neck.

I was getting so close. He continued to slowly caress me with his finger while his thumb was pushing me to my release. The burn in my stomach was coming. I threw my head back onto the tiled wall as I moaned out before crashing down around him. He leaned down to kiss me softly, biting my bottom lip as he pulled away.

"Go get dressed. We don't want to be late," he said as he stepped under the shower. I wrapped the towel around me. Flustered, I walked into the dressing room.

Oh, he liked getting his own way. I smirked and bit my lip. He did crazy things to me.

CHAPTER THIRTEEN

Carter

I smirk as I watch her pouting as she leaves the shower. I love that I can get away with anything with her. I stand a little longer under the shower before stepping out. I grab a towel and wrap it round my waist then brush my teeth. I look at myself in the mirror, my eyes glistening, my skin soft. *She makes me such a better person.* I mess up my wet, mousy brown hair before walking into our dressing room, stopping at the doorway, watching her dress. She slides her black stockings up her long legs. Last time she wore them, I handcuffed her and fucked her silly. I pull my lip in between my teeth at the thought. That was fun. I need to welcome her into that world. *Soon.* She placed her leg down and smiled at me. Fuck, she looked so hot. She was wearing a black lacy bra, a matching thong, and her stockings. It was so hard not to bend her over the cabinet in the middle of the room and fuck her.

"What are you looking at?" She interrupted my daydream.

"What do you think I'm looking at?" I asked softly.

She blushed. I loved that I still had that effect on her.

"Are you going to get dressed, Mr Cole? My parents are waiting," she asked as she smirked and pulled a few items of clothing off of her rail, then reached into her underwear drawer and pulled out her suspender belt

What is she trying to do to me? I watched her with burning eyes as she fastened the belt and slipped into a knee length skirt. I just wanted to drop to my knees, push it over her hips, and taste every inch of her. *Fuck it.*

I snaked my way over to her, her eyes wide as she knew exactly what was coming. I couldn't get enough of her. I wanted all of her. I dropped to my knees as I slowly pushed her skirt up, revealing her olive skin then planting kisses over the top of her stockings. I looked up at her through my lashes as her small hands found their place in my hair, gently tugging. I ran my nose across the lace on her panties and sniffed; she smells divine. She whimpered as I slowly ran my lips across her sensitive spot. I smile into her. I loved making her moan.

"Carter," she moaned quietly. I'd barely touched her. Listening to my name leave her full lips and innocent mouth made me hard instantly. I pulled her panties to the side and slid one finger inside her. She pressed against me and moaned out loud again.

"Shh," I demanded with a smirk. I slowly teased in and out of her, watching her come undone on each movement. I slowly stood, keeping my finger in place as I whispered into her ear. "I'm going to bend you over and fuck you."

She whimpered and panted. Oh God, she was so ready for me. I slipped my finger out of her and sucked it dry. She tasted so good. Her eyes watched me, her lips parted, chest moving faster up and down. I spun her around and bent her down over the cabinet and grabbed her thigh, lifting one leg up as I slid myself into her. I groaned as she claimed me. She tightened her grip on the edges of the cabinet as I fisted her long, auburn hair and pulled her head back as far as it would go. She was so fucking sexy and she was mine. All mine. She cried out with each thrust into her. I was so close to letting go. I needed her to find her release. I needed to claim her.

"Come for me, baby," I whispered into her ear before nipping at her earlobe. I felt her tighten around me as her body climbed, then with one last thrust, she came hard, screaming my name as she banged her fist on the table at her release. I was so turned on. I didn't give a shit if her mum and dad heard their daughter screaming; that was all me. All my doing.

"My Freya," I moaned as I found my own release, filling her with everything I had. I gave her a slap on her bare ass as she calmed her breathing. I looked at her, a red rash all over her chest. Her cheeks looked bitten, and her skirt was still bunched around her tiny waist. Her full breasts spilled out of her bra, her olive skin shimmering in sweat. Her body was breath-taking. I'd had a lot of women and no one's body came close to hers. I loved her just-fucked look. Her dark auburn hair was big and messy. How the fuck Jake could have cheated on her was beyond me. She was a goddess. My goddess. His loss was my gain.

I thought back to when I first decided my revenge path, and my eyes glazed. I would still have killed him if I saw him. He took what was rightly mine at the time. If he dared come back to get her, I would have killed him with my bare hands. The anger bit in my stomach. I could never lose her.

I was brought back to reality when she planted a soft kiss on my lips. "You okay?" she asked; clearly she had seen my expression.

"Of course I'm okay." I smiled at her, trying to shake my angry thoughts away.

"I love you," she mumbled as she put a ruffled sleeved t-shirt on and tucked it into her skirt.

"I love you more."

CHAPTER FOURTEEN

I smiled at him. He was still gawking at me with his towel wrapped around him. "Get dressed!" I shouted, then breaking into a laugh, I swatted him with my hand as I walked past. "Seriously, come on," I whined. "My poor mum and dad! You've already taken advantage of me." I pouted at him then bit my lip.

"Bite that lip again, and I will throw you on the bed and fuck you," he warned, teasing. My stomach flipped.

He walked away, dropping his towel as he pondered what to wear. Such a tease. I needed to leave. I rushed out of the room, grabbing my phone from the bedside table, and bolted down the stairs.

"Bloody hell, Freya! What have you been doing?" Mum groaned at me before tutting and looking at her watch. "Your father has disappeared into the garden again. I think we may have to leave him here! Where's Carter?" She looked past me and upstairs.

"He's coming. Just getting dressed." I knotted my fingers as I tried not to blush.

I threw my Chelsea boots on and grabbed my trenchcoat out of the closet, passing my mum her coat, then grabbed Carter's, hanging it on the stair rail. A few moments later, Carter bounded down the stairs; he looked so hot. He was sporting a camel-coloured roll neck, black skinny ripped jeans and black boots.

"Finally," my mum muttered.

I shot her a look. She was so rude when she didn't get her own way. I face palmed myself.

"Sorry, Rose. I was just seeing to something." A little smirk appeared on his face. I blushed again and he gave my mum his most dazzling smile.

"Well, I hope it was worth it because I've lost Harry again to the garden." She rolled her eyes and shook her head in disbelief.

"Oh, it was *so* worth it," he replied, looking down at his feet, his beautiful smile spreading across his face again. I snorted as I tried to hold my laugh in.

"What is it?" she asked, her eyes darting from me to him, suspicion spreading over her face.

"Nothing, just thinking about something." I pressed my lips into a thin line before opening the front door to hunt for my dad.

After about fifteen minutes, I found him wandering by the stream at the end of the garden.

"Hey, Dad!" I shouted.

He turned around and smiled, his rosy cheeks glowing, his soft grey hair blowing in the wind.

"Babyface." He beamed at me before taking me into his arms and squeezing me. "I've missed you," he whispered into my hair before kissing me on the top of my head, lingering.

"You okay, Daddy?" I looked up at him. His normally soft, olive skin looked washed out. His deep blue eyes were sad, the wrinkles at the sides of his eyes seemed so much deeper than I remembered.

"I'm okay. Well, I'm not, but I'm better now I'm with you. What an emotional few months. I don't think this old ticker of mine can take much more," he said with pained eyes.

"Oh, Daddy." I sobbed into his chest as I squeezed him tightly, his arms wrapping around me again, and he buried his head in my neck.

"I'm so sorry for everything, sweetheart," he mumbled through choked sobs. My dad had never been the emotional type, but with everything that had happened in the last few weeks, he was struggling to hold it all together.

I heard footsteps behind us on the last of the winter leaves. "Oh, Harry." I heard my mum sigh as she wrapped her arm around me, then I felt another set of arms around us. I looked up through the small gap above me and saw

Carter. He had his arms wrapped around all three of us. We stood in complete silence for a few moments.

"Anyway, enough of this." My dad looked awkwardly at all six foot five of Carter and rolled his eyes. "Let's go."

Carter chuckled a deep belly laugh as he let go of my dad, but not before giving him a soft rub on the shoulders. I watched as he and my dad walked in front, talking about God knows what while Mum and I hung back, still walking around the grounds.

"So, have you told Laura and Brooke yet?" Mum asked, searching my face when I didn't respond straight away.

I sighed. "No."

"You need to tell them, darling."

"I know, I know." I nodded, staring at my feet.

"I'm sorry this has all happened. Life isn't fair." She shrugged, taking my hand in hers.

"I know, but what can we do?" I shrugged back at her. "At least I have Carter." I smiled at her then looked at him. My eyes squinted as the low afternoon sun beamed across the grass.

"He is wonderful, Freya. He seems to be doing okay, you know, given everything," she said.

I laugh and shake my head. "He puts on a show." I nod again, my mind flicking back to how vulnerable and sad he was sitting in front of that fire.

"Really?"

"Mmhmm. We had a really bad night last night before you arrived. He really opened up about how he felt, about everything." I dropped my hand and looked at my mum, her face unreadable. She didn't say anything but twisted her mouth. I was distracted as I heard my dad and Carter laughing.

They stopped and Carter bellowed, "Come on, slow coaches!" He threw his arm in the air. I smiled and joined them. He pulled me into his embrace and kissed the side of my head before taking my hand in his as we carried on walking. I looked behind me and saw our house in the distance. I was so lucky.

***

We walked through the door early evening after a wonderful lunch in the village close to us. My mum and dad were in their room getting changed, and Carter was working, so I decided to call Laura, then Brooke. My heart was thumping and I didn't even know why.

"Hey, you! How are you? I am so done with being pregnant," Laura huffed.

I rolled my eyes. "Hey! Oh, bless you. Not long left!" I said chirpily.

"Anyway, are you okay?" she asked. My tummy was in knots. The burn in my throat began, the lump approaching a lot faster than I liked. I swallowed, trying to push it back down, but the burn just got more intense. "Freya? Are you okay?"

That was all it took. I choked out a sob, and once it was out, I couldn't stop.

"Oh, Freya," she whispered. I didn't say anything, just slid down my bedroom door and let it all out. After what seemed like a lifetime, I took a deep breath, my eyes raw. I had nothing left in me.

"It's Esme…" I trailed off, sniffing and nibbling my lip.

"What's happened?" she said, her voice quiet.

"She isn't ours. It was all part of a plan. Chloe, she, she wanted to break Carter's heart," I stammered. "How cruel can you get? Carter had to have a DNA test after Esme's birth father arrived a few days back. She was taken that day by her grandmother. Just like that, she was gone." The phone went quiet. "Lau?" I whispered. "Are you still there?" I pulled the phone away from my ear to see if we were still connected.

I heard her cough then sigh, then I heard the tremble in her voice. "Freya," she just about managed a whisper. "I… I…"

"I know. Please, you don't have to say anything. It's just… I needed to tell you."

"I love you," she said. "Tell Carter I love him too."

"Can you do me a favour please?" I asked, my voice small.

"Of course."

"Can you tell Brooke? I can't go through it again." I

immediately thought of my beautiful Esme's face. She really was perfect. A tear escaped and I wiped it with the palm of my hand.

"Sure. Yeah, that's fine," she said after clearing her throat.

"Thank you. I've gotta go. My mum and dad are here."

"Okay, hun. You know where I am. Love you," she said again.

"Love you too," I said and hung up the phone.

I sat there for a few moments with nothing but silence around me, rage building inside me. We didn't deserve any of this. Before I knew what I was doing, I launched my iPhone as hard as I could at our bedroom wall, shattering the glass. I stood up, my blood boiling as I grabbed my vase off the window sill and launched it to the other side of the room, smashing it into a thousand pieces as I screamed. It felt so good to scream, to lash out. The raw emotion of everything came back to haunt me. I fell to the floor on my knees and sobbed, uncontrollable sobbing, when I saw a blur of a figure coming towards me.

"Freya," he whispered as he fell to his knees in front of me, taking me into his arms and cradling me.

I sobbed into his knitted roll neck. I didn't know why I'd come over like that. Maybe it was Carter's chat the night before, my mum and dad being there, my dad's broken heart then telling Laura. It was all too much.

"Shit, Freya." He jolted me away from him, his eyes

wide and full of worry, I had somehow sliced my wrist, the blood all over his jumper. My lip trembled again. *Fucking idiot.*

He scooped me up as if I weighed no more than a feather as he walked me downstairs to the kitchen. My mum and dad were standing outside the door as he passed them. My mother's face was full of worry, and my dad sat on the stairs with his head in his hands because of the sight of blood. Carter sat me on the worktop as he rummaged through the kitchen units, banging them open and shut, panicked. My mum came in calmly, grabbed a bowl, and filled it with warm water. She walked out of the kitchen and grabbed a flannel from the downstairs bathroom before pressing it softly on my cut. I winced as it stung. Carter was still looking for something, I just wasn't sure what. I tried not to laugh at him.

"Where the fuck are the bandages?" he shouted.

"In the pantry, dear," my mum said, again calmly.

How the bloody hell does she know where they are? I hadn't seen Julia for a few days. Maybe Carter gave them the weekend off. I saw the annoyance on Carter's face at my mum's comment. I knew he wanted to be the one to look after me, but she was my mum. I ignored him.

He rushed back with a basket of plasters and bandages. "May I?" he said, next to my mum, his jaw clenched.

I had never seen him like that. She side eyed him and

shook her head. "Of course. I'll go and see to your dad. He went as white as a sheet. Never been good with blood." She rolled her eyes "Men." She tutted and shook her head as she walked into the hallway.

"Oh, Harry. For fuck's sake. It's a bit of blood. Get up, will you?" she scolded my dad; she *never* swears.

I looked at Carter and burst out laughing, and he laughing along with me. Oh, it was a beautiful sound. I looked at his stunning eyes; they were hooded.

"What happened? Why did you start smashing stuff?" he asked.

I sighed. "It was just everything came crashing down on me. The loss, Esme, your confessions, my mum and dad, then... my dad was just broken." I sighed again, biting my lip, trying to stop the tremble that had begun. "Then telling Laura everything, it just got too much."

He pushed my legs open slightly and stood in between them then kissed me on the forehead, taking my scent in as he did. "I'm sorry for burdening you with all of that last night," he said quietly, his eyes dark. He didn't look at me, just continued to clean my wound.

"Oh, no, Carter. You are never burdening me." I looked up at him through my lashes. "Please don't ever think that," I whispered, guilt wrecking my insides. "I want you to talk to me. I didn't mean it like that. It was just a lot to take in, that's all." I put my hand on his to stop him for a moment. "Carter, talk to me." I dipped my head, running my index finger under his chin and lifting it up so his eyes met mine. They were dull, lifeless. I could have kicked myself. "Hey, listen to me, please. I'm sorry. I didn't mean to shut you down. I was just letting you know what was going on in my head. I didn't want to lie to you. I wanted you to know everything I was feeling. I love that you told me everything last night. I feel like I love you even more than I did yesterday morning. Please believe me."

His scared, wide eyes darted back and forth to mine. I started to talk but his hands were in my hair, grabbing it as he covered my mouth with his, his kiss raw. I wanted to pull away, scared that my parents would walk around the corner at any moment, but I didn't want to push him away. I moaned quietly as his tongue explored mine. He pulled away, cupping my head in his hands. "I fucking love you," he breathed before kissing me again, quickly but hard on the lips. "Now, let me sort this arm out."

A few moments later, I was sitting on the sofa with a cup of tea and *Friends* playing. Carter walked downstairs wearing jogging bottoms, a tight t-shirt and a snapback on backwards. My mouth went dry; he looked fucking hot. I loved casual Carter. Mum and Dad had gone to bed after they knew I was okay. Carter had his arm around me, pulling me closer to him as we sat quietly, letting out muffled laughs at the familiar jokes in *Friends*.

"I've got to get my phone fixed. It's completely shattered." I sighed. "Sorry."

"It's fine. We can sort it in the morning." He kissed me on the head. "I'm so tired," he groaned as he wrapped me up and pulled me towards him, his head nuzzling into mine. "Can I just go to sleep here?" he said sleepily. *So cute.*

"Close your eyes. I'll wake you once I've finished my tea." I smiled and leant back and kissed him on the cheek.

Within minutes, I felt his head get heavy, subtle snoring in my ear. I giggled; I'd never heard him snore before.

After a couple of episodes of *Friends,* I slowly moved off the sofa. I had pushed Carter back, one of his arms above his head, his hat still on. I smiled like a fool. I placed my cup in the sink and walked back into our lounge to turn the telly off. I stood and watched him; his slight freckles on his skin, his face relaxed. I was so jealous of his long lashes.

"Carter, baby," I whispered, giving him a gentle shake. "Baby" I said a little louder in his ear.

He jumped and grabbed my wrist, panicked. I winced as his finger pressed into my cut.

"Oh, shit. Baby, I'm so sorry. You startled me." He grabbed me and pulled me on top of him. "Sorry," he whispered again, twirling a strand of my hair round his finger. I enjoyed the silence between us for a few moments, but I really wanted to get to bed. I was exhausted.

"Can we go to bed?" I groaned.

"Of course. Is your wrist okay?" he asked, panicked.

I looked down at it. Fresh blood had come to the surface. "It's fine," I said, trying to hide it, knowing full well he would make a bigger deal out of it then it needed to be. I leant down and kissed his lips before climbing off of him.

"If you weren't so tired, I would devour you right here, right now. You look delicious," he mumbled in a raspy voice. "I could fuck you all night. I can never get enough of you, Freya. Ever."

My insides squirmed. I wanted him, but I was also so exhausted.

CHAPTER FIFTEEN

"I can't believe we leave for our holiday on Sunday!" I said, excited. "It is soo needed." I neatly folded my clothes into my suitcase.

The last few weeks had flown, which was good in a way. Carter and I had been keeping ourselves busy as we adjusted to life with just us two again. We just had two more days to get through. It couldn't come soon enough.

"Erm, when will you be wearing this then?" he teased as he held up a small coral bikini.

"On the beach," I teased back as I winked at him.

"I don't think so. These little panties are for my eyes only." He shook his head while laughing as he threw them towards me. I rolled my eyes as I caught them when they flew towards me.

"What a catch!" He chuckled.

"Okay, so I'm packed. Can we go eat? I am starved."

"Sure, let me just get some last bits out of the dressing

room." He winked as he disappeared.

I zipped up my massive suitcase as he walked back in the room with that duffle bag.

"Oh," I whispered.

He ran the tip of his tongue along his top lip as a smirk spread across his face. "Don't look so surprised, you will love everything in this bag," he said in a low, husky voice. "I'll sort through it later. Don't want you seeing my bag of goodies." He smiled as he took my hand, dragging me out of the bedroom.

We sat at our dining room table as we tucked into Julia's spaghetti Bolognese. It was definitely one of my favourite dinners of hers. Each time she made it, it tasted different. I took a swig of my red wine, it was lovely and smooth.

"So, what do you wanna do when we're out there?" Carter asked.

"Relax, beach day, eat." I smiled as I twirled some pasta on my spoon. "What about you?"

"That sounds perfect." He smiled back at me as he brought his red wine to his lips. "As long as I'm with you, I don't care what we do." He placed his glass down, his eyes burning into me.

"Changing the subject slightly," he said, raising his eyebrows. "Let's get this wedding sorted. What would you like? Money isn't an option so just go wild on me. I just want you to be my wife."

"I told you. Intimate. I don't want a big wedding. As long as my nearest and dearest are there, plus your friends... who I haven't met yet." I shook my head in disappointment.

"Well... I actually arranged for us to meet them in London for a few drinks. I didn't want to tell you until now," he said with that stupid grin on his face.

"Carter! What is it with you and last minute?" I said, dropping my fork on my plate.

"Well, you know what I'm like." He shrugged as he took a mouthful of food.

"Oh God. I'm going to have to wash my hair now." I groaned.

"You look fine as you are."

"Don't lie."

"I'm not!" He held up his hands, defending himself. I rolled my eyes at him.

"I suppose I'd better go get ready then," I said as I went to stand.

"I don't think so. Sit back down," he demanded, watching me. I sighed as I slumped back into my chair. "Back to the wedding chat," he said as he finished his last bite.

"Intimate," I said bluntly.

"I get that, but where? Here in England? Abroad? A church? Registry office?"

I hadn't actually thought about it, to be honest. "Oh,

God. Give me a minute," I said, overwhelmed. I rubbed my temples with my fingers. "Right, okay. Don't laugh. Have you ever seen *Bride Wars*?"

"With Kate Hudson and Anne Hathaway?" he said confidently. I was shocked he actually knew it.

"Erm, yeah, that one," I said. "So you know they always dreamed of getting married in the Plaza?"

"Let me guess, you want to get married in the Plaza like them? Oh, and Rachel from *Friends* wanted to get married there as well," he teased, rubbing his chin with his thumb.

"No!" I shook my head. "Not the Plaza."

"Where then? I'm confused."

"The Savoy," I said. "I don't know why, I just find it breath-taking. I can't even tell you exactly why, I just do." I let my voice trail off. "I've only walked into the lobby. I get so overwhelmed."

"I wasn't expecting that," he said, taking another sip of his wine. "But it's perfect. When we get back from Cape Verde, why don't we go and have a look?" His eyes lit up.

"Yes!" I said, a little overexcited. "But just intimate, okay? Don't be getting carried away, Mister. I know what you're like."

"I promise, intimate." He nodded a little too enthusiastically. "I just can't wait to make you my wife."

"I can't wait to be your wife."

"Not long, baby, then you'll be *Mrs Cole,*" he said in a

silky voice. It sounded hot rolling off his tongue. "Then, I want you barefoot and pregnant in our kitchen," he said as he stood behind me, his hands on my shoulders as he gave them a little squeeze before kissing me on the cheek.

My heart broke a little at the thought of being pregnant again. What if it didn't work out, like before? I was snapped from my thoughts when he said. "I need you, forever, Freya," he whispered as he walked away. "You coming to get dressed?"

I nodded and grabbed his hand as we walked upstairs. I was nervous all of a sudden.

I stood under the shower and let the hot water take over me; I needed to calm down. It was Carter's friends. It would be fine. I closed my eyes and just stood, the water washing over me. I stepped out then made my way into the dressing room. Carter was already getting dressed. He was wearing a long, tight fitted khaki t-shirt, black skinny jeans, and black converse. *How can he always look so hot?* I think I fancy casual Carter so much more than suited Carter.

"Beautiful," he mumbled as he finished tying his shoes up.

"Handsome." I smiled at him. I pulled my brows together as I scanned my wardrobe. "I have nothing to wear."

"I don't believe that," Carter said as he wrapped his arms around my waist. "How about a t-shirt dress?

Causal."

"Mmm, is that not a little too casual? Plus, it's cold outside."

"Yeah, but it won't be in the car, or in the bar. And no, not too casual."

"I suppose. Oh, I don't know, Carter. Why couldn't you have told me earlier? I'm going to end up meeting you friends looking like a tramp," I sulked, pouting.

"Oh, stop it. You never look like a tramp." He shook his head.

"What about that little white t-shirt that you wore the night I asked you to be my number seven?" He stilled as he said it. My heart skipped a beat, the emotions flooding over me. I didn't reply. I just stood focusing on my wardrobe. "Shit. Sorry," he muttered.

"It's fine, honestly," I said quietly. "It's too revealing anyway. I only wore that to piss you off." I smirked as I sat down to do my make-up.

"Oh, *really?*"

"Yup," I replied. "I knew you wouldn't be able to resist, and I felt like giving you a little tease." I held out the sound of the *'se'*.

"Well, it worked. I wanted to leave dinner and just put all my time and effort into you. If I recall, it was see-through, wasn't it?"

"It was," I said bluntly. *Why am I letting this bother me?* I shook my head. After a moment, I whispered, "Sorry for being a bitch."

"You weren't being a bitch. I shouldn't have said it." He nodded at me and kissed me on the cheek. "I'll give you some time while you decide what to wear." I watched him in the mirror; his expression changed. His lips were tight, his hand running through his tousled hair as he walked out of the dressing room. I finally breathed. I didn't realize I had been holding it.

I sat and did my make-up while playing that moment over and over in my head.

"Will you be my number seven? I have flavours of the month. Shall we say, seven girls who I alternate between. The next two months will be you. I don't see any of the other girls, and you don't see anyone else. Once our two months are up, you go back to your day to day life, and once your cycle comes round again, I will call you. You will be paid generously with a wage and gifts."

I shuddered, my hair standing on the back of my neck. How had he just snapped from that man to the one I was living with? I knew a lot had happened. Maybe we had both changed a lot over the last year. I couldn't believe how far we had come. I could have never been that girl for him. I could never share him with anyone, just to be used when he wanted sex. But, to be honest, I would have had the worst of him, because I would still have wanted him. Even with that fucked up situation.

I finally decided on wet look tight leggings and an

oversized t-shirt that sat just below my hips, with my black Vans. I decided to straighten my hair. Since getting the hang of curling, I thought I would go back to basics. I ran the straighteners over my long auburn hair. I couldn't believe how long it had gotten; it sat just below my ribs. I really did need it cut. I checked my make-up one last time before heading out of the bedroom. I jumped as I saw Carter sitting on the bed, his knees spread, elbows resting on either of them with his fingers pointing up to where his chin was resting.

"Beautiful as always," he muttered as he looked me up and down. "You look so different with your hair straight. I like it." I felt his eyes undress me. He sighed and dropped his head. "You're not pissed with me, are you?" he asked quietly.

"No, and thank you." I picked up my Louis and put my make-up in there, checking I had everything I needed.

"Are you sure?" he asked again. "Because you look pissed; I can see it in your eyes."

"I was having little flashbacks. I'm just mad that we were once there," I said, looking at him.

He stood from the bed slowly. "I'm sorry for ever putting you in that situation," he said as he wrapped his arms around me and pulled me into him. "I really am. I don't know what I was thinking. I already knew I didn't want that life anymore, yet I didn't want to fool myself. I thought if I carried on, those feelings would go away because, as I said before, I didn't think I was capable of love, nor worthy of it. Especially not from you." He kissed my forehead. "Come on. We've got to go or we'll be late." He let me go before taking my hand and walking me downstairs to where James was waiting. He grabbed our coats before walking out the door. "Oh, my friends have never met a girl of mine before. This is a first for me and them." He smiled at me, nerves showing on his face.

"Now I'm even more nervous." I sighed as I got in the car next to him.

"Don't be," he said before kissing my hand. "It'll be fine."

Carter spent the duration of the journey telling me about his six friends; Louis, Tristan, Logan, Marc, Tanner, and Kel. Louis, Tristan, and Logan were married with kids; Marc, Tanner, and Kel were still single.

I pulled my compact mirror out to check my make-up again.

"Baby, you look stunning," Carter reassured me. "Plus, you only need to be worrying about what I think." He smirked.

"I know, I just want to make a good impression… and for them to like me."

"They will love you," he said as he kissed my hand. I took a deep breath as we pulled up to the kerb outside a quirky little bar in the middle of Leicester Square. "Come on, beautiful." He smiled as he took my hand and pulled me out of the car. I held on tightly as we walked through the crowds.

"There he is! The stranger of the group!" I heard a voice bellow over the low music. I peeked to the side of Carter's arm and saw a group of men standing near the bar.

"Hey, fellas!" Carter shouted out at them. They all embraced, laughing and patting each other on the back. It was weird to see how he acted around them. I studied all of them. Louis had blonde hair, was tanned, and had stunning blue eyes. Tristan had black curly hair, was pale and had brown eyes. Logan had messy copper hair and green eyes. Marc had blonde curly hair, tanned skin, and crystal blue eyes. My heart dropped slightly. He reminded me of Ethan. *I wonder how he is...* Kel was dark-skinned, and had stunning caramel eyes, and Tanner was a typical pretty boy; blonde slicked hair, blue eyes, and full of charm. I felt smug. I definitely had the best-looking one out of the group. Well, to me anyway.

"I'm so sorry, lads. This... this is my Freya," he said clinging onto my waist as he pulled me towards him. I held my breath, my eyes darting to all of them. They all chirped 'hey' in unison, then Tanner piped up "So this is the beauty that stole your heart then, eh, big boy?" He laughed as he threw me a wink. "It's nice to finally meet you." He grinned. I nodded and smiled back at him, he definitely had the charm.

"Yup, this is she," Carter said and kissed the side of

my head.

"Hey," I said quietly. My palms were sweaty. I knotted my fingers. *Why was I so nervous?*

"What would you both like to drink?" Kel asked as he stepped towards us.

"Beer for me, please," Carter replied.

"Vodka and lemonade, please," I said with a smile as I watched Kel walk into the busyness of the bar. I stood quietly watching them; they were all so different but so alike at the same time. Carter looked so carefree and young when he was with them. I wished he saw them more.

An hour later, and a few more vodkas in me, we were lost in easy conversation, mostly about the younger years of Carter.

"We used to think he was gay." Logan chuckled to himself. "Honestly, Freya, we had never seen him with a girl. He wasn't interested in anyone in high school, he just wanted to spend time with his friends and focus on his grades." He elbowed Carter. "But now look at him, engaged to you and a very successful CEO."

Carter just bowed his head and smirked, holding his glass into the air. "As I always say, I'm such a lucky bastard." He bit his lip as he looked at me and I flushed from head to toe.

"If you could excuse me, I need to use the ladies'," I said politely.

"Okay, baby. Want me to come with you?"

"No, don't be silly. You stay with your friends, I won't be long." I smiled and ran my hand across his shoulders as I stepped out of their circle.

"Cole, she is seriously fine. Maaaate, you are one lucky son of a bitch," I heard one of them say as I walked away.

"I'm warning you," I heard Carter bite back with a growl. I wanted the ground to swallow me up.

I topped my lipstick up in the mirror before heading back across to Carter and his friends; I needed another drink. As I squeezed through the crowds. I accidently bumped into a man, knocking his drink out of his hand. "God, I am so sorry," I said, voice slightly raised.

"No problems, sexy," he slurred as he turned around. "Oh, I like the look of you, you're a fiery little red-head." He grabbed my wrist and pulled me towards him. "Dance with me," he demanded, whisky on his breath.

"I'm with my fiancé," I stammered. "Let me go please."

"No chance. I think you should come home with us." He laughed before looking over at his friends. "What do you think, fellas? Shall we bring the little red-haired bitch back to ours?" They all cheered.

"Please let me go," I said again, trying to pull my arm out of his tight grip. "I want you, so you are staying. You know you'll enjoy yourself." He ran his index finger down my face. My heart beat so hard in my chest, my ears were thumping. In that moment, I didn't know what to do. I looked over to try and see Carter but I couldn't get his attention.

I leant forward and sank my teeth into his chest as hard as I could.

"Shit!" he screamed as he dropped my arm.

I ran over and threw myself into Carter. "Freya, what's wrong?" he asked, lifting my chin up. "Tell me."

"Some man grabbed me and wouldn't let me go. So, I just bit him. I didn't know what else to do," I said quietly.

Before I could calm down, Carter and some of his friends went through the crowd. Kel and Logan stayed back.

"You okay?" Logan asked me. I nodded. "It'll be okay, Freya. Stay with us," he said as he wrapped his arm around my shoulders.

I heard girls screaming. I kneeled onto the barstool so I could see over the crowds. That was when I saw Carter on top of the man that had me, throwing punch after punch at his face.

"Carter!" I screamed as I watched his friends trying to get him off, but he wasn't stopping. I jumped off the stool.

"Freya!" Logan shouted, but I ignored him.

As I got to him, I grabbed his shoulders, trying to calm him but his arm swung around and pushed me hard, sending me backwards onto the floor. I hit my head on one of the barstools, a dull ache shooting through the back of my head. It took me a moment to realize what had happened.

"Freya," Kel said as he grabbed my arm to help me up. "Are you okay? Here, sit up slowly," he said with a worried look on his face.

"Carter!" I heard one of his friends shout. I looked over at Carter, his eyes frozen on me. At that point, the bouncers had come over to grab the man off the floor, then they took Carter. I watched as he fought against them to get to me. His friends shook their heads and started making their way over. I pushed Kel off me as I scrambled off the floor and after him, my heart racing as I ran out of the bar. The cold air hit me as my eyes searched for Carter, but I didn't need to search far. He was standing on the kerb, face full of guilt as I walked towards him. I stood in front of him.

"Freya," he whispered as he took my face in his hands. "I'm sorry. I thought you were one of my fucking mates trying to get me off. I was so angry, I just lashed out." He looked down at his Converse, kicking them together. "Your wrist is bleeding." He grabbed it and held it up. "That arsehole." He growled as he went to head towards the man who was sitting on the floor, lip busted, eyes bloodshot.

"Please, can we just leave it," I said, exhausted.

"Fuck, I didn't even ask how your head is!" he said

before running his hand around the back of my head. "Forgive me?" he asked, his eyes glassy.

"Of course I forgive you, but that fighting... that was just not needed."

"He was trying to take you!" he roared. I noticed the bodyguards from the club lingering around us.

"He wasn't going to take me anywhere. God, I am capable of looking after myself!" I shouted back at him. "I got more hurt by you pushing me! I'm going inside to say bye to your friends. Call James!" I snapped and turned on my heel before hearing what he had to say.

CHAPTER SIXTEEN

I burst through our front door. We hadn't spoken on the way home which only made me angrier.

"Freya, for fuck's sake, stop!" Carter shouted as he followed me.

"No!" I shouted back. I threw my Louis on the floor as I headed for the stairs. I felt a grip on my wrist as Carter grabbed me, trying to pull me back. "Don't!" I threatened. He dropped my hand, his face like a scorned schoolboy. I ran upstairs and locked myself in Esme's nursery.

Why did I let myself get so worked up at the most stupid things?

I stopped and stared around the empty room. The hole in my chest felt like it had re-opened. I sat in the middle of the floor, not doing anything but staring, my anger slowly leaving my body. I don't even think it was the fighting that annoyed me. I just had so much pent-up anger. I scoffed that he thought I couldn't look after myself. Of course I could. I shook my head. Normally he would be looking for me, but this time, he knew he had pissed me off. I lay down on the hardwood floor and stared at the ceiling, I just needed to breathe.

I groaned as I rolled over; my back was aching. I was disorientated, not sure where, I was then I realized I was still in Esme's nursery. I got up slowly, my head throbbing as I ran my hand around to the bump on the back of my head. I walked slowly and quietly out of the bedroom and tiptoed into our bedroom. Carter was snoring on the bed, still fully clothed. I sighed as I stepped under the shower, washing the night away. I threw my hair into a messy bun before slipping one of his t-shirts on, holding it to my nose. It smelled of him; Terre d'Hermes. I smiled as I walked back into the bedroom. I un-did his jeans and slowly slid them down. I bit my lip as I marvelled at his thick, muscly thighs. I nearly came on the spot. I folded his jeans up and placed them on the ottoman at the bottom of the bed before going back over to him. I kneeled on the bed and swung one leg over him so I was sitting on top of him as I slowly ran my hands up his body, pushing his t-shirt up before lifting it over his head and folding it up. I turned around to throw it onto the ottoman when I felt his hands grab my hips. I spun back round to face him. His face was full of confusion, his eyes sleepy.

"Sorry," I whispered. "I didn't want you being uncomfortable in your clothes, so I thought I would get you undressed." He didn't say anything, his eyes on me. I gently went to push off of him when he pulled me back into place.

"Don't go," he whispered.

"Okay."

He pulled me down onto him, my head resting on his bare chest. His fingers slowly ran up and down my spine. A few seconds later, he pulled my hair out of its bun before running his fingers through my hair and pulling it to one side so it cascaded down my shoulders. His arms wrapped around my waist as we lay there, neither of us saying a word. I could feel the tension between us. I wanted to reach up and kiss him, but I didn't want to push it. I was angry at him. He was most likely angry at himself. I lay for a few moments, thinking about our night as my eyes started getting heavy. I was gone in seconds.

***

Carter

I lay still, my eyes on her the whole time. She had already fallen asleep. I wanted her so bad but she wouldn't want me. Not after tonight. I couldn't explain what came over me. I saw red. The thought of that prick having his hands all over her, trying to get her back to his just made me sick. My fear nearly became a reality; I was scared to lose her. She told me she would never leave, but what if she did? What if I pushed her to her limits? I had put her through so much already in the short time we'd known each other. Surely one little thing would tip her. I twirled her hair around my fingers. I wanted to bury myself into her, forgetting all about tonight, making her scream my name over and over again. She was my release.

I rolled my head to look at the time. *Three a.m.* I sighed. I needed to pee so bad, but I didn't want to move her. I wanted her on me. I crooked my neck to look at her perfect face, her olive skin glowing in the moonlight, her full pink lips parted as she breathed shallow, relaxed breaths. I ran my thumb over her cheek as softly as I could before running my other hand across her back. My t-shirt lifted slightly, exposing her. She was wearing a tiny thong; her arse looked amazing. I felt myself go hard just looking at her. I had never had that before. I used to have to make my girls work hard to get me off. They used to bore me, and to be honest, the sex was a lot more adventurous with the others, but with her, it was different. Fuck, I wanted to show her that world so bad, but I needed to take one step at a time, plus, I loved the sex we had. I loved her. I wanted any form of her. I sighed. I really needed to move for a piss. I gently rolled her on her side. She moaned slightly as she rolled over away from me, my t-shirt rising higher. I pulled my teeth between my lips and drew in a deep breath. *Quick, move, Carter.* I listened to my subconscious and walked into the toilet.

I came back into the room and stood at the side of the

bed, watching her. Her peachy arse hung out of her t-shirt. I grabbed myself, trying to stop my reaction. I was so moved by her; she consumed my body. Her long auburn hair splayed over her pillow. I kneeled onto the bed and kissed her softly on her cheek. As my lips touched her warm skin, I felt the electricity course through my veins, my heart racing. How could she make me still feel like that? She took my breath away. As my lips left her skin, she turned her face towards me.

"I love you," she whispered as she rolled on her back, more of her delicious skin on show, her nipples hard.

I couldn't sleep. I needed her. I reached down and kissed her lips. Her eyes opened slowly as she looked into my soul.

"Carter," she whispered as I covered her mouth again. I grabbed her hips and pulled her on top of me. She was so fucking sexy. Her sleepy eyes were brought to life when I ran my hands up her body, bunching my top up around her neck. I sat up and took her breast into my mouth, sucking and nibbling. Her head fell back as a slight moan left her body. I smirked against her skin. I wasn't spending ages doing that. I needed my release, and so did she. I put my mouth on hers as I invaded her innocent mouth with my tongue. I pressed my chest on hers, her skin on my skin. I took her breath as I took her bottom lip in between my teeth. I pulled her thong to the side, revealing every inch of her, my thumb rubbing against her. She let out a whimper as I continued to tease her. I ran my hands to her hips as I lifted her off me. She pulled my boxers down hungrily, freeing me. She didn't have to touch me; I was already so hard for her and throbbing. I lowered her back onto me as she gasped, taking every inch of me. I bit my lip as I hit her hard with my thrusts. This wasn't making love. This was a fuck. I grabbed her hair, pulling her head down, her tits forward. My thumb ran over them before grabbing her hips and slamming her into me. She bucked her hips forward, moving with me. Her moans intoxicated me; she was getting close. I could feel her tense around me. I reached up and ran my thumb across her full bottom lip and slipped it into her mouth. To my surprise, she took it and sucked it slowly, then bit the tip as I pulled it out of her mouth. I pushed her off of me and onto all fours. She looked at me over her shoulder; she was so wanting. My finger ran from her neck down to the base of her spine. I pulled her towards me as I slammed into her, taking her breath, but she moaned out for me as I filled her once more. I could never help myself. My hands were straight in her hair, pulling her head back so far I worried that I'd snap her neck, but I couldn't stop. I felt myself building. She tensed herself around me again. I loved the fact that she was still in my t-shirt, her thong pulled to the side, revealing everything. I moaned her name out as I kept up the fast rhythm. She cried out, telling me she was close. I smirked. I made her mine every single time. She came hard around me and I followed.

I lay behind her, wrapping my arms around her tiny frame and buried my head into her hair. Finally, I dozed. She was my addiction, my cure. My rough, my smooth. My heart, my soul. I could never get enough of her.

She was the one I lived for. No one else could compare to her. My love, my life, my Freya.

***

I woke hot, sweaty. Carter was entwined in me, legs and arms tangled. I wanted to speak to him about last night, to apologize but I thought we apologized in other ways. I bit my lip as I played back our moment last night. I wanted it, he wanted it, but I was scared to make the move.

It was gone eleven before we both got out of bed; we fancied a lazy morning before flying the next day. I rolled out of bed and straight downstairs where I found Julia.

"Morning." I smiled at her.

"Morning, Freya," she greeted me with a warm smile. "I'll sort some breakfast and put the kettle on," she said as she started pottering around the kitchen. "Has Carter packed?"

"I believe so. How come?"

"Normally I pack for him. He leaves it until the last minute. No worries if he has. I will check with him when I see him," she said as she switched the kettle on. "Omelette okay?" she asked as she reached for the frying pan.

"Of course. Thank you." I smiled as I sat at the breakfast bar, waiting for Carter. Julia and I sat in light conversation while I waited for him to appear. After a few moments, he came down the stairs with his jogging bottoms low, his top off. He beamed at me as he walked into the kitchen, kissing me on the forehead. "Morning."

"Hey, you okay?" I asked.

"No, I'm tired. Some little minx kept me awake last night," he groaned.

I felt myself burn with embarrassment, but fortunately, Julia didn't take any notice. I let out a sigh before swatting him with my arm as he walked behind me. I watched Julia disappear into the pantry cupboard.

"Carter!" I whispered. "Don't be saying things like that in front of Julia! It's so embarrassing."

"No it's not," he said as he grabbed my chin, pulling me towards him. "I'll take you on the breakfast bar now and she wouldn't even bat an eyelid." I swallowed, trying to bring some moisture back to my mouth. "Anyway, we okay?" he asked.

"Mmhmm." I nodded as I took a mouthful of tea.

"You sure?" he asked.

"Yes. You know, Courtney thinks I let you walk all over me." I placed my cup down. "Do I?"

"Of course you don't." he said, annoyed.

"Hmm, I don't believe you. Maybe I do let you walk all over me," I muttered. I watched as his eyes flicked to darkness, his jaw clenching. "But then maybe it's because I don't like confrontation, so if I can get something resolved without arguing, I prefer to take that route." I picked my cup back up and brought it to my lips, taking a sip. "Maybe I could do with being a bit more hard on you, not letting you off so easily." I smirked, then I was distracted as Carter slid off the breakfast bar, grabbing my arm as he did, then picking me up and launching me over his shoulder and carrying me.

"Let's go see how much I can walk over you." He growled as I giggled, trying to fight free; it was no good. As we got to the bedroom, he slammed the door, dropping me softly down and falling in between my legs. His smile consumed me, and once again, we were lost in each other.

We walked downstairs like naughty kids who had just been caught, our omelettes sitting on the breakfast bar with another plate over the top and fresh cups of tea. *Poor Julia, cooking breakfast, then us just disappearing.* We sat having light conversation about our holiday. I couldn't wait to go now. Just me and him, no distractions. I couldn't wait to have the sun on my skin, a drink in my hand, and Carter in tight swim shorts. I bit my lip at the thought.

CHAPTER SEVENTEEN

My alarm woke me at five-thirty. I rolled and woke Carter. "Hey, come on. We need to get ready to leave." I groaned. I was so tired.

He swatted me away. "Five minutes," he moaned.

I huffed as I got out of bed and under the hot shower. I threw my hair up into a high ponytail and slipped into my leggings and oversized jumper. Carter was still in bed. I stormed back into the bedroom.

"WAKE UP!" I shouted as I jumped on him.

"Argh!"

"Come on, I'm excited! Please get up!"

"Okay, okay, I'm up." He leant up and kissed me before pushing me softly off him. "I've got to go shower." He smiled as he disappeared into the bathroom.

While he was showering, I went through our bags again, making sure we had everything. I checked for our passports and boarding passes and put them in my Louis.

I sighed as I looked at my smashed phone. We never got round to getting it fixed. Carter emerged in a grey Armani tracksuit and his snapback. He was a god.

"What are you pouting at?" he asked as he sat next to me on the bed.

"We never got a chance to get my phone fixed," I muttered.

"Oh, yeah. Sorry," he said with a disappointed look on his face as he got up and walked back into the dressing room. I picked up my bag and put it by our suitcases. I looked around the room one last time, making sure I had everything when I saw Carter holding something.

"Here. Now stop pouting." He kissed me on the cheek as he handed me a brand new phone.

"What... when?" I asked.

"Don't worry about that, it's all backed up and ready to use." He smiled at me.

"Thank you."

"You ready?" he asked.

"Yup! Let's go." I grabbed my bag while he grabbed the suitcases and we made our way downstairs.

As we boarded Carter's jet, I gasped. It was stunning. It was very similar to Morgan's, but slightly bigger. We sat down and the pretty blonde-haired air hostess passed us both a glass of champagne.

"To us." Carter held up his glass.

"To us." I smiled as I clinked my glass with his. The captain came over the tannoy to advise we were taking off shortly and our flight time was approximately six hours. Six hours of just me and him on the plane and I couldn't wait.

He took my hand as we started our climb. "I can't wait for this next week. What made you choose Cape Verde?" he asked, stroking my knuckles.

"Well, it's far enough for hot weather. I wanted to go to Greece but the weather is really hit and miss this time of year. I didn't want to go too far and then waste two days travelling. I did look at the Maldives, but it was just too far." I stuck out my bottom lip.

He breathed in as he traced his thumb over my lip. "Well, we always have our honeymoon." He smiled.

"That would be amazing."

"So, when are we going to try for another baby?"

His question crushed my lungs, the breath knocked from them. It took me a moment to recover.

"I hadn't really thought about it, what with everything that happened, then with Esme. I didn't think we would be trying for a while," I said quietly. A few moments passed of complete silence, but I took a deep breath. "I'm scared," I admitted as I looked into his eyes.

"Don't be scared. It'll be okay this time. I know it." He smiled at me.

"I'm enjoying having you to myself at the moment," I

said selfishly.

"And I'm enjoying having you to myself, *believe* me," he said with a smirk, "but I also can't wait to make a baby with you. A little us running round and causing absolute carnage. You do want that, don't you?" he questioned, with doubt in his voice.

"Of course I do, I'm just afraid. Like we're trying to replace what we lost." I sniffed as the burn climbed up my throat.

"Baby, look at me." He turned my chin to face him. "No baby will ever replace our angel, but we deserve a chance at happiness as well." He kissed my forehead. "There is no rush, I just wanted to make sure we both still want it." He squeezed my hand and I nodded.

I did want a baby, I really did. Just the fear and heartache consumed too much of me to be ready to try again.

"Maybe we should make an appointment with Dr Cox. I still haven't had a period since losing the baby." I blushed. "I just want to make sure everything is working okay, just in case, especially because of the damage to my fallopian tube which will make conceiving so much harder."

"That's fine. I will sort a meeting with Dr Cox for when we get home." He kissed my temple and pulled me into him. We sat silently for a while, our conversation playing in my head. I was distracted when I felt Carter's fingers slowly running up from my knee to my thigh.

"Fancy joining the mile high club?" he whispered. My stomach flipped.

"Carter, we can't." I panicked, looking over my shoulder at the air hostess who was hovering around.

"Oh, we can. I'll pull the curtain and tell them not to disturb us. It's my plane. I can do what I want." He smirked, his eyes alight with hunger. Before I could stop him, he slipped out of his seat and walked towards the back. I watched him, eyes wide as he spoke to her. I was so nervous. He was so ballsy.

I watched her blush then nod as she pulled her curtain. I spun around in my seat and sank down in embarrassment. He walked past me and pulled the curtain by the pilot's door then walked over to me. "Now, where were we?" he teased as he kissed me, his hands clutching my chin. He pulled away then took my bottom lip between his teeth. "Slide your trousers and your panties down," he demanded in a low, husky voice and of course, I did exactly as he asked. I never wanted to say no to him.

We arrived at the hotel at eleven-thirty Cape Verde time; the sun was beaming against my skin. It felt nice. We slipped into our private transfer and made our way to our adult only hotel. We pulled up outside, and I gasped. It was stunning. Our driver unloaded our suitcases and walked them into the lobby. I stood outside the hotel just taking in the sights. I could see the beach, the crystal blue sea glittering under the sun. I couldn't wait to get down there.

Carter took my hand and pulled me inside. "Come, let's go unpack," he said quietly as we made our way up to our room. We walked into a stunning ground floor swim room with a beach view; I thought I was in heaven. It was absolutely beautiful.

"Okay, so we're unpacked, can we go eat? I'm starving," I grumbled.

"You're always hungry, Freya." He smirked. "But I love a woman who eats. I can't stand girls that sit there and stab a fork into a salad. I love a woman that wants to demolish a burger and chips." He smiled at me. "Let's go feed you before you get hangry." He laughed as we made our way to the restaurant. We decided to sit in the outside restaurant on the beach. A crisp cold bottle of white wine was served while we tucked into lunch.

"So, where first?" Carter asked with a mouthful of chips.

"How about the beach seeing as we're here," I said with a hint of sarcasm in my voice. "I'm desperate to feel the sand between my toes." I sighed. The warm sea breeze blew onto us, and I took a deep breath as I breathed the fresh air in. "Oh, I could stay here. Shall we just sell up and move abroad?" I teased.

"I would if that's what you really wanted." He took my hand and beamed his pearly whites at me.

"Well, at least we're both on board." I winked as I took my hand away to pick up my burger.

"Hey, why don't we buy a holiday home?" he asked.

My eyes widened. I couldn't respond due to the pig in me not knowing how big her mouth was. He had his silly grin on, trying not to laugh at me. It was so embarrassing. Finally, I managed to swallow everything in my mouth.

"Slow down, woman, before you choke," he teased, again chuckling to himself.

"So, yeah, holiday home?" I asked with furrowed brows. "Why are you thinking about that?"

"Why not? It'd be nice to have a base somewhere else in the world." He took a sip of the wine and nodded in approval.

"White wine and burgers. We are a classy pair." I giggled.

"Best combination." He winked at me as he took another sip of his wine. "Anyway," he said as placed his wine back down, "stop changing the subject."

"How about France? Bordeaux maybe?" I chirped. "I would say Paris but that is tarnished with bittersweet memories," I said, swirling my wine to distract my thoughts.

"Bordeaux would be nice. Not too far from home. Lots of weekend trips. I'm on board with that. Maybe we can start having a look," he said excitedly, getting his phone out and browsing properties.

"You are so impatient, Mr Cole," I mumbled shaking my head.

"I know. I can't help it." He shrugged. "I have just found the most stunning property though, look!" He shoved the phone under my nose

"Oh my God, is it a castle?"

"Erm, lemme look." He took the phone back and scrolled down. "Yup! A nineteenth century one. Let's buy it. It needs a lot of work but we can put an architect in there, make it good as new, and to be honest, you are my queen, and a queen deserves a castle." He smiled, his eyes glistening.

"Carter, do you not actually want to go and look at it? It's a lot of money to just buy from a picture," I said as I twisted my mouth.

"Well, I like it, you like it, so what's left to discuss? Plus, it's on seven acres, lots of room for the kids!" he teased.

"Carter, our house back home doesn't even have that much land! This is meant to be a holiday home, not a re-location," I said as I nicked one of his chips.

"Well, it could be a re-location, when we're grey and old and still happily in love. Our kids can bring our grandkids for the holidays. It would be amazing, just think about it. I've already sent it to Luke to see if it's available," he said, raising his eyebrows up and down.

"You are a nightmare." I giggled. "Come on, I want to

get on that beach," I said, standing up as Carter signalled the waiter. He noted down our room number and wished us good day.

I placed my hand in Carter's as we made our way to the beach. We had hired one of the big sun loungers with a canopy over if we wanted some shade. I took off my caftan and folded it into my bag.

"Oh, Freya, you…" He slid his glasses down his nose. "You look incredible." He smiled and bit his lip as he pushed his glasses back up his nose.

"So, seeing as you are Australian, can you surf?" I asked as I lay down on the bed and picked my book out of the bag.

"Oh, Miss Greene, there is so much to me you don't know. Of course I can surf," he boasted.

"Show me."

"There aren't any surfboards" he said, looking around then shrugging. "Sorry, baby. Maybe some other time."

"We should go to Cornwall, then you can surf for me."

"Another place to add to our list. I'm going for a swim, wanna join me?" he asked, holding out his hand.

"Always." I smiled at him as I placed my book back on the bed. He grabbed me round my waist and held me in his arms then ran towards the sea before throwing me into the crystal clear blue water. I gasped as I came back up, throwing myself on him using all my strength to push him under the water.

"Not going to happen, princess," he joked as he grabbed me round my waist again and threw me back into the water. He pulled me back up and kissed me hard, running his hand through my tangled locks. "I love you so much." He smiled at me before kissing me again. "Thank you for booking this." He kissed my nose then nipped my shoulder. "Let's go for a swim." He started swimming, speeding away.

"Show off," I muttered before rolling my eyes as I swam slowly behind him.

Carter was too busy swimming, so I decided to lie on the sun lounger and get lost in my book. I looked down my glasses as I saw him walking out of the sea. His shorts clung to him in all the right places, the sea water dripping off his beautiful face, his toned six pack glistening as the sun hit his skin. My mouth went dry.

"Enjoying the view?" he asked, putting his glasses on as he got to the sun lounger.

"Oh, I am. I really am." I smiled as I rolled over onto my back. "Fancy going upstairs? I need some Carter time." I bit my lip while running my foot up my calf. *Nice attempt at being sexy... or not.* I blushed once I realized how silly I must have looked.

"Oh, yeah. I need some Freya time too." He growled as he grabbed my ankle and pulled me down the bed. "Come," he said quietly.

We made our way up to the hotel room, and I dumped

my beach bag before undressing and standing under the cool shower. I hopped out and wrapped myself in a towel as I made my way through to the bedroom. I slipped on another bikini as I wandered around the suite looking for Carter. I looked outside and saw him sunbathing on the sun lounger.

"Erm, excuse me. What happened to Carter time?" I smirked at him. He looked up at me over his glasses, his long eyelashes fluttering softly against his skin as he blinked.

"I was waiting for you," he said in a raspy voice before looking me up and down. "Why are you dressed again?"

"I'm not sure." I kneeled on the sun lounger in between his legs as I slowly gripped the waistband of his bright pink shorts then gently tugged. I watched as his breath caught as I took him into my mouth, savouring every minute. There was something about being outside and getting caught that turned me on. I could hear his breathing speeding up. I moved my hand faster, wrapping my fingers tighter around his thick shaft. I loved having this control over him. He reached out to touch me which made me pull away, shaking my head slowly at him. This was his time. I needed him. I slowly took him deep into my mouth, my lips touching the base of him. He hissed and grabbed my hair as I slowly moved back to his tip, flicking my tongue across him before taking him back deep into my mouth before hearing him moan out.

"Baby, oh, I'm going to come." The saltiness of him hit my taste buds. I slowly withdrew him and pulled his shorts back up as I bit my lip. He sat up and covered my mouth with his, his tongue caressing mine on every stroke. He pulled away and stood slowly from the lounger while adjusting himself discreetly.

"Come with me," he said in a seductive tone. I followed him like a puppy, hormones racing through my body. I was so hot for him. As soon as we were in the bedroom, his mouth was on me again; my stomach ached for him. The deep burn was begging for him. He pushed me against the dresser in our room. I gripped onto the edge as he pushed himself into me. I could feel his hardness on me. He started slowly kissing my neck as one of his hands made its way to my bikini top, his fingers wrapping around the delicate material before pulling it to the side and taking one of my breasts into his mouth, sucking hard on my nipple. I whined as a pang shot through me. I watched as his tongue wickedly flicked and licked over my hard, sensitive nipples. I could have come on the spot. His free hand made its way to the apex of my thighs as he slowly rubbed the thin material of my bikini bottoms against me. He could feel how wet I was for him.

"Always so ready," he whispered against my hot, sweaty skin before biting my nipple softly. He stood back as I panted. He walked to the wardrobe and pulled out his duffle bag.

Oh.

He looked over and winked at me as he unzipped it and dug around for what he was looking for, I watched eagerly as he pulled out a vibrator and a crop. I remembered my brief encounter with that whip a few months ago. I blushed. He strode over to me, vibrator in one hand, crop in the other. He stood in front of me, my breathing heavy and harsh, my mouth dry. He ran the soft leather tip of the crop across my collarbone before moving it down to my sensitive breasts as he flicked the crop against them. The snap made me jump, throwing me off guard. He re-traced the crop over my collarbone again, but this time on the opposite side and again, slowly moved down to my breasts, snapping the crop against them once more. This time, a moan left my body. I bit my lip as he did it again then he slowly moved the crop down to my sex, running the leather tip over me in a teasing manner. He used the crop to tell me to open my legs wider as he ran the crop from my arse to my front, snapping it against me. My mouth formed am 'O' as another moan left my body.

"Carter, please," I begged in a whiny voice.

"Please what?" he teased. "Tell me you want me to fuck you." I blushed at his words then nodded eagerly as I panted. He shook his head. "No, *tell* me," he said, his eyes smouldering and dark.

"I want you," I said, trying to catch my breath. "Fuck me," I whimpered as he kissed me hard. I relaxed as his kiss got softer, before he slowly took my bottom lip in-between his teeth.

"As you wish," he whispered as he let my lip go. I let out a small sigh when I heard the vibrator come to life. "But I'm not finished with you yet," he said with a smirk on his face.

He brought the vibrator up to my hard nipples and ran it over both of them while his lips were on my neck, nipping occasionally. I could feel my climb begin; my body was being taken over. I had no control. He knew I was getting close. He pulled the vibrator away harshly and took my nipple into his mouth, devouring it and slowly nipping and sucking it before pulling away. The vibrator was soon on my skin again, this time making its way down to my sweet spot. I moaned out as soon as it hit me.

"You enjoying that?" he whispered in my ear.

"Mmhmm," was all I could manage. He pulled my bikini bottoms to the side as he slid two of his fingers inside me. "You are soaked," he said with a smile beaming across his face. I threw my head back as the sweet sensation was taking over me. I moaned as his fingers pushed deeper and deeper into me.

"I'm so close," I whimpered. He dropped the vibrator to the floor and pulled his fingers out of me quickly. His hands were on my hips as he lifted me onto the edge of the dresser unit and pulled one of my legs into his grip. I felt so exposed, but I didn't care. I needed this fire in the pit of my stomach put out and he was the only one to do it. He ran his thumb over me, making me flinch. It felt so good. He pushed two fingers back inside me as this thumb continued to stroke me.

"Watch me," he demanded.

I did as he said. I watched as he slowly pushed his fingers in and out of me, and I gasped. It was too much. I could feel myself tightening around him, his hand gripping tighter on my thigh. He whipped his fingers out of me, sucking them dry. Then, in one swift movement, he was in me, hard and fast. He started groaning as he continued to hit my sweet spot over and over again, his eyes on me the whole time. I couldn't help but watch now, and I was so glad I did because he pushed me over my edge. All that climbing and my body had finally reached her peak. It was the most intense orgasm I had ever had. My whole body stiffened while my legs were trembling. I slowed my breathing as I watched him unfold into me.

The rest of our week was perfect. I couldn't believe we were back in London already.

"Fancy a bite to eat before we go home?" I asked. "I don't want to go back to reality."

"I know. Neither do I." Carter sighed. "Back to work. Back to normality." He ran his thumb across his lip. "But, yes. Let's eat. Fancy the restaurant we went to on our first date? The Ivy?"

"Yes! Oh, that would be great." I smiled up at him.

"Good. I will tell James," he said before leaning forward and talking to James.

We walked hand in hand to the familiar restaurant, all the memories flooding back. Of course, we were sat at Carter's table. It felt weird being back there. We hadn't been there in so long. So much had happened since then.

"Hey, are you okay?" Carter asked, worried.

"Yeah, just a bit overwhelmed." I laughed before picking up my glass of wine. "Cheers."

He held up his glass and toasted to me. "Excuse me. I just need to go to the toilet," Carter said, pushing himself away from the table and giving me a wink as he stood up. I watched as he walked away. God, he was so handsome. I loved him so much. I checked my phone. I needed to give Laura a call. See how she was feeling. I aimlessly scrolled through Instagram while I waited for Carter to return. I could feel someone's eyes on me. I looked up and saw a pristine blonde lady, with legs so long they went on forever, staring at me. *I'm sure that was the woman who we bumped into last time.* I pulled eye contact and looked back at my phone when I heard Carter's voice. Slutty blonde had put her hand out to stroke his arm as he walked past. He stopped and bent down slightly so he was at eye level with her. His mouth twitched, his lips curling slightly in the corners. I kept my eyes on him the whole time. My heart was pounding, palms sweaty. His eyes flicked up to me. They were full of heat and want. There was something in them that I hadn't seen for a long time. Then it hit me, she was one of his 'flavours'. My mouth dropped open. I clung onto the stem of my wine glass too hard before smashing it in my hands. *Fuck.*

Carter came out of his trance and ran to my side. "Freya, are you okay?" He grabbed my hands, looking at the blood slowly running down.

"Fuck you!" I shouted. "Go back to your slutty 'flavour'," I shouted as I threw his glass of wine over him. I stood up, rushed out of the restaurant, and saw James sitting kerbside.

"Freya! Wait!"

"No! Don't fucking follow me!" I shouted at him as I opened the car door. "How fucking dare you? After this week, you do this to me! I saw the look in your eyes, Carter! The want, the need, the lust for her! You obviously miss it, so off you go. Go back to it. I'm done!" I slammed the door shut as I sat in the car. I finally breathed, my heart ripping out of my chest before I broke down in tears. Of course I wasn't done. I loved him with everything I had, but I couldn't do this. I needed time out.

"James, take me to the penthouse," I demanded. I needed to get my hand wrapped. "And don't tell Carter where I've gone."

I saw James' look in the rearview mirror as his lips twitched. *Of course he's going to tell him.*

"Certainly, Freya," he said before putting his eyes

back on the road.

    I just hoped he wouldn't tell Carter where I was.

CHAPTER EIGHTEEN

I ran to the elevator and pushed the button continuously until it came. I slipped in, closing the doors on James. I let out my breath.

I unlocked the penthouse door and made my way to the bathroom. I was pulling the cupboards apart, trying to find something to bandage my hand with. I finally found a bandage and some plasters. I wrapped my hand the best I could; it sucked, but it would have to do. I wandered into the kitchen, running my fingertips along the breakfast bar.

I miss it here. Everything was so much simpler when we lived here. I opened the fridge and found a bottle of chilled wine. God knows how long it had been sitting in there, but I didn't care. I didn't even know why Carter still had the place. I knew we said we would keep it for a while and maybe rent it out, but now it was just sitting there, collecting dust. I went to get a glass then changed my mind before taking a swig from the bottle. I walked aimlessly around the living room, not sure what to do with myself. I was getting more and more wound up. I had no messages from Carter, which was unlike him. Maybe James stuck to his word. Maybe he didn't tell him. I took another big swig from the bottle; it was going down too nicely.

I opened my phone and looked at my messages. Nothing. Now I was getting the hump that he hadn't text me. I turned on the TV to drown out the silence. I was lonely. I went to take another mouthful of wine but my bottle was empty. I groaned. I dragged myself up off the sofa and padded around the kitchen, looking for another bottle. The alcohol was flowing through my veins, and I was getting more frustrated as the minutes were going on. After a few moments, I found another bottle at the back of one of the cupboards. It was red. I hated red, but it was all there was. I struggled with the corkscrew but managed it eventually. I took a swig and pulled a face as the bitter taste ran down my throat.

"Oh my God, this is disgusting," I mumbled to myself. I contemplated throwing it down the sink but I needed it. I needed to sleep, and I wouldn't sleep without alcohol in me.

Another bottle of wine down, burning in my belly. I moped up to bed, defeated. Nothing from Carter, nothing from James. Not sure why I expected anything from James.

What if Carter is with the blonde? Bile rose from my

stomach up into my throat. I grabbed my phone and texted him.

Is this how much I mean to you? I haven't heard a single word from you. Too busy shagging the slutty blonde?

I instantly regretted sending it. I rolled my eyes at myself before flopping onto the bed. I had nothing to get changed into, and no toothbrush or make-up wipes. I sighed before snuggling under the duvet. I pressed my eyes shut tight, trying to doze off, but it wasn't happening. I walked into the bathroom. I was glad to see there were towels hanging on the towel rail. I turned the shower on and let it run for a while. I took my hair out of its pony tail and undressed, folding up my clothes neatly so they were ready for me to get back into. I stepped under the shower and let the water wash everything away. I was so tired. I wanted to sleep but I couldn't.

A few moments later, I wrapped myself up in the towel and looked at myself in the mirror. I looked like shit. I felt drunk, but not a happy drunk. A sad, broken drunk who didn't know which way to turn. I shook my head. One step forward, ten steps back. I was in Cape Verde that morning with the love of my life, now I was sitting in his empty penthouse, alone. Again.

I put my wet hair into a bun and climbed back into

bed. I didn't know how or if it was just my imagination, but the bedsheets smelt of Carter. His Terre d'Hermes softly scented. I found comfort and felt myself dozing.

I woke with the low sun beaming through the windows. I groaned. My head was pounding, and my mouth was as dry as a desert. I rolled out of bed and walked down to the kitchen, grabbing a pint of water and downing it as quickly as I could, water escaping my mouth and dripping down my chin. I wiped my mouth with the back of my hand before downing another pint. I felt like I was going to be sick. *Yup, here it comes.* I ran towards the downstairs bathroom and threw the contents of my stomach up, which wasn't pretty. Drinking on an empty stomach wasn't such a good idea. I sulked back into the bedroom and looked at my phone. Nothing.

I unlocked my phone and found Laura's number, I needed distraction. After a few rings I heard her voice.

"Hey, Freya." She sounded out of breath.

"Hey, you okay? Bad time?" I asked her.

"No. They think I'm in early labour."

"Early labour? Lau, you are four weeks away from your due date. Have you been to the hospital?" I asked, panicked.

"Yeah, I have. They wanted to keep me in but I refused," she said with a blunt tone. I could picture her face. Furrowed brow, pouting lips, and eyes small.

"Lau, please go back. Where is Tyler?" I asked.

"Downstairs panicking."

"Please go back to the hospital."

"I will, in a bit. I'm not ready for her yet! She isn't supposed to come yet!" she said, distressed.

"I know she isn't, sweetie, but if she's ready to come, she's ready to come. You can't cross your legs. It won't work," I said with a slight smirk on my face.

"Will you come with me?" she asked. "Tyler stresses me out, my mum will be overdramatic, and to be honest, I need some calm in this situation. And you, my love, are my calm," she said with another round of deep breaths.

"Really? I'm your calm," I said, snorting.

"Well… out of those two you are."

"Fine. I will jump on the train and meet you at yours. Get some clothes out for me. I look like shit and need a change of clothes."

"Why, where are you?" she asked.

"Erm, I'm at the penthouse."

"Why?"

"Long story. Anyway, I have no clothes, and I haven't brushed my teeth since yesterday morning. Please, sort me some bits out."

"Fine. Just hurry up and get your arse here," she demanded and hung up.

This was going to be a long day.

I stepped off the train where I used to live, and old feelings came flooding back. Part of me missed the single life, but the bigger part of me was so in love with Carter. It was ridiculous. I loved that fucking man with everything I had. I still couldn't believe I hadn't heard from him. *There must be a reason.*

I flagged down a taxi and jumped in, giving Laura's address. A few minutes later, I was there. I went to knock on the door, but as I stood there, she swung it open.

"Yup, she is definitely coming. Quick, go get changed, you tramp," she teased.

I ran past her and upstairs as I grabbed the clothes and ran into the bathroom. I grabbed the spare toothbrush and brushed my teeth as quickly as I could. I threw on a pair of Laura's old yoga pants, and a huge jumper; it must have been Tyler's. I brushed my hair and threw it up into a high ponytail. I looked a fucking mess. I ran back downstairs and jumped in their car next to Laura.

I looked at her, her eyes wide with worry. I took her hand in mine. "Hey, it'll all be okay. You can do this, my lovely." I smiled at her. Tyler eyed me in the mirror. He looked petrified as well.

We finally pulled up to the hospital; Laura said her contractions had got worse while we were driving. Tyler ran through the doors and checked Laura in. They sat her in a wheelchair and took her away.

"Freya!" she shouted. "Come on!"

Oh, God help me. She was going to be an absolute nightmare.

"Have you text your mum?" I asked her.

"Yes!" she snapped at me. I looked at Tyler, and he rolled his eyes at me.

"I'm sorry, I'm just in pain. It's making me cranky. Someone told me it was like period pains. Period pains, my arse!" she shouted at the poor midwife that was pushing her.

I bit my lip to try and stop my giggling. I couldn't believe I was there. I turned my phone onto silent. There was still nothing from Carter.

"All okay, Freya?" Tyler asked quietly as we dropped back slightly.

"Mmhmm, yup! All good!" I said, a little too enthusiastically.

"You sure?"

"No, but I don't want to talk about it." I bit my lip. "Please."

He held his hands up. "Okay, fine." He nodded and pretended to lock his lips. I giggled.

"You two having fun back there? You bunch of bellends," Laura cursed.

I grabbed Tyler's arm as I chuckled to myself; she was so funny. Tyler knew better than to laugh. She would kill him.

"Tyler! I can hear you!" she said as she tried to look over her shoulder.

"Lau, he hasn't even cracked a smile!" I said.

"I don't fucking believe you!"

We were finally at the private room that she and Tyler had booked. She waddled out of the wheelchair and slowly sat on the bed.

"I've had enough. Can I just go home?" she whined.

"No, dear. You're having a baby," the midwife said, disinterested in Laura's complaining. "Now, lie on the bed. I need to examine you," she said as she slipped her hands into a pair of rubber gloves.

I watched as Laura's eyes went wide. "You are not putting your hands anywhere near me," she said as she crossed her legs.

"Mrs Smythe, you are in premature labour. I need to check you out."

"Fine! But you two, look away," she bellowed at us.

I looked at Tyler before turning away.

"Oh, I feel for you two. It's going to be a long day for you," the midwife muttered. "Okay, you are already seven centimetres dilated. I'm calling the doctor. We need to make arrangements for little one's arrival. Keep moving. If you need anything then press the orange button on the control next to your bed." She smiled a condescending smile at Laura and left the room.

"I don't like her," Laura muttered.

"Lau, try not to focus on that. Try to focus on the fact that in a couple of hours, your perfect baby girl is going to be in the world." I smiled as I pushed her blonde hair from her face. She nodded.

"Are you are going to be okay here? You know, what with everything that has happened?" she asked quietly while eyeing Tyler who was sitting in the corner of the room on the floor, playing with his phone.

"Of course. I'm fine," I lied.

I wasn't fine. My heart was breaking all over again. This would have been me in a few months. I would have been in labour, birthing our perfect miracle, but life had other plans. Life decided to take it away from us.

I swallowed the bitter taste that was crawling up my throat. "I'm so glad I'm here with you," I said quietly as I kissed her forehead. "Let me go check on the doctors," I said before making my way out of the room. I needed a moment to gather my thoughts. I stood with my back to the wall and let out a deep sigh.

You can do this, Freya.

"Of course you can." I heard the familiar voice echo through my ears, the hairs on the back of my neck standing up. I slowly lifted my eyes from the floor and saw Carter. Still in his clothes from last night; he looked like shit. It secretly made me feel better that he also had a rough night.

"What are you doing here?" I asked bluntly, biting the inside of my cheek.

"Tyler text me," he mumbled as he looked down at his shoes.

"Oh, did he now?" I said in a high-pitched voice. *The*

bastard. It took everything in me not to barge in that room and smash him round the head with something.

"You okay? Is your hand all right?" he asked, his eyes burning into me.

"Are you fucking shitting me?"

"No," he said, kicking the ground with the toe of his Converse.

"You're a dick," I hissed. I had so much anger brewing but this wasn't the place.

"Bit harsh," he scoffed as he reached out to me.

"Bit harsh? BIT HARSH!" I screamed at him. I had lost it. Him, that place, the baby coming; it was all too much. I pushed him away with everything I had, then pushed him again as he took a step forward.

"You don't get to do this to me!" I sobbed. The tears that I had no control over were falling. I hit his chest before turning on my heel but he grabbed my arm and pulled me into him. I cried into his chest as he put his arms around me. He didn't say anything, just embraced me while I cried. I looked up when I heard the alarm from Laura's room and a group of doctors and midwives ran in.

"Shit," I mumbled as I wiped my eyes. I pulled myself out of his grip and ran into the room.

"What's going on?" I asked Tyler.

"The baby is coming," Tyler said, panicked.

"Already?"

"Yup. She is ten centimetres and wants to push,"

Tyler said with eyes wide as he watched the doctors prod and pull at his wife. Tyler ran to be next to her. As he held her hand, I stood on the other side with my hand resting on her shoulder so she knew I was there.

"Okay, Laura. I need you to push," I heard the friendly male doctor say.

"Okay!" she said through gritted teeth.

"Chin to chest, Laura," the midwife said. Laura side eyed her and nodded then, placing her chin on her chest, she pushed with everything she had.

"Wonderful, Laura. Okay, on your next contraction, I want you to give me another big push. Your baby is almost here. Now, please don't panic. When she's born, the midwives will take her, and they will check her over before bringing her over to you. Then, she will be moved down to NICU," he said, his eyes on Laura the whole time. "Okay?" he asked her. She nodded as tears started to fall down her cheeks.

"Hey, it'll be okay. They just need to check her over," I said, pushing her hair back.

"Okay, Laura. Push for me," he said. "That's it. One more and she will be out. She is crowning. Dad, do you want to see?" he asked Tyler, who was frozen to the spot, all colour drained from his face.

"Okay, Lau. One more big push, okay?" I coaxed her, and she nodded.

"Push," the doctor said as another contraction hit her

body, then the chaos stopped. The room stilled with the sound of that piercing, new-born cry. I hadn't realized, but I was crying. I looked over at Tyler who was a blubbering mess, and Laura was beside herself.

"Well done, darling," I whispered in her ear before leaning down and kissing her forehead. "Look at her. She is beautiful."

"Congratulations. You did amazing, Laura." The doctor came over, taking Laura's hand in his and rubbing the back of it. "She will be just fine." He nodded before turning to face Tyler and patting him on the back, then he left.

The midwife walked over with this tiny, pink bundle, and handed her to Laura. "Only a few minutes. We need to get her down to NICU," the midwife said quietly.

"Oh, she is beautiful." Laura sobbed as she kissed her daughter. My heart swelled then disintegrated into nothing. I longed for that, but I was so happy for them both.

"She weighs 4lb 6oz. Does she have a name?" the midwife asked Laura and Tyler.

"Yeah, she does," Tyler said, smiling at Laura. "Freya," they said in unison with beaming smiles on their faces.

"What?" I asked, confused, tears still escaping my eyes. "You... you want to call her Freya?"

"Yeah, we do. Our beautiful Freya April Smythe."

Laura beamed at me before I threw my arms around her and pulled Tyler down with me.

CHAPTER NINETEEN

I gave Laura and Tyler a hug before leaving the room. I felt exhausted and I hadn't just given birth. I walked into the hallway and took a deep breath. I saw Lucinda and Gary running towards me.

"Are we too late? Are we too late?" Lucinda asked me, panicked.

"I'm sorry." I smiled weakly at her. "Go and meet her. Congratulations, Nanny and Grandad!" I beamed at them, cuddling them both before they rushed into the room.

I smiled as I made my way down the long corridor. I felt like shit. I looked like shit. I thought Carter may have been there, but why would he have been? Probably with his slutty blonde.

I pulled my phone out and called a cab, and within a few minutes it was there.

"It's you!" he said as I stepped into the cab.

"Paul?" I asked.

"Yeah! Haha, it's me! How was Paris?" he asked as he pulled away from the kerb.

"Ah, it was amazing. Feels like a lifetime ago."

"I bet. How are the men in your life?"

"Yeah... erm, good," I said. I really didn't want to be talking to him about it all.

"Good." He nodded. He must have picked up my distant tone.

I sighed in relief as we pulled up outside the penthouse. "Thank you, Paul. Take care," I said as I handed him the cash before running into the building. I needed to go home. I needed a change of clothes, plus I had work in the morning. I unlocked the door and wandered through the empty hallway, placing my keys on the sideboard. I flicked the kettle on and made myself a cup of coffee before flopping down on the sofa. I was distracted when I heard the front door open. *Shit.* I jumped over the sofa and hid, then I realised my cup was sitting on the coffee table. I rolled my eyes at my stupidity.

"Hello?" I heard a voice, but it wasn't Carter's. I recognized it, but couldn't put a face to it. I heard their footsteps moving down the hallway then I heard the old study door go. I peeked over the top of the sofa. I needed to get out. Maybe he had rented it out.

What the bloody hell am I going to do? I jumped when I heard the smashing of furniture. *Oh my God. Was he being burgled?* I sat with my back against the back of the sofa as I unlocked my phone, and I quickly typed a message to Carter:

```
Penthouse. Help!
```

"Where the fucking hell are they?" he snarled as I heard him stomping back through the hallway. My phone beeped. *Fuck.* My heart was thumping. Why the fuck did I take it off silent? I looked down.

```
Be there in ten X
```

"Well, well, well. Look who I've found. What are you doing hiding behind there?" He smirked as he bent down and looked behind the sofa. I looked up at him, eyes wide and full of fear. It was Esme's dad. "Who have you been texting?" he asked as he bent down and grabbed my phone. "Perfect, he will be here as well." A small, twisted smile flashed over his face as he dropped my phone on the floor and stamped on it. I felt sick to my stomach. I remembered his warning. *"I'm not finished with you yet, Freya. I will come back for you. You owe me that."*

"Get the fuck up," he snarled at me, grabbing my hair and dragging me off the floor.

"Get off me!" I screamed at him as he continued to drag me along the floor. I tried to grab onto anything I could but my fingertips were like butter, slipping off everything I touched.

"Get up!" he spat as he twisted his fist into my hair, pulling me to my feet.

"Please, don't hurt me. What do you want?" I asked as he smashed me against the wall. I winced as he did.

"What do I want?" He licked his lips before breaking into a laugh. "What I want is long gone. My daughter. I will never fucking see her again because of you."

I closed my eyes as spittle left his lips and landed on my face. I was so scared; I didn't know what he was capable of. I relaxed as I saw him turn around and take a few steps away from me.

I took a deep breath. "We had no choice. She was taken away from us," I stammered.

He spun round, his eyes black and burning into me. He grabbed my cheeks so hard and pushed them together before getting in my face. "You always have a choice," he said through gritted teeth. "You thought I was gone after your precious Carter called security? The police have nothing on me. I was released with a warning." He laughed as he squeezed my cheeks even more. I grabbed his wrists and tried to pull them away. "Silly girl," he muttered as he released my cheeks. I watched as he balled his hands into fists.

Before I could shout out. I felt an almighty blow to my jaw and I fell down against the wall as the ache shattered through me.

"Get up," he said as he stood over me. I rolled on my side, trying to get on all fours to stand. My head was spinning and my eyes felt like they were rolling into my head. "I said get up!" He kicked me in the ribs. I whined as the blow hit me, taking every last breath I had, the wind knocked out of my lungs. I spent a moment trying to catch my breath. "I said get..." a stamp down on my shin bone. I heard the crack in the bone as I let out the most excruciating scream. "...the fuck up!" he yelled, the veins in his neck popping, his eyes bulging as he grabbed my hair and lifted me up, his other hand around my throat.

I couldn't focus. I couldn't breathe. His clench grew tighter and tighter around my throat. My hands moved fast up to his as I tried with every last bit of strength I had to free myself. His free hand moved slowly round to the back of his trousers and he pulled out a gun.

My eyes streamed with tears, and I felt lightheaded. "Please don't do this," I whispered.

"Sorry, I couldn't hear you." He grinned. "What did you say?"

"Please... D...do-" I couldn't get the words out. I started seeing black. My heart slowing, I was petrified. This was it. The end.

I heard the penthouse door smash open. "LET HER GO!" Carter screamed.

His grip dropped from my throat and I fell to the floor in a crumpled heap as I gasped for breath, trying to fill my lungs as quickly as I could. Pain shot through my leg; I couldn't move.

"Oh, good. You're here," Philip taunted. Carter stood in the hallway a few feet away from him, his eyes flitting from me to him. The sheer panic when he saw my face and my leg. His eyes flickered to darkness; the angry Carter was coming. I kept my eyes on Carter the whole time while they had their standoff.

"Put the gun down," Carter said calmly as he held up his hands.

"Why would I do that?" Philip joked, pushing his curled tongue through his teeth.

"Because I've asked you to."

"Oh, oh, okay, because Mr Big has asked me, I shall put the gun down," he said quietly, still smiling.

I let out a sigh of relief, and Carter dropped his hands and relaxed.

"Yeah, no thank you. I've changed my mind." Philip growled, then I heard the gun shot. Carter fell to the floor, completely limp.

"Carter!" I screamed through streaming tears, my throat burning.

"Now you, princess." He grinned. I closed my eyes and threw my arms over my head as I heard another gun shot. I gasped when I hadn't felt anything. I looked up to see James holding a gun, and Philip hunched on the floor holding his shoulder.

"Freya, call 999," he demanded. I nodded through my tears and crawled over to Carter, patting down his pockets for his phone when I came to his gunshot wound. My hands were soaked in the blood, his white t-shirt drenched as it continued to pour. I couldn't focus, my hands shaking. I looked up at James; he was already on the phone.

"Carter, baby, please stay with me." I had his head in my hands, cradling him. I was choking out sobs.

How? How had this happened.

James tied Philip up with his tie while we waited for the police. "Piece of shit" he growled as he rolled him over with his foot. He then dropped down to his knees next to Carter and felt his neck for a pulse. "He's still breathing, ambulance is on its way." He pulled off his suit jacket and ripped off his shirt then scrunched it into a ball and applied pressure to the bleed in Carter's stomach. "He will be fine, Freya," he whispered and gave me a weak smile.

"How do you know?" I cried as I leant down and kissed Carter's lifeless lips.

"Because I know my gunshot wounds," he said with a smile. "I used to be in the army. Basic training."

"Why isn't he awake?" I asked quietly.

"It's just the shock. He will come around soon." He reached out and squeezed my shoulders. "Are you okay? Your face is bruised, your lip is busted, and your leg looks broken." He shook his head in anger as he looked at Philip on the floor.

"I'm fine," I whispered. I lied. But compared to what was going on, I *was* fine.

Finally, the ambulance crew arrived. I crawled out of the way and watched as they spoke to James about what had happened while they checked Carter over and got ready to move him down to the ambulance. I was taken back to Cape Verde, us in the sea, swimming and mucking about. His kiss on my lips, his fingertips tracing every inch of my skin. My breath caught as I was pulled from my trance.

"Freya," James called out. "You go with him, I'll wait for the police. I will meet you at the hospital."

I nodded, numb. I had lost all sense of feeling.

"Baby," I heard Carter mumble as they wheeled him out the door. My heart skipped. Oh, thank God.

"Can you call Elsie, and my mum and dad, please? My phone is smashed." I trailed off as I looked around the room. I couldn't believe this had happened. I flinched as I felt a hand grab my arm.

"Hey, it's okay. Let's get you in the ambulance." A friendly blonde-haired woman tried to help me up.

"I don't know if I can walk," I muttered.

"I will support you," she said. She tried to lift me off the floor, but I couldn't move.

James came over, frustrated. "She just told you she can't walk. Sit with that prick and wait for the police while I take her down."

He stood in front of me and lifted me over his shoulder. "Hold on," he said as he made his way to the lift. I was now very aware he had no top on, but, I was so thankful he was there.

CHAPTER TWENTY

Carter

I woke disorientated, I winced as I felt the soreness of my stomach. I slowly looked up and saw I was lying in a hospital bed. My panicked eyes darted around the room when I saw my mum, and I relaxed when she took my hand into hers.

"Hey, sweetie. Are you okay? I'll get the nurse," she said as she kissed me on the forehead then left the room.

Overwhelming anxiety swept over me, my thoughts bouncing around my head. Where was Freya? Was she hurt? Had she forgiven me? I frowned at the last thought.

It wasn't what she thought it looked like. Yes, she was one of my 'flavours' but, that was all it was. She was being friendly. Okay, maybe a bit *too* friendly. I needed to apologize. She was going to be livid that I didn't contact her, but she told me not to follow her. James told me she was at the penthouse, but I didn't want her to know he had broken her trust. I just wanted to give her the space she needed. Maybe I should have text her back when she messaged me, but I just didn't know what to do. I was interrupted when my mum and a doctor walked in.

"Carter." He smiled at me. "Nice to see you awake." He came over and checked my chart.

"Just going to do a few checks, okay?" he said as he shone a light in my eyes. "Great." He took my blood pressure and temperature to make sure I hadn't caught an infection. "How are you feeling?" he asked as he sat down next to me.

"Not bad. Sore."

"Well, if you weren't sore, I would be worried. The bullet went straight through, missing your intestine and bowel by millimetres. You were very lucky. We cleaned the wound and sewed both sides. Nice little scar to show your girlfriend," he teased.

"Talking of my fiancée..." I eyed him. "Where is she?"

"She is in recovery. She suffered a nasty break to her tibia so we had to rectify that, plus stitch both wounds on her hand and wrist," he said with a grimace.

My pulse was racing, the machine beeping louder. "That bastard," I growled. "Where the fuck is he?"

"He's in custody, don't worry. They will be in to see you soon."

"When can I see Freya?" I asked impatiently.

"Once she's up from recovery, we will wheel you

round to see her. She's okay. She's still coming around from surgery. I promise, she's fine." He smiled as he stood up. "I will send the police in now, is that okay?"

"Yes," I snapped. The doctor looked at my mother and then left the room.

"Carter, don't talk to him like that," she said in her soothing voice.

"Freya is hurt because of that arsehole!" I shouted

"Language," she scolded me.

I rolled my eyes at her. "I just want to see her, Mum. You should have seen her. He had her by the throat. She was completely limp. I thought she was dead." I choked as the lump crawled up my throat. "I should have reacted differently. I should have run towards him, but he had a gun. I was scared he was going to shoot her. Her beautiful face was so swollen, her lip cut and bleeding." I took a deep breath. "I just…" I shook my head. I couldn't get the image out of my head, and now she was lying in a hospital bed. "It's my fault."

"Carter," my mum said quietly.

"No, it is. I was acting like an idiot in front of an…" I stopped myself. "An old friend." I coughed, clearing my throat. "Freya saw. I reacted in the wrong way. I let lust get in the way of everything. She stormed out, telling me not to follow her, so I didn't. I went to the hospital when I knew Laura was in labour. She didn't want to see me. She hit me and pushed me away so when she disappeared back into the room, I left. I knew she was in the penthouse, James told me, yet I still didn't go." I bit my lip as I looked at my hands. "That prick got in there and did that to her. If I was a second later, she would be dead. I would be calling Rose and Harry telling them that their beautiful, kind-hearted daughter was dead." I couldn't bear thinking about it. The hot tears rolled down my face as I faced what could have happened, all because I didn't chase after her.

My mum squeezed my hand. "Darling boy," she said as she lifted my chin to look at her, wiping my tears with her free hand. "This was not your fault. You did what she asked. You stayed away. You need to understand that she has gone through a lot these last few months. I'm not saying you haven't but she has *physically* lost. But please don't blame yourself." She stopped as she looked over her shoulder and saw a detective and a police officer come in.

"Mr Cole, can we have a minute of your time?" he asked.

"Yes," I snapped. I wasn't in the mood for this bullshit.

"I'm Detective Stone, and this is my colleague, PC Dunstable." He nodded. More like PC Dipshit. I rolled my eyes at my thought.

"We just have a few questions about the incident that took place in your home this afternoon," he said as he got his notepad out of his pocket. "What happened when you walked into the building?" he asked, eyes boring into me.

"He had Freya by the throat. She was lifeless. He was grinning. I asked him to stop."

"And did he?" he asked, jotting notes down.

"Yes," I replied.

"Then what?"

"He dropped her to the floor like a piece of rubbish and turned on me with a gun." I shook my head. "I asked him to put the gun down, calmly. He said he was going to, then, when I dropped my guard, he shot at me, then turned the gun on Freya. Then I blacked out."

"Okay, thank you. I have taken James' statement. We will need to wait for Freya to wake up before we can take hers."

"Leave her out of it. She's been through enough," I demanded.

"Mr Cole, all due respect, she is a key witness in this investigation. We need to talk to her," he said with attitude.

"Fine. Make sure that arsehole gets sent down for what he did."

"Oh, don't worry. He has a lot of charges against him because of this incident."

"Good," I growled at him.

"Get some rest, Mr Cole. We will be in touch." He smiled weakly as he and his colleague left the room.

"You hungry?" my mum asked. She looked exhausted.

"Yeah, I am."

"Good. I made pea and ham soup. Your favourite. Your grandmother's own recipe." She smiled a heartwarming smile. Her soup is the only soup I would eat; no one made it like her.

I watched as she poured the hot soup into a bowl from her flask and placed it on my bed tray.

"Thank you, Mum," I said as I took my first mouthful. "Delicious as always." I smiled.

We were lost in quiet chatter when I heard the door open. "Are we interrupting?" I heard Rose's voice as she poked her head around the door.

"No, not at all," I said as I pushed my bed tray away.

"Elsie, lovely to see you. Shame it's under difficult circumstances." She grimaced as she looked over at me. I had never seen her annoyed; she was scary. *Fuck,* I'm in trouble.

"Could I have a word with Carter please?" Harry said, short and clipped.

"Of course," Mum said. "Rose, would you care to join me in the café for a coffee?"

"Certainly," Rose said as they walked out together.

"Harry," I said sternly. I knew what was coming.

"How are you feeling?" he asked as he sat on the edge of my hospital bed.

"Not bad. Sore, but okay," I said, picking my nails.

"You know I care a lot about you. You make my Freya

very happy." He nodded as he looked at his feet, folding his farmer's cap in his hands. "But you have caused her more hurt in this last year than she has ever been through," he said bluntly, looking at me. I went to speak but he held his hand up to stop me. "I'm not finished. Carter, this needs to stop. She can't take much more. She is currently lying in a bed still under the anaesthetic. Her face is swollen, she has bruises and red marks on her throat, and her leg is pinned, plus she has ended up with twelve stitches in her hand. Did she do that earlier?"

"No," I said quietly. "I caused that. I upset her and she smashed a glass then cut her hand." I sighed.

His eyes bored into me and he shook his head in disappointment. "Carter, you can't keep causing her this hurt. I know you aren't doing it on purpose, but you need to sort this out. You're both lying in a hospital because of some maniac." He twisted his hat even tighter in his hands.

"Harry, I'm so sorry," I said. I wanted to cry but I didn't want to cry in front of him. I was too proud. *Or am I?* "I don't deserve her," I choked. "Honestly, I really don't. She is my sunrise every morning, my sunset every evening. Each day, I'm worried that it may be our last, that she will get tired of me and leave me. I have broken her heart so much, I honestly don't know how it's still beating." I sighed. "I love her, Harry. With all of my fucked up, broken, black heart. She is making it full again, turning the black back to red. She is my life. If anything had happened to her..." I choked again, wiping my eye of a stray tear. "I wouldn't have been able to go on. Please believe me when I tell you that she really is my everything. My morning, my night, my sun, my moon. My universe and everything beyond. She is my happily ever after. My something everlasting." I wiped my eyes again; they felt so raw.

He sat up straight as he cleared his throat. "Last chance with her, Carter. I can't have her go through anymore," he said as he put his hat back on. He stood and patted my leg. "Get better soon," he said as he walked out the door.

I woke from my sleep after being administered more painkillers. I slowly opened my eyes and saw my mum sitting there, waiting for me to wake. "Hey, darling. Are you okay?" she asked as she stood and walked over to me.

"Yeah, I'm okay." I reached for my water and took a big mouthful.

"Freya is awake." She beamed at me. "Want to go and see her?"

"Do you even have to ask?" I teased her. "Fetch my wheelchair."

Mum wheeled me into her room. I nodded as Rose opened the door for me.

"Carter?" Freya said quietly.

I couldn't believe my eyes. The right side of her face was swollen, and her jaw looked distorted. Her full bottom lip was even fuller and more bruised. My heart shattered when I saw her leg hoisted off the bed, pinned and casted. "Baby," I whispered.

"Are you okay?" she asked me. "Carter, I thought you were dead. If it wasn't for James…" she sobbed.

"Hey. Hey, don't cry," I whispered. "We're okay, baby. That's all that matters. Yeah, okay, I got shot, you got a broken leg. But, we are alive," I said, smiling at her.

"I can't believe you got shot. It's all my fault. If I hadn't thrown a strop, I would never have been at the penthouse." She shook her head, looking at her mum and dad.

"Can you give us a minute, please?" I asked our parents. Harry was not pleased to leave us but Rose pulled him out.

"Freya, this wasn't your fault. This was my fault. For the…" I coughed and looked over my shoulder. "The slutty blonde."

She rolled her eyes. "Don't fucking mention her again," she growled.

"I'm sorry, baby."

"Where the fuck were you?"

"I was giving you space," I said, watching her facial expression. "You told me not to follow you." I shrugged slightly, wincing as I did.

"And you listened. You never normally listen." She raised her voice.

"I know."

"Did you have sex with her?"

I scoffed and snorted at the same time. "Are you mad?"

"Answer the fucking question." She furrowed her brow.

"No, Freya. I didn't fucking have sex with her. I love you! God, no one compares to you. I mean, look at you. You even pull that hospital gown off. If I wasn't wounded, and you hadn't shattered your bone, I would climb onto that bed and devour you."

She blushed from head to toe. I loved that I still had the effect on her.

"Scoot over if you can," I said quietly. She moved over to the edge of the bed the best she could. I hissed through my teeth as I stood up slowly from the wheelchair. I slowly sat down on the bed, swinging my legs around gently. I lifted my arm up so she could snuggle in. I wasn't moving. I was staying there until we were allowed home.

"I'm sorry, Freya. I know that's all I've been saying, but I am," I whispered into her messy, bird nest of a bun.

"I'm sorry too," she said as she kissed me on the cheek.

"Once you're out of your cast, we are getting married, woman."

"Eight weeks' wait, Mr Cole," she said quietly.

"Eight weeks is nothing. I waited a year to kiss you again," I said as I turned her mouth towards me. "I love you." I kissed her softly. I felt her wince underneath me.

"Sorry."

CHAPTER TWENTY-ONE

A few weeks had passed, and things were getting easier. I was now in a sexy boot which Carter loved. Not quite sure why; maybe he was being nice. I was working from home because Carter wouldn't let me out of his sight.

"What are you doing?" he asked as he wrapped his arms around my shoulders, kissing my neck.

"I'm writing," I murmured as I looked at him. "A book."

"Are you really?" he said, surprised.

"Mmhmm."

"What's it about?" he asked, his face alight.

"An innocent woman who falls in love with a man who has never had a serious relationship, only 'flavours' of the month. Thinking of calling it *Lucky Number Seven*." I grinned before giggling.

"Seriously?" He beamed at me.

"Yeah, why not? We've been through so much so I

decided to write it down. I'm not going to pursue it, just writing more as therapy."

"I see. Well... I have a better therapy idea." He gave me a smouldering look. Before I could stop him, he swooped me up from the office chair and walked me into the bedroom. "I need some you time." He kissed my lips. "Plus, that boot really does it for me." He winked as he closed the bedroom door behind him. He un-fastened my boot and lay my casted leg down gently. "All okay?"

I nodded eagerly. We hadn't had sex since before the shooting; we were so wanting each other.

"I love that you wear shorts all the time at the moment. Easy access." He bit his lip as he traced his fingers up my thigh. I whimpered as his touch burned my skin. "Oh, I've missed you," he mumbled as he kneeled down on the floor between my legs then planted soft, wet kisses up my thighs, stopping at the apex of my thighs. He hooked his long, thick fingers around my shorts and pulled them to the side. A growl left his throat. I let out a deep sigh as his fingers slowly caressed over my sweet spot. I let out a moan as he delicately continued his soft strokes over me. "So ready for me," he groaned as he nipped my inner thigh, causing me to gasp.

"Ow!" I whined.

"Shhh," he said as he nipped again. He traced his finger down and slowly entered it into me, continuing the slow rhythm in and out of me. I felt his warm breath over my sex before his tongue brought me to life, flicking over me again and again as his fingers kept pumping into me.

"Carter," I moaned.

"Let go, baby," he whispered before taking in my taste. I could feel myself tightening, my legs beginning to shake.

"Oh," I whined out as I placed my arm over my mouth. "Keep... going," I panted as I bit my skin. I hissed through my teeth as I felt my climb, my stomach burning, needing its release. His tongue slowed as he sucked on me before flicking, one slow tongue movement. I caved, everything in me exploding as my orgasm hit me hard. He slid his finger out and sucked them dry. "Tasty as ever," he moaned, his eyes on fire, the glisten from me on his mouth. He crawled onto the bed and kissed me, his tongue invading my mouth and caressing my tongue slowly. I heard him unbutton his jeans and he pulled them down to his knees; this was going to be quick.

He grabbed my bad leg and lifted it up slightly, pushing it back past my hip. "I'll keep hold of this," he said. His other arm steadied himself over me as he slammed into me, fierce and hard. He rested his arm next to my head. "You are so beautiful." He slammed into me harder and deeper this time. I cried out as the delicious burn started brewing in my belly again. "This is going to be so quick, baby," he said through gritted teeth.

"Oh, I'm so close," I moaned. He pushed my t-shirt

up around my neck, pulling my bra down as he took my breast into his mouth, sucking hard. My tummy tightened.

"Let it go, baby. I can feel how ready you are," he said before his mouth was back on me, nipping and sucking as he filled me again and again.

"Oh," I moaned as I came hard around him. "Carter!"

"That's it, baby." He gritted his teeth as he found his high, then came crashing down around me.

We lay still for a few moments, not saying anything. His head rested on my chest as his fingers ran up and down my side. My heart thumped.

"I am so lucky to have you," he mumbled as he lifted his head and kissed my chin.

"I'm the one that's lucky," I scoffed at him. "I'm so glad you came into my office that day." I smiled at him. I loved watching his beautiful sage eyes glisten.

"I wish I didn't set out for revenge in the first place." He sighed. "I did mean what I said. I fell in love with you as soon as I saw you in that office. Your white shirt, your leather pencil skirt and those fucking hot shoes. Need to fuck you with them on once your leg is better." He stood up. "I need a shower." He kicked off his jeans and lifted his t-shirt.

I sighed when I saw the wound on his stomach. I sat up and grabbed him by the trim of his boxers and pulled him towards me. I slowly traced my finger over then round the scar. "I can't believe he did that to you." My lip trembled at the flashbacks.

"Baby, I can't believe what he did to you. But please, don't get upset. I'm fine." He leant down and kissed me. "Now, let me go shower, woman," he teased as he walked into the en-suite.

I huffed as I moved myself back up the bed. I was so fed up being in a cast. I flicked the telly on for some noise while Carter was showering. All of a sudden, I heard a noise. I muted the TV when I heard Carter singing. I smiled as I listened to the words. I recognized the song, I just couldn't think of who sang it. He then started humming. He fell silent as the shower turned off. I quickly unmuted the telly as he padded back through in just his towel.

"Nice shower?" I asked, a small smirk appearing on my face.

"Was lovely. Shame you couldn't have joined me," he said as he rough dried his hair with the towel.

"Ah, I know," I said as I bit my lip. "But to be honest, I didn't want to ruin your singing." I pulled the cushion up to my mouth as I started giggling.

He blushed then composed himself. "I have a wonderful voice. Don't be jealous, baby." He smiled at me before disappearing into the dressing room.

We had just finished dinner when my phone buzzed. "Babe, can you grab that for me, please?" I asked.

"Of course." He slid out from his chair and grabbed my phone from the side unit, passing it to me.

"Who is it?" I asked.

"I didn't look" he said as I took it from him.

"It's Mya." His head snapped up at the mention of her name. "Let me read it," I said. I could see he was getting angry

Hi Freya & Carter,

I heard what happened with Philip. My husband and I are utterly disgusted that this happened. I'm not sure if you know but Philip has been sentenced to 20 years in prison, plus another 5 on top for breaking and entering. I hope this brings you some peace.

I was hoping to speak to you in regards to bringing Esme to see you, but now under the circumstances I'm not sure if you would still like that. I was just going to drive by tonight, but didn't want to risk it.

Let me know, we can still come over tonight if you wish to see her.

Sending lots of love and strength,
Mya x

"Like fuck she is coming here!" Carter shouted.

"Carter, it's about Esme, not her!" I shouted back at him as I banged my hand down on the table then winced, forgetting it had been stitched. "She had nothing to do with it. Unfortunately, that psycho is her son. She has already told you she has nothing to do with him anymore. Please, I want to see her and I know you do too," I said with assertiveness in my voice. His eyes didn't look up from his empty plate. I reached over and grasped his hand with mine. "Please, Carter. After all of this, I really want to see her," I said in a whisper. I watched as his jaw clenched and he closed his eyes. I knew this was going to be hard for him. He hadn't even looked at a picture of her since she went. But I also knew he missed her terribly. As did I.

After a moment of silence, he let out a deep sigh. "Fine. Tell her to come tomorrow night," he snapped as he excused himself from the table.

"Bye then," I muttered under my breath. I typed a quick reply before locking my phone.

I woke early the next morning. I was tired. I couldn't remember the last time I had a full night's sleep. I could never get comfortable. I moved slowly out of bed before hobbling into the bathroom. I needed a bath. I sat waiting for my bath to run, before putting my plastic bag over my cast and sliding myself in.

Maybe on top of the uncomfortableness of my cast, it was the thought of seeing Esme that was causing my uneasy feeling. I slid myself down slightly more as my leg hung over the top of the roll top bath. I couldn't wait to get that cast off. I hated it.

I walked as quietly as I could to the bedroom and

slipped back into bed; it was three a.m. I was hoping the hot, peaceful bath would help send me back off to sleep. I lifted Carter's arm up and snuggled underneath him, taking a deep breath as I breathed in his scent. I tried what I used to do as a kid, counting sheep. It must have worked, because I don't remember what number I got to.

"Morning, beautiful. Sleep okay?" he asked as he walked in with a cup of tea.

"Mmm, I needed a good sleep," I said, hoisting myself up and resting my back against the backboard, my good leg bent up. I smiled as I accepted the cup of tea. "Thank you," I said as I brought the cup up to my lips and took a mouthful. "What time is it?"

He pulled his long sleeved t-shirt up and looked at his Rolex. "Ten forty-five." He smiled at me.

"Carter! Why didn't you wake me?"

"Because, baby, you needed sleep. You haven't been sleeping well since everything happened."

"I know. I just can't switch off."

"We've got our meeting with Dr Cox shortly. Hopefully we get some good news after the last couple of appointments." He gave a small, hopeful smile.

"Let's hope, eh? Help me up, please." I smiled as I held my hand out.

"Can I drive?" I asked as we walked to the car that Carter bought us.

"No, Freya. You have a bloody boot on," he scolded.

I rolled my eyes. "Fine. Stupid boot." I sulked. He smiled at me as he opened my door. "Always the gentleman." I beamed at him as I slid into the passenger seat. He closed the door behind me before jumping in the driver's side.

He took my hand in his and kissed it. "Try not to be nervous," he said as he started the engine.

The drive to Dr Cox's office felt like it took forever. Maybe it was the nerves that made it seem longer.

We walked hand in hand back to the same office that had broken our hearts the last two times we had been there. I saw by Carter's face he was nervous, but I didn't want to let on that I could tell. He gave my hand a squeeze as he checked us in. My arse literally just touched the seat when Dr Cox called us into his office.

"Carter, Freya. So wonderful to see you." He looked down at my boot. "What happened?"

I felt Carter's grip on my hand get tighter before hearing his wicked tone leave his mouth. "Well, Doctor, my fiancée got attacked and had her leg basically snapped in half by Esme's biological father," he snapped. "He also shot me when I tried to stop him hurting Freya." A grimace hit his face. It was like he was living it all over again.

"Oh, I'm so sorry to hear that. I hope he was dealt with accordingly," he said before giving us a weak grin then shaking mine and Carter's hands. He gestured for us to have a seat opposite his desk. "Okay, Freya, tell me. What's going on?" he asked as he pressed the tips of his index fingers into his chin. I looked at Carter and dropped my eyes to my lap before taking a deep breath. I felt shy talking about this for some reason.

"Erm, I..." I looked at Carter again then Dr Cox. "I haven't had a period since all this has happened." I blushed and knotted my fingers.

"And your last one was?" he asked as he made notes.

"Erm, November I think. I'm sorry. So much has happened. I've lost track of all days and time."

"That's okay." He nodded as he carried on writing. He placed his pen down and looked at me and Carter. "Okay, so as I said before, one of your tubes was damaged which could be the cause. But, I'll be honest, I think it is more to do with the miscarriage. It can take months for your body to get back on track."

"Okay, so how does that help us? We want to start trying for a baby soon. How can we try when she isn't having periods?" I turned to face Carter as I listened to him, his tone and manner clipped and blunt. My eyes darted back to Cox as we waited for his answer.

"Well, Carter, we are happy to run some tests, but I really do think you just need to let nature take its time."

"Right, well this was certainly a waste of time," he said as he stood from the chair, taking my hand and helping me up.

"Carter, don't..." Dr Cox said as we went to leave.

"Don't what? Stop your payments every month? I'll be honest, you have brought us nothing but bad news and heartbreak. You don't deserve anything from us. We're done." Carter snapped as he took my hand and led me out the door.

"Great, so now we have to go doctor shopping?" I teased.

"Button it," he said playfully with a wink. "You deserve the best." He kissed me softly.

CHAPTER TWENTY-TWO

"Seeing as it's been a bit of a disappointing morning, why don't we go to The Savoy? We did say we wanted to look at it, and we're close," he said with a hint of a smile on his face. He reached across and turned his music up as Dean Lewis sang through the car.

"Sure, let's go. I'm excited to see it!"

"I can't wait to marry you." He beamed at me.

"I love you." I smiled back at him.

"I love you," he said, taking my hand to his lips and kissing it. It felt weird not having James there. I got so used to him driving.

Shortly after, we drove up outside The Savoy, a massive grin sweeping across my face as we parked. We climbed out of the car and gave the keys to the smartly dressed gent in hat and tails, then walked through the revolving doors and stepped onto the black and white checked high shine tiles. I sighed. I walked quietly, not saying a word, just taking everything in. I walked down the few steps that led me to an open area with a beautiful, large flower arrangement in the middle of the floor on a dark table.

"You happy?" Carter asked as he tugged on my arm, pulling me into him, his eyes burning into my soul.

"So happy," I said, going onto my tiptoes and kissing him on the cheek.

"Good. We have an appointment with the wedding planner that I booked a couple of weeks ago. I hope that's okay," he asked, with slight uncertainty in his voice.

"Of course it is!"

"Good." He kissed my forehead.

The wedding planner's name was Anya. She was a petite brown-haired lady with beautiful hazel eyes. She was very over-enthusiastic, clapping her hands and squealing every time we made a comment on how we would like our wedding. She walked us through to one of the more intimate rooms. The ballroom was beautiful but a bit too big for what we wanted, even though I could see Carter chomping at the bit for a big, extravagant wedding. I knew he wanted it, but I didn't like the attention, or see the point of throwing a massive wedding. I wanted it to be between him and me. Anya showed us around one of the suites which was perfect. We could have our ceremony and dinner in the same room so it saved people having to move around too much. It was beautiful, with a stunning river view.

"This is perfect," I whispered as I stared out of the window at the scenery. I spun around and pictured our nearest and dearest standing there, celebrating our wonderful day. "I am so in love with this." I eyed Carter who had his most beautiful grin on, his hand rubbing his chin gently.

"Okay, Anya, what's next?" Carter said as he turned to face her.

"Fabulous!" she squealed, jumping up and down and clapping. "Okay, follow me. Let's go decide on a date."

I followed her in a daze. I was so excited. I couldn't believe we were actually booking our wedding date. It felt so surreal, but so right. I watched as she excitedly flicked through her diary.

"Okay, darlings, the first available date I have is May 6th. That's a bank holiday. How does that work?" she asked, tapping her pencil on top of the opened date.

"That sounds perfect. No one will have to take time off work. I'm happy with that." He nodded before looking at me. "What do you think?"

"That's your birthday," I reminded him.

"I know," he said with a smirk then a little laugh left him.

"Do you want to get married then? Would you not rather find another date?" I asked, looking at Anya. She took the message and started flicking through again.

"No, I want to get married on the 6th," Carter said directly to Anya.

"You sure?" I asked.

"Baby," he said, turning in his chair to face me. "I have everything I could ever wish for, except for you. That would be the best gift you could give me, to marry me on my birthday and become my wife." He winked at me, his eyes alight with excitement.

After holding my breath for a few moments, I said, "Okay," as a smile crept across my face. "Let's book for the 6th May!"

"Fabulous, darlings! Two p.m. ceremony?" she chirped.

"Perfect," Carter and I said in sync.

"Okay, Mr Cole. If you would be okay to pay the deposit that we spoke about earlier, that secures your booking." Her smile spread across her petite face.

"Certainly," he said as he stood up and pulled his wallet out. He handed over his black AMEX then signed the paperwork. "Signed, sealed, delivered," he said as he came and sat on the arm of my chair and wrapped his arm around me.

"Thank you," I mumbled as I looked up at him.

"You are most welcome. Anything for you my queen," he said, before leaning down and kissing my forehead.

"Wonderful. That's all gone through," Anya said as she put the receipt and a brochure in a bag along with some other paperwork. "If you have any questions or would like to use our recommended suppliers, please do not hesitate to contact me." She smiled as she handed over the bag to me.

"I think we would stick with your suppliers, unless Freya would like to use anyone else?" he said, looking at me.

"No. I'm happy to use suggested suppliers." I nodded as I held the bag tight.

"Congratulations again," she said as she shook both of our hands before sitting back at her desk. I couldn't believe we had just booked our wedding. This was it. I was legally going to be Mrs Freya Cole. And I couldn't wait.

We sat nattering about all the details of what we would love for our big day. It was nice to see Carter so excited and high-spirited about this, it had been such a long time since I had seen excitement on his face.

"What flowers would you like?" he asked.

"Oh, easy. Roses. They are my favourites, plus they remind me of you." I swooned, remembering the first bouquet of flowers he gave to me.

"I'm good with that. How about suits? What colour?"

"Black. You look so hot in a tux." I blushed.

"Oh, done. Nothing beats a good tux, plus you said I look hot in a tux so…" He laughed.

"Best man?" I asked him.

"Ohhh, that's hard. I love all my mates the same, but

honestly, probably Louis. We've known each other the longest. Then I would have the rest of them as groomsmen." He smiled as he tapped his finger on the steering wheel along to Nat King Cole.

"What about you? Bridesmaids?" he asked.

"Easy! Laura, maid of honour. Then Brooke and Courtney." I smiled.

"Courtney, really?" He arched a brow, surprised by my answer.

"Yes, really. She was there for me when everything happened in a way no one else was. She is my little wild one, and I love her so much."

"Okay, okay." He held his hands up in defeat before putting them back on the steering wheel.

"You going to invite Ethan?" I saw him stiffen as he asked.

"I would like to, but I doubt he would come after the way I treated him," I said and looked at my phone screen.

"Freya, you didn't do anything. You both had a moment of weakness where something nearly happened, but it didn't. I don't like that he took advantage of you like that, but it happened. You were both in different places." He raised his shoulders, shrugging. "I'm happy if you want to invite him. He is still your friend."

"Thank you. I'll think about it," I said, rubbing my thumb over my phone screen.

"Colour scheme?" he asked, changing the subject. He

was really getting into this conversation.

"Champagne. I think the champagne against the black would look lovely. Very bold." I nodded in agreement with myself.

"I think that would look nice. Very rich and tasteful." He nodded along with me.

"Okay! Songs." I flicked through his phone trying to find some. "I've always loved this one," I said as I clicked *A Thousand Years* by The Piano Guys. We both sat in silence listening to the piano and cello playing through the car. My body covered in goosebumps. I looked at Carter who was wiping his eye as discreetly as he could.

"What do you think?" I asked, eyes wide, watching him.

"I love it," he whispered.

"Yay! Okay, so what about when we're signing the register?" I asked.

"Ed Sheeran – *This*," he said quickly.

"Didn't want to think about it?" I laughed.

"No. When we broke up and I left you, I used to play the song again and again and it just made me think of you." He bit his lip. "If you don't like it we can change it," he said, looking at me.

"No, no. It's fine. Let me put it on though. I want to listen." I smiled. A few moments later, I nodded again. "Yes, I love this," I said enthusiastically. "Okay, we're flying through this. So, walking out after we're married?

Any suggestions?"

And just as that word slipped off my tongue, Nat King Cole – *L.O.V.E* started playing. We didn't say anything, just focused on the words. Once it ended, we both looked at each other and laughed; we knew that was the one.

"Okay, last one. Our first dance." He beamed. "Can I suggest one before you start looking?"

"Of course." I handed him the phone while we were stopped at traffic lights. I saw him typing and scrolling fast to find his song. He clicked play then put the phone in the centre console of the car as the music started. I scrunched my nose at first as the music started playing.

"Give it a minute," he reassured me. I listened carefully, then I realized what song it was.

"Oh my God. This is the one you were singing the other morning," I said, happily.

"Yup, it is. Because it reminds me of you, and our relationship. You never gave up on me, and I am so glad you didn't. Because, honestly, you have made me the happiest man in the world." He looked at me and sighed. "I love you."

"I love you," I said, squeezing his thigh.

I was relieved when we pulled into our gated driveway; I was glad to be home. I felt exhausted. I had lost track of what day it was since I hadn't been going into the office.

We parked up outside and Carter opened my door.

"Thank you," I said quietly.

"Can I cook dinner tonight?" he asked.

"Of course. Let Julia know though as I know she has bought this week's shopping and worked out dinners," I said as I hung my coat in the cupboard.

"No worries. Why don't you go and have a bath? If you need me to wash your back just call up." He bit his lip and winked at me.

"Thank you." I smiled at him as I hobbled up the stairs. I couldn't wait to get my cast and boot off. Only four more weeks to go. I rolled my eyes at the thought.

I wrapped my cast in its plastic bag as I slid down into the bath, resting my leg out of the top. Even though I had the bag on, I didn't want to risk getting it wet. I closed my eyes for a moment, thinking back to the car and Carter's song choices. I smiled at the thought, my heart thumping faster and harder against my chest. I couldn't wait to marry him. I reached out for my phone and looked at the time. Five p.m. Mya was coming later with Esme. I'd better remind Carter as, no doubt, he'd forgotten. I needed to wash my hair but it was so hard to do it and keep my balance. I called out for Carter but got no response so gave him a quick text. Within seconds, he was next to me. "Can you wash my hair, please?" I asked.

"Of course." He smiled as he reached for the shampoo. He ran the hand shower over my hair before lathering it up full of suds. His fingertips slowly massaging my scalp, I moaned. It felt so good.

"How did you get so good at washing hair?" I teased.

"I used to wash Ava's hair for her when she broke her arm horse riding." He laughed at the memory "I got quite good at it. She used to get the hump sitting in the tub with a swimsuit on." He shook his head as he rinsed the suds away then smothered the roots and ends in conditioner.

"You remember Mya is coming tonight, right?" I said anxiously.

"Yes. I remember. I don't really want her here, to be honest."

"It's about Esme, remember?" I reminded him, giving him a weak smile.

"I know, I know." He nodded as he rinsed the conditioner out of my hair. "You ready to get out?"

"Yea, I think so," I said, pushing myself up with my arms. I felt his arms around me, scooping me up into his chest. He walked past the towel rail, and I grabbed the warm fluffy towels and wrapped myself up as he carried me through to the bedroom then placed me on the bed.

"You okay? Can I get back to cooking dinner?" he asked in a slightly grumpy manner, but cute grumpy.

"Of course. Thank you for washing my hair. You are definitely the best washer of hair." I giggled. "Now, go cook. Your wifey-to-be is hungry." I smirked at him.

"Be done in fifteen, nice and quick." He beamed at me as he disappeared out of the room.

I flopped on the bed. I couldn't wait to see Esme. I bet she had changed so much. I sat back up and rough dried my hair before walking into the dressing room and pulling out my pyjama shorts and one of Carter's big t-shirts. I dried my long mane and pulled it into a messy ponytail. As I walked down the stairs, the smell of dinner hit me. I was so hungry. I stuck my head into the kitchen to see if he was in there, but he wasn't. The kitchen was a tip. I hoped he tidied it up. I made my way through to the dining room to see him sitting there with a smug look on his face and two large glasses of white wine.

"Smells lovely," I complimented him.

"Let's just hope it tastes good." He laughed as he pulled my chair out for me to take a seat.

He had cooked crab, chilli and lemon linguine in a creamy white wine sauce with flat bread. I took a big mouthful and groaned as the taste exploded on my tastebuds. "Oh my God, Carter. This is amazing," I groaned again in appreciation, nodding my head.

"Good. I'm glad you like it," he said, clearly chuffed with himself as he took a big swig of wine.

"I hope you're going to clean up the kitchen, Mister." I scowled at him.

"Julia will do it." He shrugged.

"Carter!" I whined. "It's not for her to do. You made the mess, you clean it," I demanded.

He rolled his eyes at me. "Fine, but she may have

already done it." He huffed as he tucked into his dinner. "I'm a fucking good cook," he boasted.

"When are you going back to work?" I asked.

"When I feel like it. I'm my own boss, remember? Plus, I have been working from home."

"I can't wait to go back," I confessed. "It's hard working from home. I find it hard to get motivated."

"I know, but you will be back before you know it." He smiled.

I cleaned up our plates and watched Carter tidying the kitchen. I was glad he was doing it and not poor Julia. I know it was her job, but he shouldn't have just expected her to do it.

I had a quick tidy around then I heard the doorbell go. My heart was pounding, the nerves creeping slowly through me.

"I'll get it," Carter bellowed from the kitchen. I walked slowly behind him as he opened the door.

"Carter, Freya," Mya said, her eyes darting to my leg.

"Come in," Carter said in a blunt voice.

"My husband is just getting Esme," she said as she took her shoes off and handed her coat to Carter. I could see him biting the inside of his lip to curb his tongue.

I watched eagerly as her husband walked in with Esme in her car chair. My heart melted as I looked at her, all wrapped up in pink with a beautiful crochet hat.

"This is Reginald, my husband," Mya said, smiling as

he walked through the door. He had grey, swept back hair and the same colour eyes as Esme. He was about the same height as Philip; I could see a strong resemblance.

"Pleasure to meet you. Wonderful home you have here," he said as he looked around the hallway.

"Thank you," I said politely.

A couple of hours had passed and the conversation was easy until Reginald brought up Philip.

"I'm so sorry to hear what you and Freya went through because of my son," he said with disappointment in his voice. I sat quietly as I cuddled Esme, her little smile breaking my heart. "We were surprised not to see you at court." He put his cup of tea on our coffee table.

"We didn't want to go. If I would have seen him, I would have killed him. Justice was served, but he should have got life," Carter snapped. "How did he turn into such a fuck up?"

Reginald and Mya looked at each other, and Mya placed her hand over her husband's. "Philip was a very bright and kind young man. When he left school, he unfortunately got in with the wrong crowd, and they then turned to drugs. We tried to help him. We sent him to the best rehab facilities all over the country but he didn't want to help himself. One day, we had to make the hard choice and let him go. He chose drugs, not us. He was our only child, our miracle, really. I couldn't carry children after him. Back then, they didn't investigate and thought the best option was to give me a hysterectomy." She sniffed. "We are truly sorry for all you have been through. We would like to keep our relationship with you for Esme's sake. We don't want her growing up without you," she said hopefully.

"I am so sorry all that happened with Philip. Some people can't be helped. And I would like that, for Esme's sake," I said. I looked at Carter, his eyes dark and fixed on Mya the whole time. "Do you want a cuddle?" I whispered to him. It took him a while for his eyes to leave her and look at me, then Esme. He didn't say anything, so I handed her over to him. I saw his jaw clench and his shoulders tense as he took her, staring deep into her blue eyes.

"Are you both free on May 6th?" I asked. I felt Carter's eyes on me, but I didn't look at him.

"Why, yes, I think we are. Why is that, dear?" Mya asked, smiling at me before taking a sip of her tea.

"We would love for you, Reginald, and Esme to come to our wedding." I smiled at her. I placed my hand on Carter's thigh and squeezed it tight to reassure him that everything would be okay.

"Oh, that would be wonderful. Thank you so much," she said, her eyes wide as she looked at Reginald, and he smiled back at her. "Absolutely wonderful."

I swallowed hard, my palms sweaty and my heart feeling like it was going to burst out of my chest. It was the right thing to do.

ASHLEE ROSE

CHAPTER TWENTY-THREE

I finally had my cast off. It felt amazing to be able to wear jeans and heels again. The wedding was only a few weeks away and I couldn't wait. We had sorted Carter's suits out, and the bridesmaid dresses. They were delicate champagne maxi dresses. Very subtle. I had my final fitting the next day; it had come around so fast. I had slowly eased myself back into work, and once I went back, so did Carter. He didn't want to leave me on my own, you know, just in case anything else happened.

"Freya, what time have we got to be at the shop tomorrow?" Courtney shouted across the office.

I rolled my eyes. I got up from my desk and stuck my head around the door. "Ten a.m.," I said quietly. "No need to shout." I smiled at her. She flipped me off with her middle finger. I shook my head.

I had Courtney, Laura, and Brooke over later for takeaway and drinks. They were staying the night, then we were heading into Surrey in the morning to go for my final fitting. My mum and Elsie were also in town.

I switched my computer off before making my way downstairs; Courtney was already waiting for me. "Ready?" I asked.

"Yup! I told Morgan to pick me up from the bridal shop," she said as she dropped her phone into her bag. She skipped out of work swinging her bag round like a baseball bat.

Carter was standing next to James, waiting for us. "Evening, ladies," Carter said.

"Evening to you too," Courtney said as she slid into the car. "Hey, you," I said, kissing him on the lips before following Courtney.

"You excited for tomorrow?" he asked. "It doesn't seem that long ago that you were doing all this for Laura."

"I know, it's flown," I agreed, nodding. "I'm super excited though. Oh my God. What if it doesn't fit?"

"Of course it will fit!" Courtney said, shaking her head. "God, woman, calm down, will you? Don't be turning bridezilla on me. How much wine have you got, Cole?" she asked, teasing him.

"Enough for you to get drunk, be sick, and go to sleep." He laughed.

"I don't do sick. I could drink you under the table," she scoffed.

"Of course you could," he replied, now really laughing

to himself. "I might go and sleep in with the housekeepers tonight. I don't know if I can be in a house with four of you, plus our mums." He looked at James, and James smirked at him in the mirror.

"Oh, stop it. You'll be fine. You'll probably join us anyway," I teased.

"Yeah, I probably will." He laughed.

I squealed when I saw Laura's car parked outside the house. I couldn't wait to see her and Brooke. Courtney just stared at me in disgust.

"Yeah, get ready for a lot of that with those three." Carter rolled his eyes.

"Great," she said, mirroring him.

"Oh, pipe down, you two, before I kick you out for the night," I said harshly before running up the stairs to the house and barging through the door. I screamed as soon as I saw Laura and Brooke. They ran to me, grabbing me and pulling me into an embrace. I had missed those girls so much. As we broke our cuddle, I saw that they had hung some hen do banners and got some beautiful balloons blown up. "You guys!" I gushed.

"Least we could do!" Laura said excitedly.

"You excited?" Brooke asked.

"Yeah, and nervous! I was saying to Courtney I was scared the dress won't fit and…" I was interrupted. I looked over my shoulder and smirked at Courtney.

"And I told her it would fit. I warned you, Freya. No

bridezilla." Courtney said.

"This, girls, is Courtney," I said.

"Hey. I'm Laura, this is Brooke." Laura smiled at her. "Nice to meet you."

"You too. Cole, go fetch the wine," she demanded, and clicked her fingers.

"Piss off, Courtney. I don't know how Morgan is at home, but I only do what my queen asks." He smirked at her.

"Useless. I'll go get it," she huffed as she walked into the pantry.

"Oh, she's nice," Laura said quietly.

"Nice? Are you taking the piss?" Brooke said.

"She is nice, you just need to get used to her." I smiled nervously.

"If you or Brooke would have asked, I would have got you the wine," Carter muttered to Laura, giving her a sneaky wink. "Anyway, I will leave you ladies to it. I'm going to get changed then head up to my office for a bit," he said as he leant over and kissed me.

"Okay. Don't work too hard." I smiled at him and watched him disappear.

Courtney came bounding through with two bottles of wine and some crisps.

"I'll go get the glasses," I said before heading into the kitchen. I wandered back into the lounge and placed the glasses on the coffee table. "I'm just heading upstairs to get changed. I won't be long, okay? Start the wine and put some music on."

I poked my head into the spare room that used to be Esme's nursery to make sure Mum and Elsie were okay. "All good in here?" I asked, smiling at them.

"Fine, love," my mum replied, snuggled under the duvet with Elsie.

"Can I get you anything before I head back downstairs?" My eyes glistened as I watched them.

"No, thank you, dear. Julia already brought us a pot of tea and biscuits. She is coming to watch *Pretty Woman* with us once she's finished work." Elsie smiled at me as she took a sip of her tea.

"Wonderful, okay. Enjoy your evening. See you in the morning." I blew them both a kiss, closed the bedroom door, then wandered into Carter's office. "Oh, it's going to be a long weekend," I groaned as I ran my fingers along his shoulders before straddling him on his office chair.

"Stay up here with me," he suggested as he kissed my neck, his teeth grazing softly along it.

"As much as that would be amazing, I can't. I just hope Brooke and Court don't clash," I said, worried.

"I'll be down soon. I'll defuse them if need be. Now, go and enjoy yourself before I fuck you here, right now, so all your friends hear," he teased, his eyes falling dark and hazy. A whimper left my mouth as I climbed off him and disappeared into my bedroom to get changed.

I finally joined the girls back downstairs. The music was on, the wine had been poured, and the crisps were open. "What's for dinner?" I asked. "What do you all fancy?"

"Chinese," Laura piped up.

"Pizza," Brooke said.

"Wine." Courtney added.

"What do you want?" Laura asked.

"Hmm, I think a Chinese." I shrugged. "Sorry, Brooke."

"That's fine!" She smiled. "Let's order then."

Two bottles of wine down and half the Chinese eaten, we were all sitting in a food coma on the sofa.

"How's baby Freya?" I asked Laura. I still couldn't believe they named her Freya.

"She is amazing. I'm tired. But she is really amazing," she said as her eyes started to go heavy.

"Hun, you can go to bed. You haven't got to stay up with us." I smiled at her.

"Would you mind? Sorry, girls. I want to make the most of a full night of uninterrupted sleep." She laughed. "Night, girls," she said as she walked up to the spare room.

"More wine?" Brooke asked.

"Please," I said.

Courtney was on her phone, smirking, obviously texting Morgan.

"Hey, Brooke, sit down. I'll grab the bottle." Carter

beamed.

Brooke slumped next to me. "I've missed you," she said as she wrapped her arms around me.

"I can't wait to see you tomorrow."

"I've missed you too."

Carter strolled back into the lounge with more wine and topped our glasses up as he slumped down next to me. "Oi, unsociable, get off your phone!" he said loudly, throwing a cushion at Courtney.

"Piss off, Carter!"

Oh my God. These two were like kids.

"Seriously, stop it!" Brooke snapped at both of them. "You're pissing me off."

"Sorry, Brooke," Carter said quietly.

Courtney just rolled her eyes. "Can you show me to my room? I want to call Morgan," she said, downing her glass of wine.

"I'll go with you. I'm going to call it a night," Brooke said as she placed her glass on the table. "Thank you for tonight, hun." She gave me a cuddle.

"No, thank you. You and Lau sorted this. It's been lovely." I smiled at her as she let me go.

"Night, bitches," Courtney called out as she started moving up the stairs, Brooke following slowly behind her.

I let out a sigh of relief when it was just me and Carter.

"I'm glad it's just us two," he said as he ran his thumb across my bottom lip.

"Me too." I nipped the tip of his thumb and smiled at him.

"I can't wait to see you in your wedding dress soon." He twirled my hair in his fingers.

"I can't wait to see you in your tux." I smiled as his hands reached up to my face and he planted a soft kiss on my lips. He made my stomach flip every time he touched me. I knew where this was going. Even though my friends were upstairs, I didn't want him to stop. I pulled myself up and straddled him. "Let's pick up where we left off," I muttered before covering his mouth with mine.

We lay quietly on the sofa, Carter just in his jogging bottoms, me lying on top of him. My hair splayed across his chest, and his heartbeat softly drummed into my ear. I slowly ran my fingers up his side while his hands ran through my hair. I loved lying like this. No noise, no one else. Just us. I frowned as my fingertip ran across his gun wound scar. I pushed myself up and stuck my bottom lip out. I slowly circled the scar, again and again. I couldn't believe Philip shot him. I thought he only had the gun as an empty threat. Not to actually harm us.

"Never had a scar before." His eyes flicked down to watch my fingers, smiling down at me.

"Neither had I until my leg."

"Well, at least we both have one," he teased. I sniffed as I ran my hand round his back and felt his second scar. "Hey, don't be sad. It could have been a lot worse, couldn't it?" he said as he lifted my chin up to meet his eyes. "The main thing is we're both here, safe. Come on. Let's go to bed. You've got a big day tomorrow." He pushed me off of him gently, then we made our way upstairs.

I was up early, not sure if it was excitement or nerves. I quietly padded from the shower to our dressing room as I decided what to wear. I rough dried my hair while staring aimlessly into my wardrobe. I still couldn't believe in two weeks we were getting married. It had flown, what with work and sorting everything for the wedding. The weather had picked up and spring was in full swing; it was my favourite time of the year. I pulled out my favourite skinny jeans and a plain black, long sleeve t-shirt and black Converse. I sat at my dressing table and styled my hair into a low bun and put a light dusting of make up on. I didn't want to overdo it. I watched Carter walk sleepily through the dressing room as I slipped my Rolex onto my wrist.

"Morning, beautiful. You look lovely, as always." He smiled and kissed me on the cheek as he wrapped his long arms around me then sniffed in my perfume scent. "Delicious." He nuzzled into my neck, and I smiled. I loved him so much. He honestly set my soul on fire. My ripped up heart was slowly mending and it was all because of him. My king.

"I wonder if the girls are awake," I said.

"I doubt it. It is super early. I was only going for a pee then saw you were out of bed."

"I just couldn't sleep. Nerves and excitement took over me."

"I hope it's excitement and not nerves, baby. It'll fit." He laughed.

"What if I don't like it now?" I asked, biting my lip.

"If you don't like it then we will get you a new one. Please stop stressing." He grinned at me as he walked into the bathroom.

I made my way downstairs and saw Brooke and Laura sitting at the breakfast bar with our mums.

"Morning," I said as I grabbed a cup of coffee.

"You hungry?" Julia asked as she was wiping down the sides.

"Erm, no, thank you." I brought my cup to my lips and took a big mouthful. "Did you all sleep okay?"

"I slept like a log." Laura beamed. "I feel so good."

"I slept well, as always." Brooke nodded as she tucked into her toast.

"Yeah, lovely," my mum chirped, and Elsie nodded in agreement. "What time is your appointment?"

"Ten." I smiled. "There's no rush. Take your time. We've still got to wait for sleeping beauty." I laughed and looked towards the stairs. If Courtney wasn't up within the hour, I would go and wake her. There was no way I would be late.

Once we finally got through the weekend traffic, the SatNav said we would get to the shop bang on time. I was driving us all. Carter was out with his friends for last minute things for them. I parked outside the shop; we were lucky to get a spot. Probably because we had the first appointment. I took a deep breath as I turned the ignition off. I looked at Courtney sulking in the boot of the car. She was the smallest so had to sit on the little chairs that fold out in the boot. I breathed a laugh before getting out and letting her out.

"Thanks," she said with a disgusted look on her face, then brushed herself off and checked her make-up in her compact mirror. I shook my head at her.

"Don't forget my shoes, Mum!" I shouted as she stepped out of the car.

"Got them!" she shouted back.

We walked into the bridal shop and were greeted by Delilah, the owner of the store. "Darling, Freya!" She walked over with her arms open, taking me into her embrace. "Are you excited to see your dress?" she asked excitedly.

"Mmhmm." I bit my lip.

"Come on through here," she said, letting me go and wandering forward into the big, mirrored dressing room. I looked behind at my mum; she was already welling up. Elsie wrapped her arm around her shoulders and comforted her. I took a deep breath as we walked through the heavy curtain and saw my dress hanging in the bag. Laura and Brooke took a seat and clapped their hands excitedly, Courtney resting up against the wall. My mum and Elsie sat on the velvet chez longue, Mum still dabbing her eyes with a tissue.

I watched Delilah as she re-adjusted the bag that my dress was in before slowly unzipping it. I focused on her, her long bleached-blonde hair. Her skinny frame but peachy bum made her slightly big dress cling to it. She was naturally pretty, and I was slightly envious. My heart was thumping when she took the bag off the dress.

I heard the girls and our mums ahhing and oohing at the big reveal.

"Okay, if you want to go into the dressing room and undress for me, then come out and I can help you into it." She smiled at me before ushering me into the dressing room and pulling the curtain. I took a moment to calm myself while listening to the quiet voices of my friends and my mum.

"Isn't it beautiful, Elsie?" she said in a hushed voice.

"She is going to look breath-taking," Elsie agreed. I could hear Laura, Brooke, and Courtney muttering to themselves, but couldn't work out what they were saying. I slid my jeans down and took my t-shirt over my head before slipping into my delicate Jimmy Choos. I smiled as I looked down at them. They were covered in diamantes with a big crystal on the front of them; they reminded me of Cinderella's glass slippers. I stuck my head out of the curtain.

"Ready," I whispered to Delilah as she opened the curtain and stood me on a raised podium. I felt embarrassed standing in my underwear.

"Okay, step into this for me," she said as she opened the dress for me to step into. My mum stood up as she held my hand to balance me and I stepped into the delicate material. My heart was thumping in my ears; I was surprised they couldn't see it coming out of my chest. I looked at the girls. They all had anticipation on their faces, waiting for me. I took a deep breath as Delilah slid the soft material up my hips then held it for me to put my arms in, then smoothed it out.

"Perfecto," she said as she brought her hands up to her chest, a big smile spreading across her face. "Oh, one last thing!" Delilah said enthusiastically. She ran out of the dressing area only to return minutes later with a veil. I bent down slightly so she could place it in my hair, then she took a step back to marvel at me.

"Oh my baby." My mum started sobbing into a tissue. I looked over at Laura, Brooke, and Courtney. They all had their arms round each other with glistening eyes brimming with happy tears.

"You look absolutely beautiful," Elsie said as she stood with my mum. "Carter is very lucky to have you."

I smiled at her, dabbing my own eyes. I took a moment to myself. I blushed as I stopped and admired the woman staring back at me then moved my eyes down to my dress. It had a delicate sheath boat neck, with capped sleeves before meeting the sleek, fitted gown which fountained out slightly at the feet. The dress had a beaded bodice. I turned slightly to look at the back of it. There was a beautiful keyhole back trimmed in covered buttons. My favourite bit was the delicate gems that attached the material at the back together. I was in love; my dress clung in all the correct places and didn't draw attention to my large bust.

"So, what do you think?" I turned slowly and faced them, my face flushed, eyes glistening.

"Breath-taking" my mum breathed. "Honestly, so stunning," she said, dabbing her eyes.

"The dress is amazing. You make a stunning bride. We can't wait for you to be a Cole." Elsie smiled at me.

Laura, Brooke and Courtney came and stood next me, Laura running her fingers delicately down my dress. "Beautiful." She smiled.

I couldn't believe this was *my* dress. Next time I would be wearing it would be when we were saying 'I do', and I couldn't wait.

CHAPTER TWENTY-FOUR

I took a deep breath as we walked into Anya's office. I couldn't believe our wedding was on Monday.

"Darlings!" she said excitedly as we took our seats. "How are you both?" she asked as she shuffled her paperwork, her eyes glistening through her long lashes. Her brown hair looked as perfect as ever.

"Good, thank you," Carter replied for both of us.

"Okay, so I won't keep you too long. Just some final things to discuss and then the last payment is due." She smiled at Carter, her breath catching as she continued to stare at my beautiful husband-to-be.

"Perfect," I snapped, bringing her eyes to mine.

"Okay, so can you just run through your song choices once more so we can make a note? I don't want to get them the wrong way around." She giggled as she passed me her notepad and pen.

"Still happy with the three we chose?" I asked Carter.

"Oh, yes," he purred as he rubbed his thumb across my thigh, electricity coursing through me. I loved that we never lost that. I jotted the songs down for her and smiled a fake smile as I passed it back to her. We went over the last details, including the flowers, centrepieces for our few tables, and the wedding breakfast. We wanted to go traditional; prawn cocktail for start, beef joint roast with all the trimmings, and wedding cake for dessert. We had chosen a lemon wedding cake; I think that was my hardest decision. I laughed to myself thinking back at it when I was distracted by Anya clapping her hands.

"All done, my darlings. We will see you on Monday. Carter, don't be late," she joked and elbowed him as she left her desk before her facial expression turned more serious. "Seriously, no later than one fifteen p.m.," she said as she tapped her long, skinny index finger on her watch.

I watched him as his eyes creased slightly, his gorgeous smile spreading across his face then breaking into a deep, belly laugh. My heart swelled as I listened to the sound; it was one of my many favourite things about him.

"I won't be late, Anya. I have waited what feels like a lifetime for this day, trust me." He took my hand, leading me out of the office. "See you on Monday, Anya. Don't be late!" He laughed, shaking his head as he did.

"Oh my God, it wasn't that funny." I laughed at him.

"It really tickled me. As if I would be late to marry

you, my love." He stopped me and swept a loose strand of hair away from my face before bringing his lips to mine. My arms moved round his neck as we shared a moment. "Not too much longer to go, then you'll be Mrs Cole." He ran his thumb across my cheek. "We better get home. Everyone is arriving this weekend. Who have we got staying again?" he asked, throwing me a wink, I knew he would forget. It was my turn to shake my head at him, before rolling my eyes.

"Laura, Brooke, Ava, Mum, Dad, and your mum," I said as we got to our car. "Can I drive?"

"Oh, what a shame, no Courtney." The corners of his mouth twitched. "And of course." He nodded, throwing me the keys over the roof of his Maserati.

"Do you not like Courtney?" I asked him as I strapped myself in and turned the ignition. My eyes widened as the roar of the engine rumbled through me.

"I do like her, she just annoys me. I think it's best she's staying at home with Morgan. What with Brooke being there as well," he said as he held on to the handle above his door.

"Seriously, holding on? I'm not that bad."

"I know, but, you know… just in case." He roared with laughter once more. I liked Carter when he was in those moods.

"Piss off, Cole." I rolled my eyes as I put the car into gear and pulled away. "I suppose it's for the best that she and Brooke only come together when they need to. I knew they weren't going to get on. They're both such hot heads," I said as I tightened my grip on the steering wheel, dropping down my gears as we slowed towards the traffic lights.

"That they are. I can't wait to see Lola in her little flower girl dress." Carter beamed. "She will look so cute."

"I know. She is going to look like a little princess. I bet Laura is looking forward to getting a full night's sleep tonight without baby Freya."

"Yeah, I bet she is grateful. Tyler probably isn't though. To be honest, I suppose Lucinda and Gary will take over anyway. I can't see Tyler being that hands on."

"Mmm, maybe," I said, letting my mind wander before sighing.

"What's wrong?" Carter asked.

"I never got an RSVP back from Ethan and what's her face."

"Baby, it's he's loss. You invited them. If he couldn't even have the decency to let you know then he doesn't deserve to be there." He shrugged it off as he ran his hands through his tousled hair.

"I know, I know. I just really thought he would have." I scrunched my nose up and shook my head.

"Anyway, we've got some open road. Put your foot down," he teased. Before I could think about it, I dropped a gear and pushed my foot to the floor, hearing the roar from the car as I opened her up on the empty road. I looked over at Carter who was smiling like the Cheshire Cat at our little speed drive. "You handle her well," he said as he patted the dash of the car.

"Why are you so surprised?" I asked as I started to slow again.

"Because I've never seen you drive." He smirked.

"Okay, but you don't judge a book by its cover. Just because you haven't seen me drive, it doesn't mean I can't." I laughed at his comment.

"How long have we got before everyone is due here?" he asks as we pull into the country lane where our home sits.

"A couple of hours." I look at the clock on the dash.

"Perfect. Time for just me and you." He grinned. I knew that grin.

"Pull into the car port," he said quietly as we drove into the gates.

"Why?" I raised my eyebrows at him.

"Stop asking questions. Just do it." I sighed and did as he said. I turned the ignition off and turned to face him. His hand slowly made its way to my thigh as it slowly ran up my denim dress, stroking me slowly over the front of my knickers. I bit my lip as the burning in my stomach started. I unbelted myself and climbed across the centre of the car before sitting on his lap. "Eager, are we?" he teased as he brought my lips to his, his tongue invading my mouth. It was hungry and harsh. But in a good way. He pushed my dress up over my hips, pulling away and biting his lip as he marvelled at me. "So fucking hot," he growled. I lifted myself up as I tackled his belt and jeans button before tugging them down as much as I could. His thick finger hooked round my lace knickers as he pulled them to the side and his thumb started delicately moving over my sweet spot. I threw my head back, a moan escaping me as he teased me. His other hand came up and pushed me back slightly so I was leaning against the dash as he slipped one finger into me, filling me while slowly pumping into me. I looked at his beautiful sage eyes, hazy with lust and want. I pushed myself into him as my hips started moving with his finger. I took his bottom lip in between my teeth, biting then sucking hard. I heard him breathe in sharply as I let go. He pulled his finger out, sucking it dry with a wicked grin on his face. He lifted himself up and pulled his boxers down slightly as I lowered myself back onto him. I gasped as the familiar feeling of him filling me completely took over me. "I love feeling every bit of you." He grunted as his hips thrust into me, both hands gripping my hips to steady me. I continued to move my hips with his, moans escaping at every hard, deep thrust into me. I was getting close. My breathing had sped up, my stomach burning so deep that I needed him to release me.

"Keep going," I moaned to him as he pressed his lips against my neck, nipping softly as he increased his pace. I felt my legs start to stiffen, my body going tight with his pleasure.

"Let it go, baby," he coaxed as he slowed his thrusts down. I leant back slightly as I kept my eyes on him; he was getting close. His bottom lip was securely between his teeth as he watched himself slide in and out of me in a slow, torturing pace. "I'm so close," he whispered as his sage eyes flicked up to meet my grey eyes. His lips parted as he tightened his grip on my hips. Just looking at him come undone underneath me pushed me over the beautiful edge which was my orgasm, ripping through me as my legs started to shake. I moaned his name as he continued pushing deep into me before finding his own release.

Once my breathing had slowed, I smirked at him. "Enjoy that?" I asked him.

"Oh, very much so," he mumbled as he ran his thumb across my bottom lip. "Give me ten and I'll take you again in the bedroom." I slowly eased off of him as I climbed back into the driver's seat. "I fucking love you, Freya."

"I love you too." I smiled at him before leaving the car. "Come on."

We walked hand in hand up to the front door when we spotted my mum, dad, Elsie and Ava.

"Hey!" Carter said with a confused look on his face. "I didn't think you were coming until five." He side eyed me.

"We weren't, but then we thought, why wait?" Elsie

said, excited.

"I'm glad you're all here." I smiled at them, accepting their embraces.

"Daddy!" I grinned up at him.

"Babyface," he said as he squeezed me again.

Julia came out and walked us into the dining room where she had prepared a late lunch. I looked at her to let her know we were still waiting for Brooke and Laura, but before I could get the words out, they bounded down the stairs.

"SURPRISE!" they squealed together. "We're early, sorry."

"Oh my God, hi!" I wrapped my arms around them both before we took our seats.

I was starving. I couldn't wait to spend the evening with my nearest and dearest. I looked up at Carter who was watching me with such love, a little smile sitting on his face the whole time. He lifted his glass and held it up before hitting the side of it with his butter knife.

"Sorry. If I could just have a few minutes of your time before you tuck into this delicious meal that Julia has made for us all." He smiled as he nodded at her, and she mirrored him.

"Thank you so much for spending our last weekend with us before we are married. We are so grateful. I can't believe we're actually here, that this is it. Me and you, baby" he said with warmth in his voice, his eyes burning into mine. "I am so lucky to have met you. I know we have had our ups and downs, but who doesn't? Freya, my queen. I love you, so very much. You have made me the happiest man in the world. If someone would have told me two years ago that I was going to meet a beautiful girl who was going to turn my world upside down, in a good way," he teased before continuing, "I would have told them to get lost. I never wanted marriage. I never wanted anything serious before you, Freya. I knew you were the one for me from the first moment we meet in Jools' office. You took my breath away. I couldn't get you out of my mind. I don't think I ever thanked you for agreeing to come out for dinner with me. If you hadn't, I wouldn't have given up on you." He winked at me, and my heart thumped in my chest. My eyes watered. "But, honestly, thank you. I can't wait to make you my wife on Monday. It will be the best birthday present I have ever received. You had me at hello, my love. Thank you for everything. I love you." He sniffed before holding his glass high in the air. "To my wife-to-be, Freya." Everyone lifted their glasses and chimed. '*Freya*' after him.

I wiped my eyes before kissing him. "Thank you for that. I love you," I said onto his lips before kissing him again, his arms sagging round my waist as we lost ourselves in each other.

I pulled away and flushed; for a moment, I forgot we weren't alone. I rubbed my lips together as I took my seat next to Carter.

"Let's eat!" he announced as everyone started tucking in. I took a moment just to reflect on everything and how far we had come. I smiled before helping myself to some food.

I was so lucky.

CHAPTER TWENTY-FIVE

Sunday evening was soon upon us; the night before the wedding. I hadn't even written my vows yet. I was starting to panic that something was going to go wrong, something that I had no control over. It was seven p.m., I was exhausted but I didn't want to leave our guests and retire to the bedroom for the evening. I slumped down on our sofa next to Carter and Laura who were in deep conversation about work. I rolled my eyes. Brooke was on FaceTime to Peter, making sure he had everything ready to bring over in the morning. Elsie and Mum were chatting, Dad was lost in conversation with James, and Ava was nowhere to be seen. I couldn't help but feel sad knowing Ethan wasn't going to be there tomorrow. I pulled my phone out of my pocket and had a quick look through my messages, just in case I had missed it, but there was nothing. My heart hurt, and my stomach was in knots.

"Hey, are you okay?" Carter asked. I nodded and

leaned into him as he lifted his arm and wrapped it around me, pulling me closer to him. I felt the weight on the sofa change. When I looked over my shoulder, I saw my mum sitting there.

"How are you feeling?" she asked with a concerned look on her face.

"I'm fine. I'm really tired, but excited." I smiled at her. "How about you?"

"I'm really excited. My baby is getting married." She beamed, taking my face into her soft hands. "I can't believe it's tomorrow," she said as she kissed me on the forehead. "You are going to be such a stunning bride."

A few hours had passed. We had been over the morning's itinerary twice already, so we all knew what time our hair and make-up was being done, and what time we had to leave by. The bouquets were coming to the house, and the rest would be waiting for us at the venue.

Everyone had started settling down for the night, so I took that as my cue to leave. I needed to wash my hair and let it dry naturally, then I wanted to just have a few moments of quiet before the madness started. I said goodnight to everyone and made my way upstairs. I could hear Carter moving around in his office, so I padded quietly down the hallway to find him.

"All okay?" I asked as I slowly leant round the door.

"Yeah. Just finishing my vows." He smiled at me. "You?"

"I'm good. I just said goodnight to everyone. I need to wash my hair." I groaned.

"Come here," he said quietly as he placed the sheet of paper into the top drawer of his desk. He pulled me into his embrace, holding me. The sound of his steady heartbeat was filling my ears. I looked up at him. "I love you," I whispered.

"I love you," he replied, placing a soft kiss on my lips. "You know what I've always wanted to do?" he mumbled into the top of my hair.

"What?" I asked, full of curiosity.

"Fuck you over this desk."

"Carter!" I slapped his hard chest before he broke into a laugh.

"What?" he said, still laughing. "It's true."

"How about it? One last time before we're husband and wife," he teased, his hands slowly making their way to the hem of my skirt.

The hairs on the back of my neck stood up, goosebumps appearing over my tanned skin. Before I could think about it he pulled me in front of his desk, pushing me down slightly then lifting one of my legs to rest on the edge of the desk.

"What a beautiful fucking sight." He sighed as he pushed my skirt up around my waist. "I like these knickers," he mumbled as he ran his index finger underneath me and along the delicate lace of my thong, then pulling it to the side. He dropped to his knees as he started kissing up the back of my thighs and he pushed one of his fingers deep inside me. I whined as the exquisite feeling coursed through me.

"Stay where you are," he demanded. My fingers were gripping the edge of the desk when I felt his tongue flicking, licking, and sucking on me. I was already at my brink when he pushed me onto the desk. His tongue continued slow strokes over me, sending a ripple through to my core. His finger continued its slow movements in and out of me. I was so close, my knuckles had turned white from gripping so tightly.

"Carter," I moaned. "I'm going to come."

Before I could try and hold it off, I felt everything tighten as I crashed down around him; the intensity of the orgasm left my legs trembling.

"Good girl. Stay there," he said with a smile in his voice. I heard him pull at his trousers as he slammed into me, hard. I moaned out as he hit me again, slowly but hard. His hand was in my hair as he pulled my head back, his other hand on my hip as he continued slamming in and out of me. "You are so fucking tight, and you are all mine. You will always be mine," he said through gritted teeth.

That wonderful burn grew deep inside me. He pushed my leg higher onto the desk before placing his hand back on my hip and thrusting me back into him.

"I'm so close," I cried. I was so consumed by him.

"Good," he said as he slapped down hard on my bare bum cheek. I heard a moan escape him as he found a release in spanking me. He did it again, this time making me moan out with him. "I want you to come all over me," he demanded in a silky voice. His grip in my hair tightened, and I knew he was getting close. He continued with his fast paced movements, each thrust hard. He was in so deep. He threw one last slap down on me and it sent my body into overdrive as I came hard for the second time within moments. I felt everything tighten around him and he came with me, digging his nails into my hips as he found his release. We were both panting and sweating. He helped me off the desk and pulled my skirt down for me.

"Well, that didn't disappoint." He grinned at me before kissing me. "Let's go shower."

I lay in bed, trying to think of what to write in my vows, I was normally so good with things like this, but I was just stumped. I started going over the past year in my head, from the first time I met Carter in my office, to our first date, our first time we slept together… I still couldn't believe I did it after our first date. I shook away my thoughts. Everything in Elsworth, the revenge, the heartbreak, the letter, Paris, the pregnancy, the engagement, Chloe, Esme. I sighed as I flopped onto the bed with my empty notepad. My mind started drifting to the book I had been writing. I definitely thought I would try and push it. Okay, I'd written about everything that had happened in mine and Carter's life, but who knew? Someone may have enjoyed it. I was interrupted from my thoughts when I heard a knock on the bedroom door. Carter walked towards me, his hair messy and still damp, his arms bulging out of his tight t-shirt and his jogging bottoms.

"Hey, baby. I just came to say goodnight." He smiled at me as he kissed me on the tip of my nose. "I know we aren't meant to sleep in the same house the night before the wedding, so I'm going to sleep in with James and Julia in their little house, okay?" He sat next to me and cuddled me.

I pulled my brows together. "But I don't want you to sleep in the housekeeper's house," I said bluntly.

"Freya, it's one night. This is the start of our forever." He smiled, kissing me on the top of my head. "Stop forcing the vows. They will come to you." He winked before standing up. "I'll see you at the altar. Don't be late, Mrs Cole," he teased as he walked towards the door.

"See you tomorrow. I love you," I breathed as he slipped out the door, blowing me a kiss.

I sulked on the bed as I heard another knock. This time, my mum walked through. "Hey, darling." She smiled as she lay next to me. "Laura and Brooke are on their way up. I just wanted to check in before Daddy and go to bed," she said as I lay under her arm and on her chest, her fingers running through my hair.

"Thank you. I am so nervous but so excited."

"I know, sweetie, but it will be fine. Everything will be perfect. Make sure you enjoy every minute as it goes so quickly," she says, still playing with my hair. "Mum, I'm sad that Ethan didn't respond."

"I know you are." She sighed. "I said that to Daddy. I knew something was wrong." I could feel her looking down at me. "But, Freya, you can't force it. This is yours and Carter's day. It's Ethan's loss. Now, I will see you in the morning. Try and get some sleep." She kissed me on the top of the head as she peeled me off her and made her way to the door. "I can hear those two giggling up the stairs. Enjoy your evening." She smiled at me as she met Laura and Brooke in the doorway. "Night, girls. Don't keep her up late."

"Frey Frey!" Laura jumped on the bed, throwing herself at me.

"Get off of her, woman." Brooke stood there with her arms folded, rolling her eyes at Laura.

"Oh, pipe down." Laura turned to me. "You okay?"

"Yeah, I'm good. I'm excited. I can't believe it's tomorrow!" I squealed, pushing the thoughts of Ethan to the back of my mind. My mum was right. It was his loss. I was marrying Carter, the love of my life, and I couldn't wait.

"How's the vow writing going?" Brooke asked sarcastically, raising her perfectly shaped and pencilled brow at the blank notepad. I huffed then groaned out as I threw my head into my pillows.

"It'll be fine!" Laura tried to reassure me. "We can help." She smiled, looking at Brooke as she threw her arms down and joined us on the bed.

"Put *Friends* on. Bit of background noise. Ooh! Put on the one where Chandler and Monica write their vows," Laura said, nodding a bit too enthusiastically which sends me and Brooke into a fit of giggles.

I look at my phone; it's eleven twenty and I think my vows are done.

"Phew," I say as I flop into bed. Laura is already snoozing and Brooke is curled up next to her, watching me. "Thanks for your help." I smiled at her as I got under the duvet.

"No problem. Glad we could help." She yawned. "Now, go to sleep, bridey. Don't want bags tomorrow," she said with a smirk on her face.

"Night," I said as I felt my lids getting heavy.

"Night, doll." Brooke barely managed a mumble.

I woke with my heart thumping, butterflies fluttering in my belly while knots tied themselves around each other. I looked over and saw Laura on her phone and Brooke was waking up.

"What's the time?" I whined.

"Eight," Laura said sharply. "Have you looked outside? It's a beautiful day." She smiled at me. I climbed out of bed quickly and pulled back the curtains. The sun was beating down into our garden. A massive smile spread across my face. "I'M GETTING MARRIED TODAY!" I screamed.

I sat and watched Brooke, Courtney, and Laura having their hair done while Vanessa was working on my make-up. I told her I only wanted subtle and natural. I didn't want a face full of make-up. The girls were having side buns, with loose bits of hair curled. The few hours flew by and my hair was just being finished when I heard a knock on the door.

"I'll get it," my mum said as she walked slowly, patting her freshly pinned hair. As she pulled the door open, I heard her gasp.

"What is it mum?" I asked, excusing myself and sliding off the stool. I walked into the hallway and my heart swelled.

His messy, curly blonde hair flopped onto his forehead, his beautiful hazel eyes were wide and bright. I watched as his smile broke. I loved his crooked smile.

"Ethan!" I screamed and launched myself at him, wrapping my arms around him.

"Hey, Freya! Surprise!" He laughed as I was squeezing the air out of him.

"You came. But you didn't reply to my invitation," I said, confused as I pulled away, looking up at him.

"I know I didn't, but Carter called me. Told me to

come, that you wanted me here. So, here I am." He smiled again. I was so caught in the moment that I hadn't realized he had brought what's her face.

"Sorry, I'm so rude. It's..." My mind went blank.

"Isabella," Ethan reminded me, rolling his eyes before laughing. She stood close to him, laughing with him.

"I'm so sorry, Isabella. I'm useless with names," I shamelessly lied, knotting my fingers.

"You look wonderful, Freya," he said quietly, his eyes trailing from my head to my toes. His eyes fixed on my still raw scar on my leg. "What happened?" he asked, his smile fading.

"Oh, it's nothing. I broke my leg," I said, swallowing, not allowing the familiar burn to crawl up my throat at the bitter memories.

"She can fill you in another time," my mum chirped. "Ethan, Isabella, please follow me. I'll make you a cup of tea before you head to the venue," she said as she walked away, Isabella following her.

"I can't believe you're here." I smiled.

"I wouldn't have missed it for the world, Freya. You deserve all of this." He smiled as he looked around our home before following Isabella.

I sat back down with Sandra, apologizing. I watched as she pinned the last few bits of hair up into a perfect chignon bun.

Hopefully I hadn't put her behind schedule.

CHAPTER TWENTY-SIX

I sat in the car with my dad while Laura, Brooke, Courtney, and Lola followed in a second car.

"Here we go," I said with nerves in my voice as we pulled up outside The Savoy. The doorman opened the car door and I watched my dad leave, holding out his hand for me. I left the car as gracefully as I could in the tight material of my wedding dress. I smiled a small smile as our photographer was snapping away. I stood on the steps and waited for my mum's car with the bridesmaids in to arrive.

"You look beautiful, babyface," my dad gushed as he wiped a tear away.

"Thank you, Daddy," I said as I snuggled into him. I smiled as I watch them pull up, the girls' champagne dresses glistening in the beautiful sunshine. Lola was excited, jumping up and down as she waited for her mum to emerge from the car. They all looked perfect.

I was interrupted when I heard Anya's voice. "Oh my

God, darling. You look absolutely breath-taking." She beamed as she looked me up and down. "Carter is waiting for you. He looks wonderful too." She eyed me as she said it, but I allowed it because he was going to be my husband in less than an hour.

"Come, come," she muttered as she pushed through the revolving doors, my dad trying hard to not stand on the long train on the dress. We stood outside the doors that were going to change my life forever. My Carter was standing there, waiting for me. I took a deep breath before breathing in the scent of the roses in my bouquet.

"Darling, are you ready?" Anya asked me as Laura and Brooke fluffed my dress out to its full length and pulling my veil out.

Courtney came and stood next to me. "I am so happy for you. You look stunning," she said, running her index finger under her eyes. I could hear the camera clicking in the background and I was grateful, because I would appreciate those photos. Anya slipped through a side door, and within moments, I heard the sound of The Piano Guys – *A Thousand Years* start to fill the room. I took a deep breath as Brooke, Lola, Laura, and Courtney stood in line in front of me, ready to walk before me. I looked up as I heard the doors open, gasping as I looked into the room.

It was just how I imagined it; roses hanging on the end of each row of seats, our close family and friends, and my handsome Carter standing at the altar, waiting for me.

His hands lapped over each other as he held them down in front of him. Louis was standing proud next to him with a beautiful smile spread across his face. I tried to slow my breathing as I watched Brooke and Lola walk out, followed by ahhs and ohhs as our intimate guests swooned over Lola. Laura soon left, followed by Courtney.

I took a deep breath. "Daddy," I mumbled.

"Yes, sweetheart," he said as he tightened his grip on my linked hand.

"Don't let me fall," I said, nerves making my voice tremble.

"Never." He stood tall and patted my hand. "Let's go."

We walked slowly down the small aisle. As soon as my eyes met Carter's, my nerves were forgotten. His eyes looked glittery as they filled with happy tears. He looked so proud. I focused only on him. I smiled as I got close to him, his eyes looking me up and down as he ran his tongue over his bottom lip before pulling it in between his teeth.

My dad kissed me on the cheek as he placed my left hand into Carter's. "Look after her, champ," he said before taking a seat next to my mum who was a blubbering mess. I smiled at her before standing and facing Carter.

"Baby, you look incredible. So beautiful," he whispered.

"You don't look too bad yourself," I teased.

He looked amazing in his black tuxedo, his black bowtie, and crisp white shirt. His hair was tousled and styled as usual. His sage eyes burned into me. I could feel everything he felt. I was so in love with him.

I was pulled from my moment when I heard the reverend say, "We are gathered here today, to witness the marriage of Carter Lewis Cole and Freya Rose Greene." He smiled down at us both. "Marriage is a wonderful, joyous occasion that should be witnessed by all who care and adore this wonderful couple. You should feel very blessed to be here today," he continued, I couldn't stop staring at Carter. I was taking everything in, like my mum said.

"Carter, would you like to say your vows to Freya?" he asked.

"Of course." He smiled as he took the piece of paper from Louis. Carter coughed slightly before unfolding the piece of paper. I had never seen him look so nervous.

"Freya," he said before taking a deep breath. "I know some people may think we are rushing into this, but I have never been more certain about something in my life. You are my world, my soulmate, my best friend. I know we have had our moments, but I honestly couldn't live without you. You are my home, my life. I vow to always protect you. I vow to always be there for you, to look after you when you need me to, and I promise to be there when words are needed and to be there when you just need me to listen. I will never let you down. Never let you go. I will love you fiercely in all your moods." The guests giggle. I continue to dab my eye with my index fingers before giggling along with them. "And I vow that we will always be together, even if things keep us apart, we will always come back to each other. My queen. I love you." He folded the paper and gave it back to Louis. I watched as his face softened and relaxed. I took a deep breath, smiling up at him.

"Freya, if you would like to now read your vows to Carter," he said.

I nodded as Brooke went to hand me my paper, but I shook my head, giving her my bouquet instead. I wanted this to come from deep down in my heart, where everything I loved about him was kept safe.

"Carter," I started, my voice shaky. He reached across and took my hands into his and gently rubbed his thumbs across the back of them.

"Love of my life, my soulmate. You're my best friend. I didn't know what love was until I found you. You brought me back to life when I didn't even know my spark had burned out. You make me feel like the only girl in the world, reminding me daily of how much you love me. A love like ours is like one out of the movies. People say that kind of love doesn't exist, but it does. I found it with you. I will be there in moments of sadness and in moments of joy. I will always be by your side. You are the person that I want to spend the rest of my life with. We will make mistakes, we will disagree, but one thing I know, we will always love each other. I will love you forever. Forever and always." I smiled up at him.

"Rings please?" The reverend said as he looked at Louis who proudly pulled out my platinum wedding band that was encrusted with diamonds.

"Now, please Carter. Repeat after me," he said.

"I give you this ring."

"*I give you this ring.*"

"As a token of our marriage."

"*As a token of our marriage.*"

The reverend smiled but then looked confused when Carter continued to speak. "Let it be a reminder that I am always by your side and that I will always be a faithful partner to you."

I smiled a gushy smile as he pushed the beautiful band onto my wedding finger. "I love you," I said as he pulled his hand away from mine.

"Okay, Freya. Now your turn." He smiled at me as Louis handed me Carter's solid platinum band.

"I give you this ring."

"*I give you this ring.*"

"As a token of our marriage."

"*As a token of our marriage.*"

I smiled up at him as I pushed the band onto his thick finger, falling in love with him all over again with this new sense of ownership I had of him. He was legally mine.

"If for any reason these two people should not be married, please speak now, or forever hold your peace."

I stood, anxiously waiting. I knew no one would, but it

was the worst ten seconds of my life.

"Okay!" The reverend clapped. "By the power vested in me, I now pronounce you husband and wife." He smiled. "You may now kiss the bride."

With that, Carter cupped my face with both of his hands before kissing me softly. The fire inside me ignited. I couldn't believe we were married. The start of our new life together. The reverend told us we needed to sign the register and that we needed to call our witnesses forward. Carter called for Ava, and I called for Laura before signing the register while Ed Sheeran – *This* played through the room. Within moments, Carter took my hand as we made our way down the aisle to the wonderful sound of Nat King Cole. I couldn't take the stupid grin off my face. I was so incredibly happy.

Carter pulled me into a side room as soon as we were out of the ceremony. "Freya, you..." He stopped and took a deep breath. "You look stunning. We did it, baby. You're mine. I'm yours." He smiled at me before kissing me again.

"I know! You're my husband. I am so lucky. Happy Birthday, hubby." I grinned at him.

"You have honestly given me the best birthday present I could have ever wished for." He smiled down at me, pressing his forehead against me.

I enjoyed the silence. I grabbed his left hand and ran my index finger along his wedding band. "You're mine now, Cole." I leaned down and kissed his wedding band.

"That I am, Mrs Cole." He beamed at me. It felt weird him calling me that now that we were officially and legally married. He pulled me tight into him and pressed his lips against my neck before whispering. "Is it wrong that I want to fuck you right now in that dress. Something about it makes you look innocent," he teased as he nipped my ear. My legs felt weak at his dirty words, the pit of my stomach alight.

"As much as I want that, we have dinner to eat. You get me for the rest of your life, plus, don't forget, we need to consummate the marriage." I winked at him.

"I can't wait." He smirked. "I will never get enough of you, Mrs Cole," he breathed before taking my hand and leading me to the bar area while they cleared our ceremony room for dinner.

The evening passed pleasantly and I sat and took in the small conversations between party guests. Carter sat next to me, running his index finger up and down my exposed back.

"This is a sexy dress," he mumbled, distracting me.

"Thank you. I didn't know if you would like it. That's what I was most nervous about," I admitted, biting the inside of my cheek.

"Why the hell would you worry about that?" He looked confused. "Freya, baby, you would look good in a black bag. Honestly, if I could have chosen a dress for you, it would have been this." He looked deep into my eyes as I leant up and kissed him. I didn't want to pull myself away, I wanted him to take me to our room and devour me. I blushed at my thoughts as we were pulled from our moment by the DJ announcing that it was time for our first dance. I smiled as I heard Kodaline – *The One* playing as Carter wrapped his arms around me, pulling me close. I draped my arms around his neck and watched his eyes the whole time. They seemed lighter than usual, glistening under the lights in the room. I was so in love with him. I never knew love like that before. I liked having moments like that, just us.

"Was it everything you dreamed of?" he asked as we swayed side to side.

"It was more," I gushed at him. "It really has been the most amazing day," I said as I leaned up to kiss him again.

"I'm glad. I have had the best day. And the best birthday. You are my wife, my beautiful, smart, funny, sexy wife." He grinned at me, showing his perfect white teeth. "Also, how does it feel to be rich beyond your means?"

"Carter, it's never been about the money. I have my own money. Okay, granted, not as much as you, but I like to pay my way." I nodded at him and looked as everyone else joined us on the dance floor. "Please don't think for one second it was about money."

I looked at him, worried, as I watched him burst into a deep laugh. "Of course I don't. Honestly, woman. You're rich, just deal with it." He chuckled again before resting his head on mine. "Our forever starts today." He smiled before slowly reaching down and kissing me once more. I would never get enough of him. He was my life, my soul, my king and I would always be his queen.

He was my something everlasting.

EPILOGUE

Carter

"Come on, baby, keep going," I said to her. I felt helpless, fucking useless in that situation. I watched her, her beautiful auburn curls pushed off her face, her glistening grey eyes on mine the whole time, and her tanned skin beaded with sweat.

"I can't do it anymore," she cried out to me. "Please make it stop."

I watched as the midwife shook her head and laughed. "Freya, we can't stop. The baby is coming. You are so close. I think two to three more pushes and the baby will be here. I promise."

I wiggled my fingers under her tight grip. They had gone red where she was squeezing them so hard, but I didn't care. If it helped her, that was fine. It was the least I could do.

"Carter, another contraction is coming," she wailed.

"It's okay, baby. You've come this far. You are so close, baby." I reassured her. I felt awful. My heart was thumping. I wanted to take it all away from her. We had waited so long for this moment that neither of us could quite believe it had happened.

"Okay, great, Freya. Chin to chest, darling. Baby is starting to crown. One more push and they'll be out." She nodded as the other midwife grabbed the tiny plastic cot and wheeled it over. I watched, with the realisation that I would soon be a daddy, and Freya would finally become a mummy.

"Do you want to watch, Dad?" the midwife asked me. I nodded eagerly but Freya pulled my arm back then grabbed the front of my t-shirt and pulled me down to her sweaty, beautiful face. "Don't you fucking dare. You aren't going to look down there! You will never want to come near me again. Keep your head up this end!"

"One more push, Freya," the midwife shouted. I watched in awe as her body took over, her chin to her chest and pushing our beautiful baby into the world. I was pulled from her when I heard a piercing cry fill the room.

"Congratulations. It's a beautiful baby boy," the midwife proudly stated as they placed him onto Freya's chest.

"A boy," I whispered, shocked. We kept the sex a secret, but I honestly thought the baby was a girl.

"Well done, darling. You did so well. Congratulations," she said as she walked away and started noting things down.

"Oh my God," I said as happy tears had escaped without me realising. "He is amazing. You were amazing, baby. God, I didn't think I could love you anymore than I did, but I do. I am so madly and deeply in love with you." I gasped as I leant down and kissed her plump lips.

"I love you," she cried as she looked deep into my eyes before cradling the tiny new-born on her chest.

"Daddy, do you want to cut the cord?" the midwife asked, holding the equipment in her hand.

"Of course!" I said, wiping my eyes with the palms of my hands. I held my breath as I clamped down, cutting the supply that once connected Freya and the baby.

"Do we have a name?" the midwife asked as she filled out the baby's ankle tags.

"Parker Harry Cole," we said at the same time. We decided to dedicate the baby's middle name to Freya's dad. The midwife came and lifted Parker off Freya's chest.

"Where are you going with him?" she asked, panicked as she watched the midwife walk off with her baby.

"We are just weighing him and putting his hat and tags on," the midwife reassured her. Within minutes, she walked over to Freya, placing him back in her arms.

"Perfect baby Parker weighs 7lb 4oz and was born at 00:06 am on the 6th May." She smiled before going back to her notes. I watched as Freya started giggling.

"Happy Birthday, baby, and happy first wedding anniversary," she said.

"What a wonderful birthday and first anniversary gift." I smiled down at her, placing my hand on her face and kissing her. My life was complete.

ACKNOWLEDGEMENTS

Thank you Leanne, once again for being so wonderful and helping me when I got stuck, and also helping me with the new covers for my series! You are a saint. Also, thank you for making my book look amazing.

Thank you Karen for editing my book so quickly once again.

And last but not least, thank you to my following who once again have been so supportive on this adventure. I am so grateful to you all, you are all amazing.

I hope you enjoy the last book of the Entwined In You series, I can't believe it's the end already.